VERDICT IN BLOOD

OTHER JOANNE KILBOURN MYSTERIES
BY GAIL BOWEN

Deadly Appearances
Murder at the Mendel (U.S.A. ed., *Love and Murder*)
The Wandering Soul Murders
A Colder Kind of Death
A Killing Spring

VERDICT IN BLOOD

A Joanne Kilbourn Mystery

Gail Bowen

M&S

Canadian Cataloguing in Publication Data

Bowen, Gail, 1942-
  Verdict in blood

"A Joanne Kilbourn mystery".
ISBN 0-7710-1487-2

I. Title.

PS8553.08995V47   1998   C813'.54   C98-931135-X
PR9199.3.B68V47   1998

We acknowledge the financial support of the Government of Canada through the Book Publishing Industry Development Program for our publishing activities. We further acknowledge the support of the Canada Council for the Arts and the Ontario Arts Council for our publishing program.

Typeset in Trump Mediaeval by M&S, Toronto

Printed and bound in Canada

McClelland & Stewart Inc.
The Canadian Publishers
481 University Avenue
Toronto, Ontario
M5G 2E9

2 3 4 5   02 01 00 99 98

For

Bert Bartholomew
June 12, 1913 – April 9, 1997

Hazel Wren Bowen
June 12, 1914 – February 26, 1998

and

Madeleine Wren Bowen-Diaz
born, Palm Sunday, April 5, 1998

"A time to mourn and a time to dance"

∼

With thanks to Jennifer Cook, R.N. and Mickey Rostoker, M.D., for advice on medical matters; to Heather Nord, B.A. LLB, for wise counsel on the law, and to Ted Bowen, for thirty years of friendship, laughter, and love.

CHAPTER

1

When the phone on my bedside table shrilled in the early hours of Labour Day morning, I had the receiver pressed to my ear before the second ring. Eli Kequahtooway, the sixteen-year-old nephew of the man in my life, had been missing since 4:00 the previous afternoon. It wasn't the first time that Eli had taken off, but the fact that he'd disappeared before didn't ease my mind about the dangers waiting for him in a world that didn't welcome runaways, especially if they were aboriginal.

I was braced for the worst. I got it, but not from the quarter I was expecting.

My caller's voice was baritone rubbed by sandpaper. "This is Detective Robert Hallam of the Regina City Police," he said. "Am I speaking to Hilda McCourt?"

"No," I said. "I'm Joanne Kilbourn. Miss McCourt is staying with me for the weekend, but I'm sure she's asleep by now. Can't this wait until morning?"

Detective Hallam made no attempt to disguise his frustration. "Ms. Kilbourn, this is not a casual call. If I'd wanted to recruit a block captain for Neighbourhood Watch, I would have waited. Unfortunately for all of us, a woman's been murdered, and your friend seems to be our best bet for establishing the victim's identity. Now, why don't you do the sensible thing and bring Ms. McCourt to the phone. Then I can get the information I need, and you can go back to bed."

Hilda was eighty-three years old. I shrank from the prospect of waking her up to deal with a tragedy, but as I walked down the hall to the guest room, I could see the light under her door. When I knocked, she answered immediately. Even propped up in bed reading, Hilda was a striking figure. When the actress Claudette Colbert died, a graceful obituary noted that, among her many talents, Claudette Colbert wore pyjamas well. Hilda McCourt shared that gift. The pyjamas she was wearing were black silk, tailored in the clean masculine lines of women's fashions in the forties. With her brilliant auburn hair exploding like an aureole against the pillow behind her, there was no denying that, like Claudette Colbert, Hilda McCourt radiated star power.

She leaned forward. "I heard the phone," she said.

"It's for you, Hilda," I said. "It's the police. They need your help." I picked up her robe from the chair beside the window and held it out to her. "You can take the call in my room."

She slipped into her robe, a magnificent Chinese red silk shot through with gold, and straightened her shoulders. "Thank you, Joanne," she said. "I'll enlighten you when I'm enlightened."

After she left, I picked up the book she'd been reading. *Geriatric Psychiatry: A Handbook.* It was an uncharacteristic choice. Hilda was a realist about her age. She quoted Thomas Dekker approvingly, "Age is like love; it cannot be hid," but she never dwelled on growing old, and her mind was as sharp as her spirit was indomitable. While

I waited for her, I glanced at the book's table of contents. The topics were weighty: "The Dementias"; "Delirium and Other Organic Mental Disorders"; "Psychoses"; "Anxiety and Related Personality Dysfunctions"; "Diagnosing Depression." Uneasy, I leafed through the book. Its pages were heavily annotated in a strong but erratic hand which I was relieved to see was not my old friend's. The writer had entered into a kind of running dialogue with the authors of the text, but the entries were personal, not scholarly. I stopped at a page listing the criteria for a diagnosis of dementia. The margins were black with what appeared to be self-assessments. I felt a pang of guilt as sharp as if I'd happened upon a stranger's diary.

Hilda wasn't gone long. When she came back, she pulled her robe around her as if she were cold and sank onto the edge of the bed.

"Let me get you some tea," I said.

"Tea's a good idea, but we'd better use the large pot," she said. "The detective I was speaking to is coming over."

"Hilda, what's going on?"

She adjusted the dragon's-head fastening at the neck of her gown. "The police were patrolling Wascana Park tonight, and they found a body sprawled over one of those limestone slabs at the Boy Scout memorial. There was nothing on the victim to identify her, but there was a slip of paper in her jacket pocket." Hilda's face was grim. "Joanne, the paper had my name on it and your telephone number."

"Then you know who she is," I said.

Hilda nodded. "I'm afraid I do," she said. "I think it must be Justine Blackwell."

"The judge," I said. "But you were just at her party tonight."

"I was," Hilda said, stroking the dragon's head thoughtfully. "That book you're holding belongs to her. There'd been some disturbing developments in her life, and she

3

wanted my opinion on them. I left your number with her because she was going to call me later today."

"Come downstairs, and we'll have that tea," I said.

"I'd like to dress first," Hilda said. "I wouldn't be comfortable receiving a member of the police force in my robe."

I'd just plugged in the kettle when the phone rang again. It was Alex Kequahtooway. "Jo, I know it's late, but you said to call as soon as I heard from Eli."

"He called you?"

"He's back. He was here when I got home."

"Oh, Alex, I'm so glad. Is he okay?"

"I don't know. When I walked in, he'd just got out of the shower. He went into his room and started taking fresh clothes out of his drawers. Jo, he didn't say a word to me. It was as if I wasn't there. At first, I thought he was on something, but I've seen kids wasted on just about every substance there is, and this is different."

"Have you called Dr. Rayner?"

"I tried her earlier in the evening. I thought Eli might have got in touch with her, but there was no answer. Of course, it's a holiday weekend. I'm going to call again, but if I don't connect, I'm going to take Eli down to emergency. I hate to bring in another shrink, but I just don't know what to do for him, and I don't want to blow it."

"You won't," I said. "Eli's going to be fine. He's come a long way this summer. Most importantly, he has you."

"And you think that's enough?" Alex asked, and I could hear the ache.

"I know that's enough."

For a beat there was silence, then Alex, who was suspicious of words, said what he didn't often say. "I love you, Jo."

"I love you, too." I took a breath. "Alex, there's something else. About ten minutes ago, Hilda got a phone call from a colleague of yours. There was a murder in the park tonight.

It looks like the victim was Hilda's friend Justine Blackwell. I'm afraid Detective Hallam – that's the officer who's coming over – is going to ask Hilda to identify the body. I don't want her to have to go through that."

"She shouldn't have to," Alex said. "There are a hundred people in this city who know Justice Blackwell. Someone else can make the ID – I'll take care of it. And, Jo, pass along a message to Hilda for me, would you? Tell her not to let Bob Hallam get under her skin. He can be a real jerk."

"I'll warn her," I said. "Alex, I'm so thankful that Eli's back."

"Me too," he said. "God, this has been a lousy night."

As I poured boiling water into the Brown Betty, Alex's words stayed with me. It had been a lousy night, which had come hard on the heels of a lousy day. The problem was, as it had been so often in the past few months, Eli.

He was a boy whose young life had been shadowed by trouble: a father who disappeared before he was born and a temperament composed of equal parts intelligence, anger, and raw sensitivity. Driven by furies he could neither understand nor control, Eli became a runaway who spattered his trail with spray-painted line drawings of horses, graffiti that identified him as definitely as a fingerprint. His capacity for self-destruction seemed limitless. He was also the most vulnerable human being I had ever met. Alex told me once that when he'd heard a biographer of Tchaikovsky say that the composer had been "a child of glass," he had thought of his nephew.

From the day he was born, the centre of Eli's life had been his mother. The previous May, Karen Kequahtooway was killed in a car accident. Eli had been sitting in the seat beside her. His physical injuries healed quickly, but the lacerations to his psyche had been devastating. The child of glass had shattered. For weeks, Eli's anguish translated itself into a kind of free-floating rage that exploded in graffiti and hurled itself against whoever was luckless enough to cross his path. On more than one occasion, that person was me. But as the summer days grew shorter, the grief and fury that had clouded Eli's life began to lift. For the first time since Karen's death, Eli appeared to be seeing a future for himself, and Alex and I had allowed ourselves the luxury of hope.

Then everything fell apart.

At first, it seemed as if the gods were smiling. When she arrived for the weekend, Hilda surprised Alex and Eli and my kids and me with tickets for the annual Labour Day game between the Saskatchewan Roughriders and the Winnipeg Blue Bombers. As we settled into our seats on the fifty-five-yard line, Alex and I grinned at each other. The seats were perfect. So was the weather, which was hot and still. And on the opening kickoff, the Riders' kick returner broke through the first wave of tacklers and scampered into the endzone for a touchdown. All signs pointed to a banner day.

From the beginning of our relationship, Alex and I had been careful not to use the fact that Eli and my son, Angus, were both sixteen as justification for asking them to move in lockstep. We had hoped for the best and left it to them to find each other. That Sunday, they were sitting a few seats away in the row behind us, and as their game patter and laughter drifted towards us, it seemed our strategy was working.

At the beginning of the third quarter, Angus announced that he and Eli were going to get nachos; they bought their food and started back, but somewhere between the concession stand and their seats, Eli disappeared. There were twenty-five thousand people at Taylor Field that day, so looking for Eli hadn't been easy, but we'd done our best. After the game, we checked the buses on the west side of the stadium. When we couldn't find Eli, we went back inside the stadium and waited until the stands emptied. There was always the possibility that he had simply lost track of where we were sitting. But we couldn't find him, and as we walked through the deserted parking lot it was clear that, as he had on many occasions, Eli had simply run away. The rest of the day was spent in the dismally familiar ritual of checking out Eli's haunts and calling the bus station and listening to a recorded voice announce the times when the buses that might have carried Eli away from his demons left the city. Now, without explanation, he was back, and it seemed that all we could do was hold our breath and wait until next time.

Detective Hallam arrived just as I was carrying the tray with the teapot and cups into the living room. On my way to the front door, I caught a glimpse of my reflection in the hall mirror and flinched. I was tanned from a summer at the lake, and the week before I'd had my hair cut in a style which I was relieved to see fell into place on its own, but after I'd talked to Alex, I only had time to splash my face, brush my teeth, and throw on the first two items I found in the clean laundry: an old pair of jogging shorts and a Duran Duran T-shirt from my oldest daughter's abandoned collection of rock memorabilia. I was dressed for comfort not company, but when I opened the door, I saw that Hilda's caller was dapper enough for both of us.

Robert Hallam appeared to be in his mid-sixties. He was a short, trim man with a steel-grey crewcut, a luxuriant bush of a moustache, and a thin, ironic smile. It was a hot night, but he was wearing meticulously pressed grey slacks, a black knit shirt, and a salt-and-pepper tweed jacket. He nodded when I introduced myself, then walked into the living room ahead of me, checked out the arrangement of the furniture, dragged a straight-backed chair across the carpet and positioned it next to the couch so he'd be able to look down at whoever sat next to him. He turned down my offer of tea, and when Hilda came into the room, he didn't rise. As far as I was concerned, Detective Hallam was off to a bad start.

He motioned Hilda to the place on the couch nearest him. "Sit down," he said. "Inspector Ke-quah-too-way has informed me that we don't need you to make the ID any more, so this may be a waste of time for both of us."

Hilda remained standing. From the set of her jaw as she looked down at the detective, I could see that she had missed neither Robert Hallam's derisive smile when he mentioned Alex's rank nor the exaggerated care with which he pronounced Alex's surname. She shot him a glance that would have curdled milk, then, with great deliberation, she walked to the end of the couch farthest from him and sat down.

The flush spread from Robert Hallam's neck to his face. He stood, grabbed his chair, and took it to where Hilda was sitting. Then he perched on the edge and pulled out a notepad.

"I'll need your full name, home address, and telephone number," he said tightly.

After Hilda gave him the information, he narrowed his eyes at her. "How old are you, Ms. McCourt?"

"It's *Miss* McCourt," Hilda said. "And I don't see that my age is germane."

"The issue is testimonial capacity," he snapped. "I have to decide whether I can trust your ability to make truthful and accurate statements."

Hilda stiffened. "I assure you that you can," she said. "Detective, if you have questions, I'm prepared to answer them, but if you wish to play games, you'll play alone."

Detective Hallam's face was scarlet. "How did Mrs. Kilbourn's phone number get in the dead woman's jacket pocket?" he rasped.

"Justine Blackwell put it there herself," Hilda said.

"Yesterday I drove down from Saskatoon to attend a party celebrating her thirtieth year on the bench. Afterwards, at Justine's invitation, I went to the hotel bar and had a drink with her. Before we parted, she asked for a number where she could reach me. I gave her Mrs. Kilbourn's."

"How would you describe your relationship with Justine Blackwell?"

"Long-standing but not intimate," Hilda said. "She rented a room in my house in Saskatoon when she was in law school."

"And you've kept in touch all these years?"

"We exchanged holiday cards. When either of us visited the city in which the other lived, we had dinner together. But as I said, we were not intimate."

"Yet you drove 270 kilometres on a holiday weekend to come to her party. That's a long drive for a woman your age."

Hilda's spine stiffened with anger, but she didn't take the bait. "I came because Justine Blackwell telephoned and asked me to come," she said.

"How was Judge Blackwell's demeanour at her party?"

Hilda didn't answer immediately. Robert Hallam leaned towards her, and when he spoke his tone was condescending. "It's a simple question, Miss McCourt. Was the judge having the time of her life? Was she miserable? In a word, how did she *seem*?"

Hilda sipped her tea thoughtfully. "In a word, she seemed contumacious."

Detective Hallam's head shot up.

Hilda spelled the word slowly for him so he had time to write it in his notepad. "It means defiant," she added helpfully.

"She was defiant at a party celebrating her accomplishments?" Detective Hallam was sputtering now. "Isn't that a little peculiar?"

"It was a peculiar party," Hilda said. "For one thing, Justine Blackwell threw the party herself."

Robert Hallam cocked an eyebrow. "Wouldn't it have been more natural for the other judges to organize the tribute?"

"In the normal run of things, yes." Hilda said. "But Madame Justice Blackwell's thinking had taken a curious turn in the last year."

"Describe this 'curious turn.'"

"I can only tell you what Justice Blackwell told me herself."

"Shoot."

"Justice Blackwell had come to believe that her interpretation of the law had lacked charity."

"After thirty years, this just came upon her – a bolt from the blue?"

"No, she'd had an encounter with a prisoners' advocate named Wayne J. Waters."

Detective Hallam narrowed his eyes. "That man is lightning in a bottle. What's his connection here?"

"Justine told me he'd accosted her after a young man she'd sentenced to prison committed suicide. Mr. Waters told her that he held her personally responsible for the man's death."

"I suppose the lad was as innocent as a newborn babe."

Hilda shook her head. "No, apparently there was no doubt about his guilt. But it was a first offence and, in Mr. Waters' opinion, Justine was culpable because she had failed to take into account the effect the appalling conditions of prison would have upon a sensitive young person."

"Justice without mercy," I said.

My old friend looked at me gratefully. "Precisely. And according to Mr. Waters, that particular combination was Justine's specialty. He told her that her lack of compassion was so widely recognized that prisoners and their lawyers alike called her Madame Justice Blackheart."

"That's a little childish, isn't it?"

Hilda nodded. "Of course it is, and considering the source, the appellation didn't bother Justine. She'd been called worse. But she was woman who held herself to very rigorous standards, and she needed to prove to herself that the charge was unwarranted. She went back to her office and began rereading her old judgments. When she saw how uncompromising her rulings had been, she was shaken."

"Wayne J. had scored a bull's-eye?"

"He had indeed."

"Was Mr. Waters at the party last night?"

Hilda nodded. "Oh yes. He and Justine had an ugly confrontation."

Detective Hallam's eyes narrowed. "Describe it."

"It was at the end of the evening," Hilda said. "I'd gone to the cloakroom to pick up my wrap. By the time I got back, Justine and Mr. Waters were *in medias res.*"

"In the middle of things," Detective Hallam said.

This time it was Hilda's turn to look surprised. "Exactly. Mr. Waters was accusing Justine of failing to honour some sort of agreement. He stopped his diatribe when he saw me, so I'm not clear about the nature of the transaction. But his manner was truly frightening."

"Did Justice Blackwell seem afraid of him?"

"I don't know. The incident was over so quickly. But it was an unsettling moment in a very unsettling evening."

"Go on."

"Over the past year, Justine had made an effort to get in touch with everyone with whom she felt she had dealt unfairly. She'd sent some of them money and offered to do what she could to help them re-establish themselves. Last night was supposed to be the final reconciliation."

"Sounds like the judge got religion," Detective Hallam said.

Hilda ignored his irony. "Not religion, but there was an epiphany. Detective Hallam, in the past year, Justine's entire way of looking at the world had altered. She even looked different. She'd always been a woman of great style."

"A fashion plate," he said.

"Hardly," Hilda sniffed. "Fashion is ephemeral; style is enduring. Some of Justine's suits must have been twenty years old, but they were always beautifully cut, and her jewellery was always simple but elegant. I was quite startled when I saw her last night."

"She'd let herself go?" he asked.

"To my eyes, yes, but I don't imagine Justine saw it that way. She was wearing bluejeans that were quite badly faded and one of those oversized plaid shirts that teenagers wear. Her hair was different too. She's almost seventy years old, so for the last couple of decades I've suspected that lovely golden hair of hers was being kept bright by a beautician's hand; still, it was a shock to see her with white hair and done so casually."

"Was her hygiene less than adequate?"

Hilda shook her head impatiently. "Of course not. Justine was always fastidious – in her person and in her surroundings."

Detective Hallam's pen was flying. "Have you got the names of any of the other people at the party?"

Hilda looked thoughtful. "Well, Justine's children were there. She has three daughters, grown, of course. There was a man named Eric Fedoruk, whom Justine introduced as a friend of long standing. There were perhaps seventy-five other guests. None of the others was known to me."

"What time was it when you last saw Justine Blackwell? You can be approximate."

"I can be exact," Hilda said. "It was midnight outside the Hotel Saskatchewan. We'd had our drinks, and Madame

Justice Blackwell came outside and waited with me until a cab pulled up."

"When you left her, did she give you any indication of her plans for the rest of the evening?"

Hilda shook her head. "She said she was tired, but she thought she should go back inside to say goodnight to a few people before she went home."

"And that was it?"

"That was it."

"Is there anything you'd care to add to what you've already told me?"

For a moment, Hilda seemed lost in thought. When she finally responded, her voice was steely. "No," she said. "There is nothing I would care to add."

Detective Robert Hallam snapped his notepad shut and placed it in the inside pocket of his jacket. "Thank you for your time, Miss McCourt. You've been very helpful." He bobbed his head in my direction and headed for the door.

After he left, I turned to Hilda. "You *were* helpful," I said. "Surprisingly so, after you two got off to such a rocky start."

Hilda shuddered. "The man's an egotist," she said. "But I couldn't let my distaste for him stand in the way of the investigation of Justine's murder. This news is so cruel. It's barbarous that Justine should die not knowing . . ." She fell silent.

I reached over and touched her hand. "What didn't Justine know?"

A wave of pain crossed Hilda's face. "Whether she was in the process of losing her mind or of finding a truth that would make sense of her life," she said.

"That book on geriatric psychiatry you were reading tonight was Justine's, wasn't it?"

Hilda nodded. "She gave it to me last night. Joanne, the information I gave Detective Hallam was accurate but not complete. Out of deference to Justine's reputation, I didn't divulge the nature of our final conversation. It was a deeply distressing one. Justine said she didn't know who to trust any more. Certain people, whom she did not name, were concerned about her mental competence. She wanted me to read through the diagnostic criteria for a number of conditions and, in light of what I'd learned, tell her if I believed she was in need of psychiatric help."

"She wanted you to reach a verdict about her sanity?" I asked.

"That's exactly what she wanted. And she wanted to make certain I had the evidence I needed to reach a just verdict." Hilda slipped a hand into her pocket and withdrew a cream-coloured envelope. She took out a single piece of paper and handed it to me. The letter was dated the preceding day, handwritten in the same bold, erratic hand I'd seen in the margins of the book on geriatric psychiatry.

Dear Hilda McCourt:

As you know, I have become increasingly concerned about my mental state. I require your assistance to determine whether I am still mentally competent. Therefore, I am concurrently executing a Power of Attorney appointing you as my attorney with all necessary powers to investigate and examine my past and current affairs, including the right to access and review all financial records, personal papers, and any and all other documents that you deem relevant in order to determine my mental competency. Further, should you determine that I am not mentally competent, then I authorize you to apply to the court pursuant to the Dependant Adults Act to have me declared incapable of managing my personal affairs, and furthermore, to have you appointed as both my personal and property guardian. Incidentally, my trusted friend, I want to inform you that I have previously executed my will, appointing you as my Executrix.

The signature was Justine Blackwell's.

I felt a coldness in the pit of my stomach. "I can't think of many things more frightening than not knowing if I was losing touch with reality."

Hilda's voice was bleak. "In all the years I knew her, I never saw Justine unsure of herself until last night. When she handed me this letter, there was something in her eyes I can't describe – a kind of existential fear. From the moment I heard about her death, I haven't been able to get that image out of my mind. There's a story about Martin Heidegger."

"The philosopher," I said.

Hilda's nod was barely perceptible. "A policeman spotted him sitting alone on a park bench. He appeared so desperate that the officer went over to him and asked him who he was. Heidegger looked up at the man and said, 'I wish to God I knew.'" Hilda's eyes were bright with unshed tears. "Joanne, can you conceive of a fate crueller than dying without knowing who you are?"

I thought of Eli Kequahtooway, the child of glass. "Only one," I said. "Living without knowing who you are."

CHAPTER

2

When I awoke the next morning the sun was streaming through the window, and our golden retriever, Rose, was sitting beside the bed, looking at me accusingly. It was 7:00 a.m. Our collie, Sadie, had died in June, and Rose, in her grief and confusion at losing her lifelong companion, had become a stickler about adhering to the old routines. By this time, she and I were usually halfway round the lake. I rubbed her head. "Cut me a little slack, Rose," I said. "It was a long night, and I don't bounce back the way I used to."

Fifteen minutes later, we were on our familiar route. For the first time in weeks, Wascana Park wasn't throbbing with the drums and shouts of a team getting ready for the Dragon Boat Festival. The exuberant event had become a highlight of our city's celebration of the last weekend of summer, but now the paddlers had gone home, and the only sounds on the lake were the squawks of the geese and the shouts of the men loading the last of the big boats onto trailers.

The races had been held all day Saturday. A crew from "Canada Tonight," the TV show on which I appeared every weekend as a political panellist, had drawn a position in one of the first heats, and Alex and Eli and my kids and I had gone down to the lake to offer moral support. We found a clearing on the shore where we could see the finish line, and after the "Canada Tonight" team came in dead last, we cheered for whoever struck our fancy until we got hungry and decided to cruise the concession stands. After we'd sampled everything worth sampling, we came back to my house, dug out the old croquet set, and played until it was time to eat again, and Alex had barbecued burgers while I served up potato salad and slaw. When the sun started to fall in the sky, the five of us walked back to the lake and watched the final heats of the race.

The evening had been flawless. As the sun set, the lake glittered gold, transforming the dragon boats into sampans, those magical vessels that sailed through the China of fairy tales, a land of sandalwood, silk, and nightingales whose silence could break the heart of an emperor.

For the first time I could remember, the five of us seemed to be in a state of perfect harmony. On the way home, the boys talked about getting a team together to enter the race next year. My daughter, Taylor, who was two months shy of her seventh birthday, was adamant about being included.

Her brother winced, but Eli was gentle. "Sure we'll need you, Taylor. Somebody has to sit at the front of the boat and beat the drum. You'll have the whole winter to practise." When Taylor crowed, Eli looked at me anxiously. "That'll be okay, won't it?"

"Absolutely," I said. Then, tentatively, I'd let my hand rest on his shoulder. In all the time I'd known him, Eli had never permitted physical intimacy. When he smiled at me, I thought that, at long last, we might be home-free. Yet not even a day later, he'd run away again. It didn't make sense.

A cluster of dog-walkers had gathered along the shore. They were looking out at the lake. I joined them. A few metres out, police frogmen were diving.

"What's happening?" I asked.

A man with a black standard poodle half-turned towards me. "You heard about that murder last night?"

"Yes," I said. "I heard."

"Apparently, they're looking for the weapon."

I gazed out at the lake. It shimmered sun-dappled and inscrutable: a place for secrets.

"The woman was killed up there at the Boy Scout memorial," the man with the poodle continued, pointing towards the path that ran from the clearing where we were standing up towards the road. Between us and the road was the Boy Scout memorial. A handful of curious joggers were checking out the yellow crime-scene tape which roped off the area.

"You can take a look if you like," the man with the poodle said. "But there's not much to see."

"I think I'll give it a pass," I said. At the best of times, the monument gave me the creeps, and this was not the best of times. Both my sons had been Boy Scouts, so I knew that the memorial, a central stone circled by nine smaller stones, was a representation of the sign Scouts leave at a campsite to indicate to others that they've gone home. But these stones were as large as tombstones, and they were engraved. The chunk of marble in the middle was inscribed with the Boy Scout emblem and motto; each of the more modest stones encircling it was etched with one key word from the laws that stated what a Boy Scout should be: Obedient, Cheerful, Thrifty, Clean, Trustworthy, Helpful, Brotherly, Courteous, and Kind.

Tired of waiting, or perhaps responding to some atavistic urge the presence of death stirred in her, Rose began to whine.

I tightened the leash around my hand. "I'm way ahead of you, Rose," I said, and we headed for home.

When I came in, Alex and Taylor were sitting at the kitchen table reading the comics in the newspaper. It was a homey scene, but Alex's shoulders were slumped and his exhaustion was apparent. I said hello, and he looked up at me through eyes so deeply shadowed that I went over and put my arms around him.

Taylor looked at us happily. "This is nice," she said.

"I agree," I said. And for a while it was nice. We had breakfast, then Taylor took Alex and me out to the sunroom to look at the painting she was working on. She had started using oils that summer, and her talent, a gift from her birth mother, the artist Sally Love, was declaring itself with a sureness that filled me with awe. The picture on her easel was of Angus, Eli, and Taylor herself watching the dragonboat races, and it throbbed with the energy of the contest. Spikes of light radiated from the sun, and as the dragon boats slashed through the water, they sent up a spray as effervescent as joy.

Alex gazed at the painting thoughtfully, then he took Taylor's hand in his. "Nice work," he said.

She scrutinized his face carefully. "You *really* think it's okay?"

"Yeah," Alex said, "I *really* think it's okay."

Content, my daughter picked up her brush and began shading the underside of a cloud.

I looked at Alex. "I don't think we're needed here," I said.

He grinned. "I think you're right."

I made us a pitcher of iced tea. We took it out to the deck and sat on the steps.

Alex closed his eyes and touched his cold glass against his forehead.

"Headache?" I asked.

"It's manageable," he said.

I turned to him. "Ready to talk about Eli?"

Alex shook his head. "There's not much to say. It's as if he's decided to shut down. He doesn't talk. His face is a mask. Even the way he moves is different – as if suddenly his body doesn't belong to him. The psychiatrist who's taking Dr. Rayner's emergencies is going to see him this morning. The new guy's name is Dan Kasperski, and he specializes in adolescents. I like his approach. When I started to tell him Eli's history, he asked me to wait and tell him later. Kasperski says it's best to start with a clean slate, no pre-conceptions; that way he can put himself into the patient's situation and pick up on what Eli thinks is important."

"It sounds as if Eli's in good hands," I said.

Alex sipped his tea. "Let's hope."

"I haven't thanked you for stepping in last night," l said. "Going downtown to identify her friend would have been very painful for Hilda."

"And unnecessary," Alex said. "Justine Blackwell had three daughters. They did their duty. Apparently it was quite a scene."

"The daughters made a scene?"

"No. From what I hear, they were quite businesslike. The problem was with the pathology staff. They were tripping all over one another to gawk at Lucy Blackwell."

"It's not every day you get a chance to gawk at a legend," I said. "When I was in my twenties, I was so proud that a Canadian girl was hanging out with Dylan and Joan Baez. I think I've got all of Lucy Blackwell's old albums. It's funny, I hadn't thought about her for ages, then I heard her interviewed on the radio this summer. She's just come out with a CD boxed set. It's called *The Sorcerer's Smile*. I've asked Angus to get the word out that's what I want for my birthday."

20

Alex laughed softly. "Angus has already got the word out. I might even be able to get you an autograph. Sherm Zimbardo is the M.E. on this one, and he said that Lucy Blackwell was very co-operative."

I shuddered. "Poor woman, having to go down to the morgue and see her mother like that."

"At least she was spared the crime scene." Alex's face was sombre. "Justine Blackwell did not die easily. She was bludgeoned to death. We haven't recovered the weapon yet, but Sherm thinks she was probably killed on that big flat stone at the centre of the monument." He looked at me questioningly. "Do you know the one I mean? It's got the Boy Scout motto on it."

"I know the one," I said.

"Sherm thinks that after the first couple of blows, Justine Blackwell fell back against the centre stone. The killer finished her off there, then dragged her over and propped her up where we found her."

"You mean the killer deliberately moved her to one of those stones with the Boy Scout virtues on them?" I said.

"Is that what they are?" he asked. "We didn't have a Boy Scout troop out at Standing Buffalo."

"Too bad," I said. "You would have looked mighty fetching in those short pants."

Alex's face was pensive. "I wonder what we're supposed to make of the stone Justine Blackwell was propped up against?"

"Which one was it?" I asked.

"'Trustworthy,'" Alex said drily.

It was almost 9:30 when Alex left. I walked him to the car and watched as his silver Audi disappeared down the street. Angus was waiting for me in the front hall when I went inside.

"Has anybody heard from Eli?" he asked.

"He's back," I said. "Too bad you didn't get up earlier. Alex was here. He could have filled you in."

Angus looked away. "I was waiting till he left."

"Waiting till Alex left? Why would you do that?"

"Because I need to talk to you alone."

"Okay." I put my arm around his waist. My son had shot up over the summer. He was close to six feet now, but he was still my baby. "Let's sit down in the kitchen so we can look each other in the eye."

As a rule, Angus met problems head on, but it took him a while to zero in on this one. He went to the fridge, poured himself a glass of juice, drained it, and then filled his glass again. Finally he said, "Something happened at the football game yesterday that I should have told you and Alex about."

"Go on," I said.

"You're not going to like it." He leaned forward. "Mum, when you asked me why Eli ran off at the game, I said I didn't know."

"But you did."

He nodded. "Remember those college kids who ran out on the field just before half-time?"

"Of course," I said. "I was surprised they didn't get thrown out. They were pretty drunk."

"But everybody thought they were funny," Angus said. "Those guys sitting behind Eli and me were really cheering them on."

"They weren't exactly sober themselves," I said.

Angus traced a line through the condensation on his glass. "When Eli and I were coming back with our nachos, another man ran out on the field. The guys in the row behind us started to cheer – the way they'd done for the college kids. Then one of them said, 'It's only a fucking Indian,' and everybody stopped cheering."

"And Eli heard them."

Angus nodded. "At first, I thought he was going to cry. Then he just went ballistic. Do you know what he said, Mum? He said, 'Sometimes I'd like to kill you all.'"

I felt a sudden heaviness in my limbs. "He didn't mean it, Angus. I've blown up like that when I was mad. So have you. It's just a figure of speech."

Angus shook his head dismissively. "I know he didn't mean it. Eli wouldn't *kill* anybody. What pissed me off was the way he just lumped me in with those jerks. I was ready to go up and pound those mouthy guys into the ground, but Eli didn't give me a chance. He acted as if we were all the same."

"Well, we're not," I said. "But Eli will never know that if you bail on him now."

After Angus went upstairs to shower, I poured myself another glass of iced tea and turned on the news. There was nothing there to cheer me up. The media had discovered Justine Blackwell's murder, and judging from the play it was getting on the radio, her death was going to be the biggest story to hit our city in a long time. A breathless account of the bizarre circumstances in which the body was discovered was followed by an obituary which moved smoothly from the highlights of Justine Blackwell's legal career to a synopsis of the life and loves of her celebrated daughter, Lucy. Finally, there were excerpts from a press conference with Detective Robert Hallam in which he announced that the police were following up a number of leads and asking for the public's help.

The saturation coverage of Justine Blackwell's death didn't leave much time for the other big news story, the heat. At mid-morning the temperature in Regina was 32 degrees Celsius and climbing. The last day of the holiday weekend was going to be a sizzler, and there was no relief in sight. I turned off the radio, called Taylor, and told her that if she wanted to hit the pool for her daily swimming lesson, now was the time.

When I'd been looking for a larger place after I adopted Taylor, one of the features that had made this house affordable was its backyard swimming pool. By the mid-nineties, prudent people had filled in their energy-wasting pools, but the owners of this house hadn't been prudent, and I'd been able to snap it up at a bargain price. Angus and I had counted it a privilege to be able to swim whenever the fancy struck us, but no one took greater pleasure in the pool than Taylor. All summer, she had been working to transform her exuberant dogpaddle into a smooth Australian crawl. She was no closer to her goal when we came home from the lake than she had been on Canada Day, and that morning she splashed so much that Rose, who was getting fretful with age, thought she was drowning and jumped into the pool to save her. After Taylor and I had helped Rose out of the water and praised her for her heroism, my daughter decided we'd logged enough pool time. She pulled a lawn chair into a shady spot, plunked herself down, and announced that she needed to rest. I grabbed a chair, sat down beside her, closed my eyes, and gave myself over to the rare pleasure of a silent moment with my little girl.

It wasn't long before her flutey voice broke the stillness.

"Was my mum a good swimmer?" she asked.

"Let me think," I said. "When your mum and I were growing up, we always spent summers at the same place, so all the holidays sort of blend together, but I think when she was your age your mum swam pretty much the way you do."

"Not great," Taylor said gloomily.

"Not bad," I said. "And she got better."

Taylor slid off her chair and came over and sat on my knee. She smelled of chlorine and sunblock and heat, good summer smells. "When Eli's mum was ten years old, she swam almost the whole way across Echo Lake."

"That's impressive," I said. "Echo Lake's big."

"And she could run," Taylor said. "Eli says she could have been in the Olympics."

"When did Eli talk to you about his mum?" I asked.

"That night at the lake when we had the corn roast. He told me his mum liked to cook her corn with the skin still on, then he just kept talking about her."

I pulled my daughter closer. "Do me a favour, Taylor. Do what you can to *keep* Eli talking about his mum. He misses her, and it helps him to talk."

"Sure. I like Eli."

Taylor wriggled off my knee. The subject was closed. "I'm going in now," she said. "I've got to find some shorts and a T-shirt to wear to school tomorrow. If I wear that back-to-school outfit we bought at the mall, I'll *boil to death*."

I lay back and closed my eyes again. I didn't intend to drift off, but the heat and the broken sleep the night before caught up with me. My dreams were surreal: Lucy Blackwell was there, singing with Bob Dylan, and Karen Kequahtooway was dancing to their music. Detective Hallam was trying to focus a spotlight on them, but he kept shining it on me by mistake. The glare hurt my eyes, but every time I tried to get out of the way, the spotlight followed me. Finally, someone tried to pull me out of the light's path, and I woke up.

The sun was full in my face and Hilda McCourt was bending over me with her hand on my shoulder. She was wearing a lime-green peasant skirt and a white cotton blouse with her monogram embroidered in lime green on the breast pocket. Her face was creased with concern.

"I hate to awaken you, Joanne, but I was afraid you were getting sunburned."

"I'm glad you did," I said thickly. "What time is it?"

Hilda looked at her watch. "It's a little after twelve," she said. "Why don't I make us all some lunch while you give yourself a chance to wake up?"

I stood up. "I feel like I've been hit with the proverbial ton of bricks," I said. "I think I need a shower."

"Before you hop in," Hilda said, "there was a telephone call for you from Jess's mother. She wondered if they could take Taylor to a movie with them this afternoon. Your daughter was at my elbow, militating for a positive answer, so I said yes, conditional upon your approval, of course."

"You've got it," I said. "I don't want Taylor racing around outside in this heat."

After I'd showered, I towelled off, spritzed myself with White Linen, slipped on my coolest sundress, and revelled in feeling fresh. The pleasure was short-lived. By the time I got to the kitchen, I could feel the rivulets of sweat starting. In ten minutes, my sundress would be sticking to my back. Hilda was sitting at the kitchen table, cutting salmon sandwiches.

I leaned over her shoulder. "Those look wonderful," I said.

"Angus thought so," she said. "These are my second attempt. He ate the first plateful. Incidentally, he's going to be gone this afternoon, too."

"Did he say where he was going?"

"No, but he did he say he'd be home for dinner."

"That's a good sign."

"Is something wrong with him, Joanne? He was uncharacteristically quiet when I saw him."

"He's worried about Eli," I said. "So am I. He ran away again yesterday. You'd already gone to Justine's party when we got back from looking for him, so I didn't have a chance to tell you. He showed up at Alex's late last night."

"Is he all right?"

"I don't know."

Hilda gave me a searching look. "I gather you'd prefer that I not press you for details."

"It's not that," I said. "I just don't know very much. At the moment, all we can do is be here if he needs us." I smiled at her. "Now, it looks like you and I are on our own this afternoon. Anything special you'd like to do?"

"I'm afraid we aren't quite on our own, Joanne. While you were sleeping, I checked the message manager on my phone in Saskatoon."

I couldn't help smiling. Hilda noticed. She lifted her hand in a halt gesture. "I know I said those machines were cold and impersonal and would erode even the small amount of civility we're still clinging to, but they really are handy, aren't they? Mine certainly proved useful today. I had a message from Eric Fedoruk. Do you remember my mentioning his name to Detective Hallam?"

"I remember," I said. The name had seemed familiar to me at the time, and it nagged at me still, but I couldn't place it.

"At any rate," said Hilda, "I returned Mr. Fedoruk's call. It turns out that he was Justine's lawyer as well as her friend. We had a very curious conversation." She frowned. "I'm still not quite sure what he wanted. He kept circling around the question of my relationship with Justine. For a man trained in the law, he was quite imprecise."

"Law schools aren't exactly breeding grounds for clear expression," I said.

Hilda gave me a wry smile. "True enough," she said. "But I had the sense that Mr. Fedoruk's obfuscations were deliberate. My reading of the situation is that he was less concerned with giving information than getting it."

"You think he was on a fishing expedition?"

"Exactly," she said. "And I don't like being baited. So, to stand your metaphor on its head, I reeled Mr. Fedoruk in. He's coming here at two o'clock. I hope you don't mind, Joanne. I know it's a breach of etiquette to invite a stranger into a home in which one's a guest."

I picked up a sandwich. "Hilda, you're not a guest; you're family. Besides, you've made me curious."

Hilda handed me a napkin. "Wyclif thought 'curiouste indicated a disposition to inquire too minutely into a thing,'" she said, "but I have a premonition that it's going to be impossible to inquire too minutely into the circumstances of Justine Blackwell's death."

As soon as I opened the front door and saw Eric Fedoruk standing on the porch, I knew why his name had rung a bell. In the late seventies, Eric Fedoruk had played for the Toronto Maple Leafs. He was a prairie boy with a slapshot that could crack Plexiglas and a smile as wide and untroubled as a Saskatchewan summer sky. The man offering his hand to me was a boy no longer: his crewcut was greying and the athlete's body had thickened with middle age, but as we introduced ourselves, it was obvious Eric Fedoruk's smile hadn't lost its wattage. He was wearing black motorcycle boots and he had his helmet in his hand. Over his shoulder I could see the kind of sleek, lethal cycle that Angus lusted after. I thanked my lucky stars he wasn't home.

"I apologize for barging in on you like this," Eric Fedoruk said. "Holiday weekends should be off limits to everybody except family and friends. But Justine's death has thrown everything off balance, at least for me." His sentence trailed off, and he shook his head in disbelief.

"Come inside where it's cool," I said. "Or at least *cooler*. Isn't this heat unbelievable?"

"And getting worse, according to the last weather report I heard," he said. "Mrs. Kilbourn, could I trouble you for a glass of water? I've been out riding, and throwing a six-hundred-pound bike around in this heat really takes it out of you."

I led him into the living room where Hilda was waiting. When I came back with the water, I started to excuse myself, but Hilda motioned me to stay. "Joanne, if you have a moment, I'd like you to hear this."

Eric took the water and gulped it gratefully. "Thanks," he said. "I was just telling Miss McCourt that I've been on the phone all morning with Justine's colleagues. I think we're all just beginning to realize how completely we failed her."

I sat down beside Hilda. "In what way?" I asked.

"Isn't it obvious? Someone should have stepped in – faced the fact that Justine's mind was deteriorating and forced her to get some professional help. As people who work in the legal system, we were all aware of how dangerous that crowd she was associating with were." His gaze was level. "Mrs. Kilbourn, I know there are some ex-cons and gang members who turn their lives around but, believe me, they're in the minority. I don't know whether it's bad genes, bad breaks, or bad judgement, but many criminals simply lack the kind of control they need to keep their violence in check. Look at them sideways and they snap."

"And you think one of them snapped and killed Justine Blackwell."

"I've talked to the police. Justine was bludgeoned to death. Doesn't that sound like the murderer just went crazy? We blew it. We should have intervened. I guess we just didn't want to deal with what was happening to Justine. I know I didn't."

"Because you and she were so close," Hilda said.

A look of pain crossed Eric Fedoruk's face. "Not as close as I wanted to be. Justine didn't let anyone get too close. It's just that I can't remember a time in my life when she wasn't there. I grew up in the house next door to hers on Leopold Crescent; I articled with her old firm after I graduated from law school; I represented clients in her courtroom. She was absolutely brilliant. That's why all this is so . . ." He fell silent, fighting emotion.

In the course of her professional life as a teacher of high-school English, Hilda had dealt with more than her share of the agitated and the overwrought. When she spoke, her voice was as crisp as her monogrammed blouse. "Mr. Fedoruk, I understand that you've sustained a loss, but you don't strike me as the kind of man who would come to a stranger's home to vent his grief. What is it that you want from me?"

He flinched. "All right," he said. "Here it is. Miss McCourt, last night at the party, Justine told me she was going to ask for your help with a certain matter. Did she have time to talk to you about it?"

"You'll have to be more explicit," Hilda said. "Justine and I spoke about many matters last night."

Eric Fedoruk hesitated. I could see him calculating the odds that, in divulging information to Hilda, he might lose his advantage. Once he'd made his decision, he waded right in. "What Justine said was that, as her lawyer, I should be aware that she was about to ask you to assess her capacity to handle her personal affairs. *Did* she ask you to make that assessment?"

This time it was Hilda's turn to deliberate before answering. When she finally responded, her voice was firm. "Yes," she said. "Justine did ask me to intervene in her life.

She gave me a medical text on geriatric psychiatry and a handwritten letter authorizing me to evaluate her mental competence."

"May I see the letter?"

"In due time," Hilda said. "Now, I have a question for you, Mr. Fedoruk. What's your interest in this?"

"I'm Justine's lawyer. I need to know . . ." He was faltering, and he knew it. He took a deep breath and began again. "My interest is a friend's interest," he said. "In the past year, Justine Blackwell was not the woman she'd always been. Miss McCourt, you remember what she used to be like. She was so . . ." He shrugged, searching for the right word. Finally, he found it. "She was so *elegant* in everything she did: the way she wrote judgments; the way she dressed; the way she arranged her office; even the way she smoked a cigarette was stylish – the way actresses in those old black-and-white movies used to smoke." He smiled at something he saw in my face. "Oh yes, Mrs. Kilbourn, until last year Justine was a two-pack-a-day smoker. Quitting smoking was another of her changes."

"A positive one," Hilda said drily.

"Maybe," he said. "But if it was, it was the only one. Of course, Justine saw quitting smoking as just one of many positive changes she made in her life after she met Wayne J. Waters. Did she talk to you about him?"

Hilda nodded.

"Then you know what an impact he had on her. It was insane. Justine had always had a built-in radar for bullshitters, but Wayne J. seemed to slide in under the beam. She told me that meeting him was her 'moment of revelation.' I tried to make her see how nuts that was. 'Like Paul on the road to Damascus,' I said. I was sure she'd laugh. Justine didn't have much use for religion."

"But she didn't laugh," I said.

He sighed. "No," he said. "She was very earnest. She said, 'If you consider the moment on the road to Damascus a metaphor for a life-altering experience, then your comparison couldn't be more apt.'"

To this point, Hilda had been silent, taking it all in. When she spoke, I could hear the edge in her voice. "So Justine *was* aware that her life had altered radically. She didn't just slide into this new pattern of behaviour."

"Oh no," he said. "She was fully aware that things were different."

"Then your assessment that Justine wasn't in complete possession of her faculties hinges solely on the fact that you found the choices she was making repellent."

Eric Fedoruk grinned sheepishly. "You would have made a dynamite lawyer, Miss McCourt." He got to his feet. "Now, I really have taken up enough of your time. I'm sorry to have cast a shadow over the last long weekend of summer, but I needed to know how things stood."

He started for the door, but Hilda laid her hand on his arm, restraining him. "I wonder if you could leave me your business card, Mr. Fedoruk."

He pulled his wallet out of his back pocket, took out a card and a pen. "I'll jot down my home phone number too. I'm not always the easiest guy in the world to get hold of." He scrawled his number on the card and handed it to Hilda.

She looked at it thoughtfully. "You'll be hearing from me," she said. "Last night, Justine Blackwell asked a favour of me. Her death doesn't nullify that request. She wanted me to look after her interests, and that's exactly what I intend to do."

Eric Fedoruk furrowed his brow. "We *are* on the same side in this matter. I hope you understand that."

"Allegiances are earned, not assumed," Hilda said. "I hope *you* understand that." She smiled her dismissal. "Thank you for coming by. Your visit was most instructive."

When the door closed behind Eric Fedoruk, I turned to Hilda. "Were you throwing down the gauntlet?" I asked.

She shook her head. "Just alerting Mr. Fedoruk to the fact that I'm a woman who takes her responsibilities seriously." She squared her shoulders. "If your afternoon's clear, Joanne, would you be willing to join me in paying a condolence call? I telephoned Justine's daughters while you were napping. They're expecting me at two-thirty. It would be good to have a companion with me whose judgement I trust."

CHAPTER

3

Half an hour later, we were on our way. Hilda had replaced her peasant skirt with a seersucker dress the colour of a ripe apricot and covered her fiery red hair with a summer hat, a straw boater with a striped band that matched her outfit. I was wearing a white linen shirt and slacks. When I came downstairs, Hilda nodded her approval. "Very nice. Thank heavens we've jettisoned that hoary rule about summer's colours being appropriate only during the weeks between May 24 and Labour Day." She picked up her clutch bag from the cedar chest in the hall. "Now, it's already two-fifteen, so I suppose we'd better step lively."

From my kitchen window I could see the creek that separated my neighbourhood, Old Lakeview, from Justine Blackwell's, an area of handsomely curved, pleasingly land-scaped streets known, accurately if unimaginatively, as The Crescents. Justine Blackwell's home was almost at the end of Leopold Crescent. I had walked by her place a hundred times, and I'd never ceased to admire it. It was a heritage house and unique: cobalt-blue Spanish-tile roof, white stucco walls artfully studded with decorative tiles, and windows of styles so varied and delightful that I'd once taken a book on turn-of-the century architecture out of the public library just to look them up. Their names had been as evocative as the windows themselves: Oriel, Lancet, Mullioned, Œil-de-bœuf, Catherine wheel.

The front door of 717 Leopold Crescent was oak, framed at the top by a graceful semicircular window that my reading had taught me was known as fanlight. The effect was, as Eric Fedoruk would have said, elegant.

From the moment Hilda suggested paying a condolence call on Justine's family, I had felt an adolescent thrill at the prospect of meeting Lucy Blackwell face to face. Her name summoned forth a kaleidoscope of images that were part of the cultural history of every woman my age. In the youthquake of the late sixties, Lucy had been a Mary Quant girl in thigh-high clear plastic boots and leather mini, her eyes doe-like behind the kohl eyeliner and fake eyelashes, her hair ironed into smooth sheets the colour of pulled taffy.

She had been a ripe sixteen when she recorded the first song that brought her recognition. The song was called "Lilacs," and she had written it herself. Its subject, the painful process of losing a first love to a heartless rival, was an adolescent cliché, but Lucy's treatment of the angst-ridden convention rocked between low farce and elegy, and her voice was a husky sensation.

In the seventies, shod in sandals hand-tooled in Berkeley by people who'd got their priorities straight and wearing granny gowns of hand-dyed batik, Lucy had woven flowers in her hair and sung songs of misplaced faith and love gone wrong that became anthems for a generation of middle-class kids raised in the warm sunshine of Dr. Spock but yearning for the storm of sexual adventure. We mined the lyrics of each new song for autobiographical details. Was that "singin' man" who left her on the beach, "cryin' and dyin' as the tide washed in," James Taylor or Dylan? When she sang of "that small white room where I left behind a gift I could never retrieve," was she remembering the abortion clinic in which, it was whispered, she had gone to have Mick Jagger's baby cut away? It was heady stuff.

When the decade ended, she settled down somewhere on Saltspring Island with a man none of us had ever heard of and announced she was going to raise a family and write an opera for children. For a time she disappeared, and it seemed Lucy Blackwell was destined to become a candidate for a trivia-quiz answer. Then, in the early eighties, she surfaced again. She was alone and empty-handed: no man, no babies, no opera, but there was savage light in her eyes and a new and feral quality in her voice. Within a year, she'd written the score for a movie and the music for an off-Broadway show; both were hits. She was back, and with her beautiful hair permed into an explosion of Botticelli curls, her body hard-muscled from feel-the-burn exercise, and her voice knife-edged with danger, she was the very model of the eighties woman.

For three decades, Lucy Blackwell had been the first to catch the wave, but the woman who stood before me that Labour Day afternoon seemed to have left trendiness behind. She was barefoot, wearing bluejean cut-offs and a man's white shirt, with the sleeves rolled up to reveal a dynamite tan. Her eyes were extraordinary, so startlingly green-blue that they were almost turquoise, and her shoulder-length hair shone with the lustre of dark honey. Lucy was a Saskatchewan-born forty-five-year-old, but she had the long-limbed agelessness of the prototypical all-American girl.

"Thank you for coming," she said, extending her hand. She was holding an old-fashioned scrub brush, and when she noticed it, she laughed with embarrassment and lifted it in the air. "Trying to fix what can't be fixed," she said distractedly. "I'm Lucy Blackwell. Won't you come in?"

Hilda and I followed her through the entranceway and down the hall. The parquet floors along which we walked were scuffed and sticky underfoot, and the air was heavy with the rotting-fruit smell of forgotten garbage. "I hope you don't mind if we visit in the dining room," Lucy said. "My mother had some curious guests in the last year. The dining room's the only room in the house that doesn't look as if 2 Live Crew has been playing a concert in it."

The room was a damaged beauty. A wall broken by lancet windows looked out onto the yard. The shell-pink silk curtains that bracketed the view were coolly ethereal, but they were stained at child level. A rose Berber carpet that must have cost a king's ransom was discoloured by the kind of patches that are left by dog urine. Lucy motioned us to sit down at the mahogany dining table. The creamy needlepoint on the backs and seats of the chairs was soiled, but the wood gleamed and there was a scent of lemon oil in the air. A bucket of soapy water rested on a stool near the sideboard.

"I've been scouring away in here all day," Lucy said. "But no matter what I try, nothing seems to help." She pointed with her brush. "Look at them," she said, indicating walls covered in silk of a pink so delicate the colour seemed almost illusory. Figures were woven into the fabric: Rubenesque women, epicurean and lush. The wall-covering must have been a treasure once, but someone had desecrated the women's bodies. Crude breasts and genitalia were drawn in marker over the delicate lines in the fabric. Lucy had obviously been scrubbing at them; the places where she had worked were marked by ugly spoors of damp colour.

"When we were young, my mother wouldn't allow us to eat in this room. It was for adults only," she said. There was an intimate teasing quality in Lucy's voice that seemed to draw us into her orbit. "But if my parents had a dinner party," she continued, "my father would call us down to meet the guests. It was so exciting. Of course, my sisters and I would be all shined up for bed. I can still remember how soft the rug felt under my bare feet when we trooped in to be introduced. It was always so shadowy and scary in the hall, but the candles in here would be blazing."

"'Three little girls in virgin's white, swimming through darkness, longing for light,'" I said.

Lucy shot me a radiant smile. "You remembered."

"'My Daddy's Party' is a pretty memorable song," I said.

"Thanks. That means a lot. Especially now." She looked around the room, and when she spoke again, her voice quivered with rage and hurt. "I haven't been in this room in years. Somehow, I'd hoped on this visit . . ." She swallowed hard. "Too late now. We'll never get things back the way they were. Metaphors aren't much fun in real life."

"Perhaps you should get professionals in to do this work," Hilda said gently. "As you're discovering, a home is a powerful symbol for those who live within it."

Lucy ran her fingers through her hair. "I guess that's why my sister Signe thinks trying to put things right in these rooms is good therapy for me. My other sister says it's a way of making up for my sins of omission."

"What do you think?" I asked.

"It doesn't matter what I think. The prodigal daughter doesn't get a vote." She laughed sadly. "I'm forgetting my manners. Can I get you a drink? The Waterford crystal my father bought my mother on their honeymoon is pretty much a write-off, but there must be a jam-jar or two around."

"We're fine," Hilda said. "Mrs. Kilbourn and I aren't planning to stay, but, Lucy, there is something I'd like to talk to you and your sisters about. Will they be able to join us?"

"Signe will. Tina isn't seeing people right now."

Lucy left to get her sister, and I walked over and looked out at the scene framed by the window. Zinnias, asters, and marigolds, prides of the late summer garden, shimmered in the gold September haze. A boy pushing a power-mower made lazy passes across the lawn. Heat hung in the air. Hilda came and stood beside me. The scene was idyllic, but I could feel my friend's fury.

"Why would anyone set that poor woman the Sisyphean task of cleaning up this disaster and tell her it was her way of making up for what she did or failed to do?" she asked.

"She does seem to be near the breaking point," I said.

"My sister doesn't break."

The voice, as huskily melodic as Lucy's, came from behind us. I turned, expecting to greet a stranger, but I knew the woman standing in the entrance to the dining room. Eli Kequahtooway had introduced us. She was his therapist.

"Hello, Dr. Rayner," I said.

She gazed at me, perplexed. "You'll have to forgive me," she said, "I don't remember . . ."

"There's no reason to," I said. "We only met once – at the Cornwall Centre. I'm Joanne Kilbourn, a friend of Eli Kequahtooway's."

"Of course," she said. "I remember thinking Eli must be fond of you to bring you over to me."

"I hope he is," I said. "I'm certainly fond of him. Dr. Rayner, this is my friend Hilda McCourt."

She took Hilda's hand. "It's Signe – please. My mother spoke of you often, Miss McCourt, and always with great respect."

"I'm flattered," Hilda said evenly. "Your mother was an extraordinary woman."

Signe Rayner gave Hilda an odd little smile. "There's no disputing that," she said drily. She gestured towards the dining-room table. "Shall we continue this conversation sitting down?"

Her offer seemed to be as much for her benefit as ours. She was a large woman, as tall as Lucy but much heavier, so heavy, in fact, that standing for any length of time must have been uncomfortable for her. She was wearing an ivory-and-black African-print gown which had affinities to both the muumuu and the caftan without being either. She had been wearing the garment's twin, in shades of coffee and taupe, the day Eli introduced her to me in the mall. Signe Rayner had impressed me then as a woman of self-confident authority, but it appeared her ability to dominate situations didn't extend to her family.

Lucy Blackwell came back into the room just as her sister pulled out a chair at the head of the table. As Signe settled in, Lucy's smile was wicked. "You'll notice how Signe chooses the seat of command. She's a psychiatrist, so watch your step."

Hilda's eyes widened. "A psychiatrist," she said, settling into the chair to Signe's right. "Your mother presented me with a book last night: a review of geriatric psychiatry. It was a medical text. Did you give it to her?"

Signe Rayner met Hilda's gaze. "I did. At her request."

"When did she ask you for it?"

Signe rubbed at a whorl in the mahogany table with her fingertip. "At the beginning of August. We have a family cottage up at Little Bear Lake. We take turns using it, but we always reserve the first weekend in August to be together – just the four of us. I'd been concerned about my mother's behaviour for months. I'd suggested she see a colleague of mine who specializes in geriatric patients, but my mother refused." Signe's brow furrowed. "She was quite vehement. She insisted that a change in the way one chose to live one's life was not necessarily an indicator of a progressive dementing disorder."

Hilda leaned forward with interest. "Did she use that term?"

"Oh yes," Signe said. "When it came to areas that touched her life, my mother believed in acquiring expert knowledge."

"Oedipus had great knowledge too," Hilda said gently. "He was even able to solve the riddle of the Sphinx, yet he never truly knew himself. That was the source of his tragedy."

Lucy twisted a hank of her hair around her finger. "Do you think my mother didn't know herself?"

Hilda smiled enigmatically, then she turned to Signe Rayner. "Perhaps you have an opinion?"

Signe shrugged. "I was trying to formulate one up at the lake. There are a number of standard tests that are used to determine mental status."

"And Justine agreed to be tested?" Hilda asked.

Signe Rayner looked rueful. "She wasn't supposed to notice. I was trying to be unobtrusive."

"Blending into the wallpaper isn't exactly your strong suit, Signe." Lucy Blackwell pushed back her chair and drew up one of her legs so that its heel rested on her other leg. Her legs were beautiful, long and shapely. The pose seemed deliberatively provocative. She was, I realized, one of those people whose every encounter is surrounded by an erotic haze. She gazed at her sister with interest. "To be fair, the time for subtlety did seem to be over. I hadn't seen Mummy since the summer before, but her life really had become quite bizarre."

"That's why Tina and I had been calling you for almost a year asking you to come back," Signe said.

"I had obligations."

"We hoped your obligation to your family might take priority."

"Families," Lucy said. She shot me a conspiratorial glance; then, in a voice that was thrillingly familiar, she sang, "'*You can slam the door and walk away, but you're still trapped in their photo albums.*'" She looked at me expectantly.

"'Picture Time,'" I said. "From the first album."

Signe glared at me. "Don't encourage her," she said sternly. She turned to Hilda. "Miss McCourt, you said Mother gave you my handbook on geriatric psychiatry. Did she explain why she wanted you to have it?"

"Justine wanted me to decide whether her mental faculties were intact."

"Isn't the fact that she dragged you into this proof that her mental faculties *weren't* intact?" Lucy's frustration was evident. "I mean no disrespect, Miss McCourt, but from what Signe tells me, you weren't that close to my mother. She had friends and family here. Doesn't it strike you as bizarre that she felt she couldn't go to the people who knew her best?"

"Not at all," Hilda said flatly. "It strikes me as eminently sensible. Your mother knew me as a person of probity who had no axe to grind. Now, let's deal with the situation at hand. When Eric Fedoruk came to see me this afternoon, we talked about the task your mother set me."

"*Eric* came to see you?" Lucy leaped to her feet. She seemed close to tears. "He hasn't even returned our calls."

Signe Rayner half-rose from her chair. "Lucy, don't."

"Why not? What did he tell you about us, Miss McCourt?"

"That's enough, Lucy." Signe's voice was commanding. "We can talk about this later."

Lucy walked over to Hilda. "Miss McCourt, don't believe everything you hear."

At close to five-foot-eleven, Lucy was almost a foot taller than my old friend, but Hilda took charge of the situation. "I've learned to make my own assessments of people, Lucy. Now, while I'm truly sorry for your loss, my purpose in coming here this afternoon is not simply to commiserate. Last night, when your mother gave me Signe's book, she also gave me a note authorizing me to do what I deemed necessary to protect her interests." Hilda turned to Signe. "I came here today to let all of you know that's exactly what I plan to do."

Lucy and Signe exchanged glances, then Signe thanked us, quite formally, for coming, and she and Lucy saw us out.

Silenced by the misery we had felt in Justine Blackwell's home, Hilda and I walked down the front path. Out of nowhere, another image from "Picture Time" flashed through my mind. "*Our last smiles frozen in Kodachrome.*" As we turned onto the sidewalk, I found myself thinking that there wasn't much about painful leave-takings that Lucy Blackwell didn't understand.

Hilda's musings had obviously been running parallel to mine. "Two very unhappy women," she said. "And I don't believe the genesis of their problems was their mother's death."

"No," I agreed. "Whatever's troubling the Blackwell sisters goes way back."

Hilda touched my arm. "And there's more trouble coming to them," she said. "Look over there."

A van painted in the style of comic-book high realism that Taylor's art teacher called jailhouse art had pulled up across the road. The vehicle was, by anyone's reckoning, a mean machine, and as its driver bounded out and started towards us, there was no denying that he was one tough customer. He was of middle height, with a shaved head, a full moustache, and the powerful physique of a bodybuilder.

As he brushed past us, I saw that the parts of his skin not hidden by his Levi's and white V-necked T-shirt were purpley-blue with tattoos. He vaulted up the front steps of the Blackwell house and knocked on the door.

"Another condolence call," I said.

"I wonder what the Blackwell sisters will make of this one?" Hilda said. She turned to me. "I assume you can guess at that man's identity, Joanne."

"Wayne J. Waters?"

"In the flesh," Hilda said.

Patient as a choirboy, Wayne J. waited for someone to respond to his knock on the door. When it was apparent that no answer was forthcoming, he pounded his closed fist into the open palm of his other hand and headed back down the walk.

As his van screeched back towards Albert Street, the words painted in red on the back of the vehicle leaped out at me: "Every Saint Has a Past. Every Sinner Has a Future." It seemed Lucy Blackwell hadn't cornered the market on folk wisdom.

That night, after Taylor's school clothes were laid out for the next day her backpack filled with her new school supplies, and she'd been bathed and tucked into bed with her cats, Bruce and Benny, and Hilda had been rung in to tell the next adventure in the ongoing saga of Sir Gawain and the Green Knight, I drove over to Alex's apartment on Lorne Street, and we made love.

When I was twenty, I had believed that the pleasures of sex were aesthetic and athletic. Then, the prospect of being physically intimate with a man when I was past fifty and my body was no longer a delight to look at or a joy to manoeuvre had filled me with alarm. I'd been wrong to worry. With Alex, I was enjoying the best sex of my life: by turns passionate, tender, funny, restoring, and transcendent. That September night, we managed four out of five. When we'd finished, our bodies were slick on the tangled sheets, and we were at peace.

It was good to be back in the apartment. Since his nephew had come to live with him, Alex and I hadn't spent much time there, but tonight we were alone. Declaring that Eli was in need of chill-out time, Dr. Kasperski had decided to keep him in the hospital overnight. As I looked at the lines of worry etched in Alex's face, I thought the man I loved could use a little chill-out time himself. The events of the past twenty-four hours had taken their toll. Through the open window of the bedroom, I could see the plaster owl a previous tenant had anchored on the rail of the balcony to scare off pigeons. Alex called the bird his sentinel, and we had joked that as long as the bird was there, no intruder could disturb our delight in one another. As I felt the tension returning to Alex's body, I knew I had to face the fact that even plaster owls had their limits.

I moved closer to him. "Talk to me about it," I said.

"There's not much to say. I had a quick visit with Dan Kasperski after he saw Eli this afternoon. Considering Eli's his patient only until Dr. Rayner gets back to her practice, Kasperski's giving a lot of thought to the case. He says his first task is to get Eli to see him as an ally who can help him find a way to deal with all the things that are troubling him."

"That makes sense to me," I said.

Alex's dark eyes were serious. "Everything Dan Kasperski says makes sense. The amazing thing is he looks like he's about seventeen years old. Maybe that's why Eli's responding so well to him. This afternoon, when Kasperski came in, I could see the relief on Eli's face."

"Maybe you should ask him to take Eli on as a patient. In

the next few weeks, Signe Rayner could have her hands full just dealing with her own life."

"What do you mean?"

"Did you know she's Justine Blackwell's daughter?"

"You're kidding."

"No. Hilda and I went over to Justine's house today to pay a condolence call, and Signe Rayner was there. Alex, how does Eli get along with her? She seems so . . ."

"Forbidding? I know what you mean, but she came highly recommended, and she did get Eli to open up about the guilt he feels about Karen's death."

"Guilt? You never said anything about him feeling guilty."

"It was Eli's story to tell or not tell. Besides, he seemed to be dealing with it."

"Why would he feel guilty? Nobody can prevent a car accident, and from what you've said, Eli really loved Karen."

"He did love her, but he also caused her a lot of grief. I never could figure out why. Karen was about the best mother any kid could ask for: very devoted, very involved with the culture. But as great as Karen was, when Eli was about ten the graffiti started, and the running away to the city."

"Did something happen?"

"No. Eli just got mad at the world. I went through the same thing when I was his age."

"You straightened out," I said. "Can't get much straighter than a cop."

Alex drew me closer. "I was lucky," he said. "My mother didn't die when I was sixteen. By the time my mother died, I'd had time to show her I valued the things she'd taught me."

"But Eli never had that chance," I said.

"No," Alex said, "he didn't. And it's eating him up. Has he ever said anything to you about Karen?"

"Never," I said. "But he did talk to Taylor about her."

"To Taylor? She's the last person I'd have thought he'd open up to."

"There's a certain logic there, I guess. Taylor lost her mother too, and of course she's so young, Eli doesn't have to worry about being a tough guy in front of her. Just this morning, Taylor was telling me that she and Eli had talked about what a great swimmer Karen was."

In the moonlight, Alex's face grew soft. "She *was* a great swimmer. We used to tell her she was part otter. She loved that lake. We had this old canoe. When Karen was four, she went clear across the lake in it. She was so little, she could barely hold the paddle." His voice broke. "And could she ever run. Some of those hills we've got out at Standing Buffalo are steep, but that never stopped Karen. It seemed like every time my brother and I were supposed to be watching out for her, she'd take off on us. We always knew where to look for her – right at the top of the biggest hill she could find. As soon as she saw Perry and me, she'd start to run to us. We'd yell at her to slow down because we were afraid she'd break her neck, and then we'd catch hell. But she never slowed down. And she never fell."

For a long time, we were silent. Finally, Alex said, "The only thing that ever scared my sister was thinking about what could happen to Eli. When she died, I promised myself that I'd do everything I could to make sure he had a good life. Damn it, Jo, until yesterday, I thought Eli was going to be okay. What would make a kid take off like that, for no reason?"

I sat up. "He had a reason," I said.

As I told Alex about the incident at the Rider game, I could see the cords in his neck tighten, but he didn't say anything until I'd finished. Then, under his breath, he murmured a word I'd never heard him use before, and I could feel the barrier come between us. I went into the bathroom to get ready to go home. After I'd dressed, I looked out the bathroom window. On the balcony of the apartment across the alley, a man and a woman, who looked to be about my age, were having a late supper. There were candles on the table and fresh flowers. As I watched, the man leaned towards the woman and touched her cheek. When she felt his touch, the woman covered his hand with her own. That unknown couple might have had a hundred secret sorrows but, at that moment, I envied them their uncomplicated joy in one another. Moonlight and unspoken intimacies: that was the way love was supposed to be.

Alex walked me down to my car. I slid into the driver's seat. "Tell Eli the kids and I will come by and visit him tomorrow after school," I said.

"Considering the circumstances, maybe you'd better wait a while," Alex said.

"Whenever you think he's ready," I said.

I waited as Alex opened the front door of his building and walked inside. He didn't look back. His apartment was on the third floor at the corner. I knew exactly how long it took to reach it. I watched as the lights went out in his living room, and a few seconds later in his bedroom. Miserable at the thought of Alex sitting alone in the dark, his only protection against the vagaries of the world a plaster owl sitting sentry on a balcony railing, I took a deep breath and turned the key in the ignition.

CHAPTER

4

I slept deeply that night and awoke thinking about Alex Kequahtooway and Martin Heidegger and the question of whether any of us ever truly knows who we are. It was gloomy pondering for 5:00 a.m. on the first workday after a holiday weekend, and I was relieved when the phone rang and I heard my older daughter's voice. Mieka was twenty-four years old, and she had a great marriage, a career she loved, and a first child due any minute. To my mind, the only problem about Mieka's life was that it was being lived in Saskatoon, 250 kilometres away from me.

"I knew you'd be up," she said. "No baby news. I'm just calling to whine."

"Whine away," I said.

She took a deep breath. "Well, for starters, I don't think this baby is ever going to be born. My doctor says if I don't get cracking by next weekend, they're going to induce me. Is it just an old wives' tale that painting the kitchen ceiling gets baby moving along?"

"I don't know about kitchen ceilings," I said, "but I do

know that going out for Chinese food works. That's what your dad and I did the night before you were born."

Mieka laughed. "Tucking into a platter of Peking duck does sound more appealing than clambering up a ladder to slap on a coat of flat white." She sighed heavily. "Mummy, I'm so discouraged. I haven't slept through the night in eight months, I haven't seen my feet since Canada Day, and I've got a seductive line of black hair growing from my breast-bone to what used to be my organs of delight."

"It'll be over soon," I said. "I just wish I was there with you."

"But you will come when the baby's born?"

"Wild horses couldn't keep me away."

After we hung up, I reached under the bed and pulled out the cradle board that Alex had made for Mieka and Greg's baby. The hide bag stitched to the board was as soft as moss, and it smelled of woodsmoke. A newborn would feel safe in its snug confines. Later, the cradle board would hold the baby tight against its parent as it learned to keep a careful eye on the wonders and the terrors of the world.

I slid the cradle board back under the bed and walked downstairs. The heat and the humidity in the closed-up house were almost palpable, and I opened the front door to let in some fresh air. On the cedar chest in the front hall, Taylor's new tartan backpack bulged, waiting to be grabbed by its owner as she sped out the door, eager to seize all the learning and fun Grade 2 had to offer. Ordinarily, I loved fall days with their heady mix of elegy for the summer past and anticipation of adventures to come, but this September was different, and as Rose and I headed for our run around the lake, I wondered if the heat would ever stop pressing down on us, making our nerves jump and our spirits sink.

By the time we got back, my hair was curling damply, and

my clothes were soaked with sweat. I grabbed the newspaper off the porch and went inside to get Rose a bowl of fresh water and to plug in the coffee maker. As I waited for the coffee to perk, I glanced at the front page. The story of Justine Blackwell's murder was above the fold. The picture the editors had chosen was a formal one of Justine robed for court. With her fair hair swept back into a smooth chignon and her coolly intelligent gaze, she seemed an unlikely candidate for grisly murder.

The story accompanying the photograph was circumspect and predictable: a dry but factual account of the murder, a review of Justine's legal career, a brief history of her personal life. No surprises, but the final sentence of the piece *was* unexpected: "Longtime friend Hilda McCourt announced that funeral plans for Madame Justice Blackwell were pending."

When Hilda came in, I held the paper out to her. It was 6:45, but she was already dressed for the day in a trim mint sheath, with a mandarin collar and neck-to-knee mother-of-pearl frog fastenings.

"You're famous," I said.

She took the paper, glimpsed at the story, and frowned. "I was afraid my name would be mentioned."

"How did the paper get hold of you?"

"Lucy Blackwell gave them my name and your number," Hilda said. "Joanne, I apologize for yet another intrusion in your home. This is becoming a distressing pattern."

"Don't give it a second thought," I said. "But I don't understand why Lucy would decide that you should be the one dealing with the press."

Hilda sighed. "Neither do I. But according to Lucy, I was the unanimous choice. Apparently, Tina Blackwell is having a difficult time accepting her mother's death. Her sisters think she's in no state for media scrutiny. They've concluded that since Justine asked me to protect her interests, I might as well act as an intermediary with the press."

I felt a rush of annoyance. Hilda was a wonder, but she was an eighty-three-year-old wonder, and she had just been handed an open-ended duty.

As always, Hilda was quick to read my face. "You're not convinced I'm the best choice."

I shook my head. "As far as I'm concerned, you're the best choice for any job you choose to undertake. I'm just not certain you should have been asked to undertake this one."

"It's been busy, I'll grant you that. Just after you left to meet Alex last night, I had a call from the journalist who is responsible for this." Hilda tapped the Blackwell story with a fingernail freshly painted in her favourite Love That Red. "Later, there were other members of the press. I'm afraid your house was photographed, Joanne."

I felt a stab of irritation, not at Hilda, but at the intrusion. "Don't worry about it," I said, but my voice lacked conviction.

Hilda leaned towards me. "Maybe it would be easier all around if I went back to Saskatoon. With facsimile machines and my message manager, I could handle everything from there, and you'd be spared the prospect of living in a circus."

"Don't be silly," I said. "In a day or two, there'll be another story for the media to chase. Besides I love having you here. You know that."

Taylor's ginger cat, Benny, padded into the room. As usual, her tortoiseshell, Bruce, followed meekly. My daughter wasn't far behind.

"I like it when you're here, too," Taylor said. She bent, grabbed Benny, hefted him under one arm, and scooped up Bruce. Then she twirled so Hilda could check out the back of her head. "Are my braids okay?" she asked.

Her braids were, in fact, okay. So was her face, which was clean, and her runners, which matched and were tied. What wasn't okay was the T-shirt she was wearing, which had a picture of a bull on it that bordered on the obscene, and an eyebrow-raising caption: "Bottlescrew Bill's Second Annual Testicle Festival – I Went Nuts."

I knelt down beside her. "T, you look great, but you're going to have to find another shirt."

"But this one's so funny. You laughed when Angus brought it home from the garage sale, and everybody at the cottage thought it was good."

"It was good for the cottage," I said, "but not for school."

"Why?"

"Because wearing that shirt to school would be like wearing tap shoes to church."

"Dumb," she said.

"Not dumb," I said. "Just not your best choice. Now come on, let's go upstairs and find a shirt that isn't going to get you thrown out of Grade 2 before the end of the day."

Taylor went off to school wearing a white cotton blouse and the intricately beaded barrettes Alex had bought the day we went to a powwow out at Standing Buffalo. They were reserved for special occasions, but she and I agreed this occasion was special enough. After she left, Bruce looked so miserable I gathered him up and began scratching his head. Benny came over, rubbed against my ankle and howled. Benny and I had never been close, but it was a day to put aside old enmities. I bent down to pick him up too. "She'll be back," I said. Benny shot me a look filled with contempt and streaked off; then Bruce, who was sweet but easily led, leaped out of my arms and dashed after him.

When I finally got around to showering and dressing, I was running late. I knew that if I didn't make tracks, I wouldn't be on time for the early-morning meeting the Political

Science department always held at the Faculty Club on the first day of classes. I decided to skip breakfast, grabbed my briefcase, hollered at Angus to get moving, called goodbye to Hilda, and raced out the front door and straight into the wall of muscles that was Wayne J. Waters.

At close range, he was even more intimidating than he had appeared at a distance. He was not a tall man; in fact, he wasn't much taller than I was, five-foot-six. But he was tattooed to terrify. On his arms, jungle beasts coupled ferociously; savage mastiffs chewed on hearts that dripped blood; buxom women straddled unidentifiable animals and embraced crucifixes. It was the Garden of Earthly Delights envisioned by a lifer. I couldn't stop staring, and Wayne J. Waters caught me.

"Better than an art gallery, eh?" His voice was deep and surprisingly pleasant. "Are you Hilda McCourt? That reporter who came to interview me did the usual half-assed job those media types always do – told me where to find Hilda but didn't give me a whiff about how to recognize her."

"I'm not Miss McCourt," I said. "But she is staying with me. I'm Joanne Kilbourn. Can I help you?"

"We'll give you a try. My name's Wayne J. Waters," he said. "I wanted to talk to Hilda about the funeral she's got pending." He shook his head and laughed. "The way we word things, eh?" he said. "Anyway, you get the drift." He stepped closer. His aftershave was familiar and distinctive. Old Spice. "So is Hilda around?"

My first thought was to lie, to simply say that Hilda had left town. In his sleeveless muscle shirt, Wayne J.'s upper arms were grenades, and Hilda's account of his nasty confrontation with Justine the night of the party leapt to my mind. But my friend was not a person who took kindly to having decisions made for her; besides, the rumble of Wayne J.'s laugh was reassuring, and there was something in his eyes which, against all logic, inspired trust. It was a tough call. Luckily, while I was vacillating, Hilda appeared and made the call for me.

As soon as he saw her, Wayne J. introduced himself and held out his hand. Hilda's response was icy. "Mr. Waters, when I've satisfied myself that you had nothing to do with Justine Blackwell's death, I'll take your hand. Until then . . ."

Hilda's blue eyes were boring into him, but Wayne J. Waters didn't flinch. "Fair enough," he said. "Do you want to talk out here, or can I come inside?"

Hilda shot me a questioning look.

"It'll be easier to talk where it's cool," I said.

As we walked back inside, Wayne J. glanced at the briefcase in my hand. "Decided to play hooky, Joanne?"

I shook my head. "Decided not to leave until you do, Wayne J."

He put his head back and roared. "Who could blame you?"

Wayne J. Waters might have had his troubles with the law, but somewhere along the line he had come up with some personal rules about how to treat a lady. He waited until Hilda and I were seated before he lowered himself into my grandmother's Morris chair. Once seated, he got right to the point.

"To set your mind at ease," he said, "I had nothing to do with Justine's death. If I have to give you specifics I will, but for now, I hope it's enough to say that she was the classiest woman I ever knew, and she was a good friend to me and to a lot of other people I could name."

Hilda adjusted the mother-of-pearl button fastening at the throat of her dress. "Yet you quarrelled with her bitterly the night of her party."

Wayne J. Waters put the palms of his hands on his knees and leaned forward. "Didn't you ever fight with a friend?" he asked softly.

Hilda wasn't drawn in. "Not one who was murdered a few hours after our dispute," she said.

Wayne J. reddened. "You were lucky. I'd serve ten years of hard time to see Justine walk into this room. But that isn't gonna happen. As they say, all we can do is honour her memory." He squared his shoulders. "That's why I'm here. Hilda, will the people who Justine helped out at the end be welcome at her funeral?"

Hilda's brow furrowed. "Provided it's not a private service, I see no reason why anyone who chooses to attend wouldn't be welcomed."

Wayne J. sighed heavily. "That's all I needed to know," he said, standing up.

"Wait," Hilda said. "I answered your question. Now please answer mine."

He turned and looked at her expectantly.

"What was the cause of your quarrel with Madame Justice Blackwell?" she asked.

The question could hardly have been a surprise, but as Hilda posed it, the pulse in Wayne J.'s neck began to beat so noticeably that the wings of the eagle tattooed on his neck appeared to flutter. I remembered Detective Hallam's one-phrase description of him: lightning in a bottle.

"Money," Wayne J. said, biting off the word.

"Can you elucidate?" Hilda asked.

He eased himself back into his chair. "Justine had promised to give some money to Culhane House – it's a prisoners' support group some of us started up for cons and ex-cons.

"Culhane House, as in Claire Culhane?" I asked.

He gave me a sidelong glance. "She was another classy

lady," he said. "Justine suggested the name." He turned back to Hilda. "Prisoners' rights aren't exactly a hot ticket now. Most people seem to think the only choice society should give a con is permanent incarceration or the end of a rope."

"But Madame Justice Blackwell believed there were more humane alternatives," Hilda said.

Wayne J. shrugged. "You could say that, but I wouldn't. I think for Justine it was more a practical thing."

"Practical in what way?" asked Hilda.

"Like in the way that, most of the time, prisons just don't do what solid citizens want them to do. All prisons are good for is pissing away lives and pissing away money. You can make semi-good people bad in prison, and you can make bad people worse, but you never make anybody better. And I'll tell you another thing, Hilda. They may be hellholes, but I've never seen a prison yet that made anybody scared to come back. Every time I hear some expert running off at the mouth about that three strikes and you're out crap, I want to laugh. The only guy who's scared of going to prison is a guy who's never been there. Any ex-con knows that he might as well be in prison as anywhere else. Justine finally figured that there was a cheaper, better alternative to prison, and she was prepared to use her chequebook so that other people could figure it out too."

"But she withdrew her offer of financial support," Hilda said.

Wayne J. gripped the arms of his chair. Until that moment, I hadn't noticed how big his hands were. They were huge, and they were taut with the effort to maintain control. "God damn it, she didn't withdraw the offer," he said furiously. "She just decided to fucking reconsider."

The rage in his voice was a shock; so were his eyes, which had darkened terrifyingly. The Old Spice and the self-deprecating chuckle had lulled me, but there was no disputing the fact that only an act of will was preventing the man in front of me from springing out of my grandmother's chair and smashing everything in sight. My grandmother would have said I had been six kinds of fool to invite Wayne J. Waters into my house, and she would have been right. I began to run through strategies to get him out of the house. Just when I'd decided that none seemed workable, the storm passed.

Wayne J. hung his head in an attitude of abject apology. "Sorry about the language, ladies," he said. "It's just that there were so many people pushing Justine to 'withdraw' her offer. Miss McCourt, I don't know if she had a chance to tell you this the other night, but since Justine decided to support Culhane House, people have been lining up to tell her how crazy she is – *was*." He made a fist with one hand and pounded it repeatedly into the palm of his other hand. It was the same gesture he'd made when no one answered the door the day he went to Justine's house on Leopold Crescent. "They tried to tell her she was losing it because she was getting old, but she wasn't losing it, she was finding it." He looked at me. His eyes were black and mesmerizing. "Does that make sense?"

Almost against my will, I found myself agreeing. "Yes," I said. "It makes sense."

"Good," he said. "Because no matter what people said, Justine was with the people at Culhane House 110 per cent."

I narrowed my eyes at him. "Absolutely trustworthy," I said.

He didn't blink. "Except for that last night, absolutely."

When Wayne J. left, I followed him out. I'd decided to skip the meeting at the Faculty Club and concentrate my efforts on getting to the university in time for my first class. I backed the Volvo down the driveway, but as I turned onto the street, Wayne J. came over. I cranked down my window.

"I forgot to say thanks," he said.

"For what?"

"For letting me into your house. A lot of ladies wouldn't have had the balls." He realized what he'd said and grimaced. "Whoa," he said, "that didn't come out right."

"I took it as a compliment," I said.

He touched an imaginary cap. "That's how I meant it."

I got to the university just in time to run to the Political Science office to check my mail and pick up my class lists. Rosalie Norman, our departmental administrative assistant, was lying in wait. She was dressed in her inevitable twin sweater set, this time the colour of dried mustard. As it had been every morning since I'd come to work at the university, Rosalie's greeting was minatory.

"It helps to let me know ahead of time if you're not going to show up for a meeting. That way I don't order extra at the Faculty Club."

Wayne J. Waters might have seen me as a lady with balls, but dealing with Rosalie always unmanned me. "I'm sorry," I said. "Something came up at home. I hope you were able to find someone to eat my bran muffin." I looked down at my class list for Political Science 110. There were 212 students registered, twice as many as usual. I held it out to her. "Rosalie, something's wrong with this list."

She didn't even favour it with a glance. Instead, she tapped her watch. "Well, you're going to work it out yourself. When a person decides to come late, she can't expect the rest of us to pick up the pieces."

The day continued to run smoothly. My hope that the problem on my list was clerical rather than actual was dashed as soon as I walked into my classroom. More than two hundred students were jammed into a space with desks for a hundred. A computer glitch had timetabled two

59

sections of Political Science 110 together, and by the time I had separated the classes, half the period was over. In the afternoon, my senior class informed me sulkily that their text wasn't in the bookstore. When I got back to my office, the telephone was ringing, but it rang its last as I unlocked the door. I checked my voice mail. My first two callers invited me to start-up meetings of organizations I had no intention of joining; my third caller was Alex, asking a favour. He had been phoning Eli's school all day, but hadn't been able to connect with Eli's teacher. Now he had a meeting that would run all afternoon, and he wondered if I could get in touch with the school and fill them in. I hung up the phone and grabbed my briefcase. Suddenly I had a legitimate excuse to get out of the office early, and I snatched it.

Gerry Acoose Collegiate was an inner-city experiment: an old secondary school that the community had convinced the Board of Education to give over to those who believed First Nations' kids might thrive on a curriculum that reflected their cultural history and an attendance policy that took into account the realities of adolescent life in the city's core. As I pulled up in front of the school, I thought about the new-model cars that lined the streets near my son Angus's south-end high school.

The students at Gerry Acoose weren't kids whose parents handed them the keys to a Nova on their sixteenth birthday. These young people had seen a lot more of life than the shining-eyed innocents who clutched Club Monaco book-bags in the back-to-school ads. Among other innovations, G.A.C. had a program for teen mothers, and as I waded through the students lounging on the front steps, I passed a number of girls, barely into puberty themselves, who were clutching babies. The only student who reacted to my presence was a whippet-thin boy with shoulder-length hair, worn in the traditional way. He gave me a half-smile, which encouraged me enough to ask him for directions to the principal's office.

The halls of the school were filled with student art: some good; some not so good. On the wall outside the gymnasium, there was a life-sized painting of a white buffalo that was absolutely breathtaking. I thought of Eli's spray-painted horses; this looked like a place where they might find a home. The principal wasn't in his office, but the school secretary, a motherly woman in a flowered dress, pink cardigan, and sensible shoes, checked the computer and directed me to Eli's homeroom.

At the back of Room 10C, a young woman in bluejeans and a T-shirt was stapling a poster of an aboriginal man in a white lab coat to the bulletin board. She didn't look old enough to be the one in charge of the staple-gun.

I coughed to get the woman's attention, but she didn't respond. Finally, I said, "I'm looking for the homeroom teacher."

"You're looking *at* the homeroom teacher," she said, without turning. "Hang on. I'll be right with you."

As I waited for her to finish, I glanced around. It was a pleasant room, filled with that gentle hazy light that comes when afternoon sun filters through chalk dust. There was a hint of sweetgrass in the air, a starblanket against the far wall, and a bank of computers in front of the windows. Posters brightened the other walls: a hockey player, a powwow dancer, an actor, a playwright, and an orchestra conductor – all aboriginal.

When Eli's teacher turned and saw me, her face was as impassive as those of the kids outside. "I'm Anita Greyeyes," she said, not smiling. "What can I do for you?"

"I wanted to tell you why Eli Kequahtooway wasn't in class today," I said.

Anita Greyeyes moved to the desk at the front of the room and motioned me to the chair opposite hers. "Are you his social worker?" she asked.

"No," I said. "I'm a friend. Of Eli and of his uncle." As I explained the situation, Anita Greyeyes' gaze never left my face.

When I finished, she said, "What's Eli's prognosis?"

"I don't know," I said. "But, Ms. Greyeyes, he's very bright and he has a close relationship with his uncle. We're hopeful."

She looked at me thoughtfully. "I take it that your relationship with his uncle is also close."

"Yes," I said.

"Any chance that's the problem?"

"I don't know," I said. "I hope not."

Anita Greyeyes went to a table near the window that was loaded with texts. I watched as she chose a selection for Eli. She had small hands, blunt-fingered and efficient. As she recorded the titles in a record book, her precision-cut black hair fell forward against her cheekbones. She wrote assignments out in a small spiral notebook, put it on top of the books, and slid the stack to me. I noticed that one of the books was Eden Robinson's *Traplines*.

I picked it up. "Good choice," I said.

Anita Greyeyes didn't respond. "If it looks as if Eli's absence is going to be long-term, come back and we'll work something out."

"Thanks," I said.

I was just about out the door when she called to me. "Tell Eli that there's no shame in what he's going through."

"I will."

She was leaning forward, hands on the desk. "And tell him that it may be hard to believe right now, but life will get better." She paused. "I know because I've been there."

"I'll tell him." I offered a smile, but she didn't return it. Somehow, I wasn't surprised.

I was in the garden, making a desultory pass at propping up my tomato plants, when Taylor got home from school. She burst through the back door with Bruce and Benny in hot pursuit. She kissed me, bent to nuzzle her boys, as she had taken to calling them, and began her monologue. By the time I'd threaded the last yellowing leaf through the tomato cage, the salient facts had emerged: there were two new girls in the class and one new boy. The Grade 2 teacher's name was Ms. Jane Anweiler, and she had silver earrings that were shaped like dinosaurs. Ms. Anweiler also had a Polaroid camera with which she had taken pictures of everybody in the class. The pictures were mounted on a bulletin board outside the classroom, under a sign reading: WELCOME TO THE HOME OF THE GRADE 2 ALL-STARS!!! The letters were made out of baseball bats except for the O's, which were baseballs. Taylor would be allowed to sit beside her best friend, Jess, as long as she remembered not to talk. The Lakeview School year was, it seemed, off to a dazzling start.

Angus didn't get home from school till dinner time. I was making a salad when he came into the kitchen, poured himself a glass of juice, and started to leave.

"Hang on," I said. "Whatever happened to 'hello' and 'how are you'?"

"Sorry," he said. "Hello and how are you?"

"Fine," I said, "but you look a little down. Back-to-school blues?"

He shook his head. "No," he said. "School's okay. Actually more than okay. It looks like it's going to be a good year."

"So why the long face?"

"I went down to the hospital to see Eli."

"Was he still mad at you about what happened at the game."

My son's face was perplexed. "No. When I got there, Eli was the same as he'd been before. I thought he was just ignoring what happened, and for a while I went along with him. Then I decided it would be better if we talked about it." Angus put his glass down and came over to me. "Mum, Eli doesn't remember what happened at the game. He doesn't remember anything from the time he took off till he saw his shrink yesterday."

"That's twenty-four hours."

"I know. So does Eli. He's really psyched about this. Mum, could you go see him?"

"Do you think it would help? Eli has never been exactly easy with me."

"It'd help. He likes you. I think he just kind of resented you."

"Because of my relationship with Alex?"

Angus frowned. "I never thought it was that. I always thought it was just that you were our mum and, every time he saw you, it reminded him of what he didn't have."

That night, after supper, Taylor and I drove to the hospital with the books and assignments Anita Greyeyes had given me. I was tense as we approached Eli's room, but he seemed genuinely pleased to see us. Physically, he was an immensely appealing boy: graceful, with the brooding good looks of a youth in an El Greco painting. He tried a smile of welcome, then stood aside so we could walk through the doorway. He was wearing brand-name sandals, khaki shorts, and a pressed white T-shirt, an absolutely normal sixteen-year-old boy, but one of his slender wrists was ringed with a hospital ID band, and his brown eyes were troubled.

Taylor immediately staked out one of the visitor's chairs

for herself; Eli directed me to the other one and sat on the edge of his bed. For a moment, there was an awkward pause, then Taylor took charge. She amazed me. She didn't prattle about her cats or her school; instead, she asked Eli very seriously about what they did to help him at the hospital and whether he'd made any friends. Even more surprisingly, she waited for his answers, which came, at first haltingly, then with more assurance. When she told him a story about Bruce and Benny, Eli laughed aloud, and the melancholy that had hung in the air, heavy as the hospital smell, seemed to lift.

I wasn't as successful with Eli as Taylor had been, but I did my best. I told him about Gerry Acoose Collegiate and his homeroom. As I described the starblanket on the wall and the bank of computers by the window, Eli's eyes moved with interest towards the textbooks we'd brought. When it was time to leave, he gave Taylor an awkward one-armed hug, then he and I stood side by side in his doorway and watched as she wandered down the hall towards the elevators. It was a rare moment of connection for us.

Eli seemed to feel the closeness too. "Thanks for bringing the school stuff by," he said.

"It's a good school, Eli. You could be happy there."

For a moment he was silent. Then he said, "Do they know about me being in the hospital?"

"Your teacher does," I said. "She seems pretty decent. She said to tell you you're not the only person who's ever needed time to work things out."

"You mean this has happened to other kids in that class?"

"I don't know about the other kids," I said, "but I have a feeling Ms. Greyeyes has had some problems in her life. She asked me to give you a message."

His look mingled hostility and hope. "She doesn't even know me."

"Maybe not," I said, "but she says she understands what you're going through because she's been there."

"And she's all right now?" he asked. The question was barely a whisper, but I could hear the yearning.

"She's fine," I said. "And you're going to be fine, too. A lot of people care about you, Eli."

Riding down in the elevator, Taylor was quiet. As we walked towards the parking lot, she said, "When's he getting out?"

"Soon, I hope," I said. "But I don't know."

"I'm almost finished that painting of us watching the dragon boats."

"Good."

"Do you think Eli would like it as a present?"

I smiled at her. "I know he would," I said.

When we got home, the dishes were done, the kitchen was shining, and the table was set for breakfast. I pointed Taylor towards bed, stuck my head into the family room where Angus was listening to a CD, and went out to the backyard. Hilda was sitting on the deck with a gin and tonic.

She raised her glass when she saw me. "I bought a bottle of Beefeater this afternoon. Will you join me?"

"Absolutely," I said. "But I don't think I've ever seen you drink gin before."

"It's been a gin kind of day," Hilda said.

I poured myself a drink and went back outside. It was a beautiful night. The air smelled of charcoal and heat, and from the park across the way we could hear the sounds of an early-evening ball game. I sipped my drink. "The house looks wonderful," I said. "I love it when you stay with us. Everything seems to run so smoothly."

"I don't do much myself, you know. Your children are very cheerful about pitching in."

"Only when you're here," I said. "The rest of the time, they pitch in, but I wouldn't characterize their attitude as cheerful." I smiled at her. "You're kind of like Mary Poppins."

Hilda winced.

"You don't like the comparison?" I said.

"Not much," she said. "But I am relieved to hear that you welcome my presence, because I'm going to ask if I can stay a few days longer."

"You can stay as long as you want to," I said. "You know that. Has something come up?"

She sighed wearily. "This business with Justine," she said. "I can't seem to extricate myself from it."

"Do you want out?"

"I don't know," she said. "I went to see Eric Fedoruk this morning. My intention was to tell him that, after giving the matter some thought, I'd concluded my responsibility to Justine Blackwell was discharged."

"That's an about-face, isn't it?"

Hilda turned towards me. "It is, but there are times when reversal is the only sensible course. Joanne, I went to Eric Fedoruk's because it seemed that my commitment to Justine was a problem for you."

"Hilda, you could never be . . ."

She made a gesture of dismissal. "I know what you're about to say, but I saw your face last night when I told you a TV crew had interviewed me at your house, and I saw you change your plans this morning when Wayne J. Waters turned up on your doorstep. This business with Justine has simply become too much of a burden on you, and that's what I intended to tell Eric Fedoruk."

"You were going to step aside?"

"I was. This morning after you went to the university, I sat down with Justine's letter. I read it many times, and as far as I could ascertain, I had honoured my commitment. The power of attorney she gave me ended with her death, and when I called Eric Fedoruk to ask if Justine had named me executrix of her will, he said she hadn't. He told me he had the will on the desk in front of him, and it named him executor. I went down to his office this morning fully intending to tell him that I'd satisfied myself there was nothing more I could do for Justine, and that I was going home to Saskatoon."

"But something made you change your mind," I said.

"Not something . . . someone. More accurately, several someones. Joanne, when I got to Eric Fedoruk's office, the Blackwell sisters were there. From what Tina let slip, I gathered they'd come about the will. They certainly had some agenda in mind. As soon as I came into the room, they began apologizing. Lucy said they were wrong to shirk their obligations to their mother. Signe said they should never have asked me to act as their intermediary with the press. Even Tina Blackwell chimed in; she said she was wrong to put her need for privacy ahead of my right to live my own life." Hilda frowned. "Although having finally met her, I can understand why Tina Blackwell wouldn't want to be photographed."

I was baffled. "Hilda why wouldn't she want to be photographed? She's on TV all the time. She's the anchor on the CJRG six o'clock news."

"With all that scarring?"

"What scarring? I don't watch that station much, but over the years I've caught their news a few times. Tina Blackwell's a very attractive woman."

"No one would describe the woman I saw this morning as attractive." Hilda's voice was thoughtful, then she added briskly, "But Tina Blackwell's appearance isn't the issue.

68

The issue is whether my continuing to work on Justine's affairs is going to be a problem for you."

"It won't be a problem. But, Hilda, have I missed a step here? What did the Blackwell sisters do to make you change your mind about bowing out?"

"They nettled me." Hilda's blue eyes were dark with anger at the memory. "They treated me as if I were an old family retainer who was, oh so reluctantly, being relieved of her duties. Lucy offered the usual sweet female banalities: "It was too much to ask anyone outside the family to do." Signe Rayner wondered, *sotto voce*, whether the fact that I lived in Saskatoon would prevent me from acting effectively in a Regina-based case."

"I take it you countered their arguments," I said.

"I most assuredly did," Hilda said. I reminded the Blackwell women that their mother had asked me to protect her interests and that we lived in the age of technological wizardry. There was no disputing either argument. That's when Signe Rayner turned cruel."

"Towards whom?"

"Towards me and towards the memory of her mother. Dr. Rayner said that psychotic patients can often be quite charismatic, especially with elderly people. In her view, psychotics often infect those around them with their delusions. I asked her if she thought her mother had infected me. She said that, in her opinion, my determination to take on this commitment bordered on the obsessional."

"But she and her sisters asked you to handle the funeral arrangements."

"A decision they apparently regret," Hilda said tartly. "Dr. Rayner's attack on me was personal and it was vicious."

I shook my head. "All this from someone whose profession involves teaching other people to handle their anger."

Hilda sniffed. "Dr. Rayner didn't bring much honour to her profession today. At one point, Eric Fedoruk literally jumped between us. He was quite sensible. He said that things were being said that could not be unsaid, and that perhaps we should go to the restaurant on the main floor of his building and have a drink."

"Did you go?"

"No. At that point, I'd had enough. But when I started to say my goodbyes, Lucy Blackwell came over and put her arms around me. Joanne, it was the strangest thing. She was almost weeping, and she said, 'Hilda, don't be mad at us. It's for your own good. My mother left everything in such a mess, and my sisters and I would feel terrible if anything happened to you.'"

I looked across at her. In the dying light, a truth that I tried to banish was apparent. While Hilda's spirit was as robust as ever, there was no denying that physically she was becoming more fragile. I didn't want anything to happen to her either.

"Let's go inside," I said. "Even on a night like this, it's possible to get a chill."

CHAPTER

5

The next afternoon, when Taylor came home from school she grabbed an apple and her cats and headed out to her studio to work. She went back after dinner. She continued the pattern all week. "I want the painting to be ready for Eli as soon as he comes back," she said.

Taylor wasn't the only busy member of our household. As the first Friday after Labour Day approached, it was clear that the aimlessness and languor of summer was well and truly over. Angus's football team started practice, and his girlfriend, Leah, came back from theatre school in Toronto. I sorted my classes out and began to lecture in earnest. We all took turns visiting Eli.

Hilda spent Wednesday and Thursday downtown, continuing her investigation into Justine Blackwell's affairs. She described her movement back and forth between the courthouse on Victoria Avenue and the shabby storefront offices on Rose Street that harboured Culhane House as spider-like. In her attempt to connect the disparate strands in the complicated web of relationships that Justine had established in her life, Hilda talked to everyone she could find who had known the dead woman, from the small circle of colleagues, family, and friends who had watched with dismay as she metamorphosed from figure of judicial rectitude into eccentric advocate for prisoners' rights, to the ex-prisoners and their families and lawyers who exulted as Justine embraced their cause.

Often Hilda arrived hard on the heels of the police, whose frustration as they continued to come up empty-handed in their own investigations was growing. They weren't short on suspects. Justine Blackwell had spent the last night of her life in a room filled with people she had sent to prison. The final year of Justine's life might have been given over to making amends, but delayed charity can be cold comfort. Most of the guests at Justine's party would have known only too well the truth of the old saw that "a man that studieth revenge keeps his own wounds green." They would have known, too, that in the course of history few places have proven themselves more congenial to the study of revenge than the slammer.

The theory that Justine's death had been an act of prisoner vengeance was given credibility by the nature of the weapon the police now believed had been used to kill her. On the night of Justine's final party, Eric Fedoruk had presented her with handsomely engraved marble-based scales. The doorman at the hotel had seen Justine put the scales on the seat beside her when she stepped into her BMW, but they were nowhere in evidence when the police examined the car after Justine's body was found. The scales still hadn't been recovered, but the forensics unit, having examined both Justine's injuries and photographs of Eric Fedoruk's presentation at the banquet, had concluded that the marble base could have inflicted the fatal wounds. A healthy percentage of those who had watched the presentation had proven themselves adept at the art of assault with a deadly weapon. An equally healthy percentage had no alibi whatsoever.

The police weren't alone in feeling disappointed that the truth about Justine was eluding them. Friday morning, when I came back from taking Rose around the lake, Hilda was sitting at the dining-room table surrounded by library books.

"What's up?" I asked.

"I'm trying to unearth a few appropriate passages for Justine's memorial service. It's tomorrow."

"I saw the notice in the paper." I sat down in the chair across from her. "Do you realize we haven't really talked about Justine all week?"

"You've had enough on your mind with Eli," Hilda said. "Besides, all I'd have had to contribute was a litany of failures. I can't even succeed at this." She picked up the letter Justine had written her and slipped it into the book she was reading.

I glanced at the book's title. "Montaigne's *Essays*," I said. "Searching for insights?"

"That's precisely what I'm doing. Lucy asked me to choose some readings that would sum up her mother's life."

"Another task," I said. "The Blackwell sisters must have decided you're too useful to alienate."

"That possibility has occurred to me as well," Hilda said. "But their motives don't interest me a whit. I've undertaken this assignment for Justine. I just wish I were making a better job of it. How can anyone sum up a life, if she's not certain what that life truly added up to?"

"You're no closer to understanding what Justine's state of mind was in the last year of her life?" I asked.

Hilda frowned. "It's as if I'm hearing about two separate and distinct human beings. Justine's legal colleagues speak of her with pity and anger. The people at Culhane House talk about her as if she were a saint." Hilda shook her head in a gesture of disbelief. "Joanne, I know that human beings contain multitudes, but as a rule one can reconcile the disparities."

I poured myself a cup of coffee and sat down opposite her. "What was Justine like when you knew her first, Hilda?"

"Bright, independent, ambitious." Hilda smiled. "I don't mind admitting that I saw a great deal of myself in her. She was, as my beloved L.M. Montgomery's Anne would have said, 'a kindred spirit.'"

"Then I would have liked her," I said.

Hilda took the compliment coolly. "Yes, you would have liked her. There was no reason not to. We met in 1946. I'd just bought my house on Temperance Street. It was a chaotic time, Joanne; the universities were jam-packed with returned soldiers. It was wonderful, but it was madness: students sitting atop radiators, on window-ledges, in the aisles, and still spilling out into the halls. Of course, housing was at a premium. That September, I decided that by offering room and board to a woman student, I could do a good deed *and* expedite the process of paying off my mortgage. I put a notice on the bulletin board in the administration building at the university. Within an hour, Justine, or Maisie, as she was known then, was standing on my doorstep."

"Justine changed her name?" I asked.

"Justine changed *both* her names," Hilda said. "She was born Maisie Wilson. Blackwell is her married name; Justine was her *nom de guerre*. The choice was a wise one. By the time I met her, it was plain that she saw her destiny as going far beyond that of a Saskatchewan farmgirl. For the future she had in mind, Justine was a much more suitable name than Maisie.

"I expect you can tell from the photographs in the paper that Justine was attractive, but in 1946 she was ravishing, no other word for it. Her hair was white blonde, and she wore it in a pageboy, as young women did in those days; it was immensely flattering. Her skin was flawless, and her eyes were the same colour as Lucy's. Since the advent of contact lenses, I've seen a number of young women with those aquamarine eyes, but the shade of Justine's was God-given. She had the same generous mouth Lucy has, and the same dazzling smile. When she asked me about the room, my first thought was that my house would be overrun with eager young men, so I asked her straight out how serious she was about her studies. She assured me there would be no late-night visitors, because her only goal in life was to graduate at the top of her class in law school."

"I take it she realized her goal."

"She did indeed. Top of her class. But she worked hard for it: left the house at seven sharp every morning; took one hour off for supper at five; then back to the library till it closed. It was a monastic life for such a handsome young woman."

Hilda seemed about to let the subject drop, but I wanted to hear more. "You *did* like her, though," I said.

Hilda seemed perplexed. "I'm not sure 'like' is the word I would use. I respected her. Justine knew what she wanted, and she went after it."

"Dedicated and persistent," I said. "She does sound like you."

Hilda laughed. "Justine made me look lackadaisical. There was an incident the first year she lived in my house on Temperance Street that revealed her measure. I owned a gramophone and an extensive library of recordings, and when Justine moved in I invited her to make use of them. She never did. Then one day, I came home and found her listening to *Manon Lescaut*. She was reading the libretto, taking notes. She didn't appear to be enjoying the music much, so I asked her if she liked Puccini. Justine said she didn't have an opinion one way or the other, but one of the men in her class told her that the senior partner in Blackwell, Dishaw and Boyle, the law firm with which she planned to article, was an opera lover, and she wanted to be prepared. Three years later, when she walked into Richard Blackwell's office, Justine Wilson could have won the Metropolitan Opera's Saturday-afternoon quiz."

"And she married the senior partner?"

"She did indeed – a month to the day after their first meeting. Richard Blackwell was twenty-five years older than Justine. He'd never married, and he was eager for a family. Justine complied. Signe was born in 1950, and the others followed. Justine never seemed very interested in motherhood. She was combative by nature, and she loved the rough and tumble of the courtroom. Richard retired to raise those children. He and his little girls became quite a well-known sight in Saskatoon."

"A wife with a high-powered career and a husband who stays home with the kids – the Blackwells were about forty years ahead of their time," I said.

Hilda's face grew sad. "From what I saw, Richard Blackwell relished every moment he spent with his daughters. It's too bad he didn't have longer with them."

"When did he die?"

"In 1967. I remember because he died at one of the banquets we had in Saskatoon that year for Canada's Centennial. The Blackwells had moved to Regina by then. Justine had already made a name for herself as a criminal lawyer, but she was ready for the next stage. She wanted to be noticed by those who influenced judicial appointments. Richard had come back to Saskatoon for the dinner. I was there. It was terrible. There were hundreds of people in the room. Everyone was rushing about, trying to summon help.

But nothing could be done. It was a heart attack. Massive. The worst thing was that Lucy was with him. Richard had brought her over for a chat when they came in. She would have been about fifteen, I guess, and she was so proud of being at a grown-up event with her father. Then, in an instant, he was gone. I've often wondered if that trauma spawned the need to be surrounded by men which seems to have been so much a part of her life."

A line from one of Lucy's songs came back to me. *He painted a rainbow and took me along, then lightning split us, shattered my song.* I turned to Hilda. "I think that's probably a pretty solid observation."

Hilda's voice was thoughtful. "Justine didn't appear to suffer any permanent ill effects from her husband's death. Not long after Richard died, she was appointed to the bench. As I told that odious Detective Hallam, Justine and I lost touch except for the occasional lunch and holiday letters. Of course, Saskatchewan is a small province, so it was impossible not to hear news of her."

"From farmgirl to Justice on the Court of Queen's Bench," I said. "Justine put together quite a life for herself."

Hilda looked at me approvingly. "Thank you," she said. "It's amazing how often simply talking a problem through can help one solve it." She picked up the book of Montaigne essays and read aloud. " 'What? Have you not lived? That is not only the fundamental but the most illustrious of your occupations. . . . To compose our character is our duty. . . . Our great and glorious masterpiece is to live appropriately.' " She cocked an eyebrow. "Well, is that quotation equivocal enough?"

I smiled at her. "As equivocations go, I'd say it's almost perfect." I touched her hand. "Hilda, let this be the end of it. You've already done more than Justine would ever have asked of you."

Hilda shrugged. "Perhaps I have, but it's still not enough. Joanne, you know as well as I do that fine words butter no parsnips. Montaigne's *Essays* may get us through the funeral, but unless I discover the truth about Justine's state of mind in the last year, her enduring epitaph will be written in tabloid headlines. She deserves better."

"So do you," I said, and I was surprised at the emotion in my voice. "Hilda, don't let them draw you into this. Murder spawns a kind of ugliness that most people can't even imagine. It's like a terrible toxic spill. Once it splashes over you, you're changed forever. Believe me, I know. Don't let it touch you."

Hilda's expression was troubled. "It already has, my dear. Maybe that's why I can't just walk away. What kind of woman would I be if I just turned my back and let the darkness triumph?"

"There's nothing I can say that will dissuade you?"

"Nothing."

"Then at least promise me you'll be careful."

"I may be stubborn, but I'm not stupid," she said curtly. "I've been given a long and healthy life, Joanne. I'm not about to jeopardize what any sensible person would realize is a great blessing."

When Jill Osiowy, the producer of "Canada Tonight" and my friend, called my office later that afternoon, I was deep in weekend plans. Except for the usual round of Saturday chores, the next couple of days were clear, and I aimed to keep them that way. Our summer at the lake had been straight out of the fifties: canoeing, canasta, croquet, and a calm broken only by the chirping of crickets and the reedy voices of little kids calling on Taylor. I had come back from the lake with a tan and an overwhelming sense of peace. The tan was fading, and the events since Labour Day had made some major inroads on my tranquility, but in my estimation two days by the pool would go a long way to restoring both. If I was lucky, I'd be able to convince Hilda to join me.

"I hope you've got nothing more on your mind than chilled wine and serious gossip," I said.

Jill laughed. "We have a little task first. How would you like to look at some videos of men doing interesting things?"

"It depends on the men," I said. "And on the interesting things."

"These men are auditioning for the chance to replace Sam Spiegel on our political panel," she said. "I've tried to talk him into staying, but Sam says retirement means retirement from everything."

"I'm going to miss him," I said.

"Me too," Jill said, "but, ready or not, life goes on, and some of these new guys might work out. The network's narrowed it down, but I'd appreciate your input. Glayne's still in Wales but she says she trusts your judgement." Jill's voice rose to the wheedling singsong of the schoolyard. "I'll buy you a drink afterwards."

"Okay," I said. "And I'll take you up on that drink. You and I haven't had a chance to really talk all summer."

"Good. I'll meet you at the front door of NationTV at two o'clock."

I'd barely hung up the phone when it rang again. It was Alex, and he sounded keyed up.

"Jo, I have another favour to ask. I just got back to the office and there was a message here from Dan Kasperski. He thinks Eli's ready to come home."

"That's good news, isn't it?"

"It is, except I have to go to Saskatoon. The cops there have a suspect they think I can help them nail. If I catch the seven-ten plane tonight, I can check out this creep and be back tomorrow afternoon. I hate to ask, but could Eli stay with you tonight?"

"Of course, as long as it's okay with Eli."

"It will be. Eli tells me he got pretty tight with you guys this week."

"We enjoyed being with him, too. Look, why don't you two come for an early supper? I could barbecue some of that pickerel we caught at the lake. A last taste of summer."

"Can we bring anything?"

"Just yourselves. And Alex, tell Eli I'm really looking forward to seeing him."

I hung up. I thought about my tan and my peace of mind. Both would have to wait. As Jill had said, ready or not, life goes on.

When Alex and Eli arrived, Eli was carrying his gymbag and a box of Dilly Bars from the Dairy Queen. He handed them to me. "Uncle Alex wanted to get an ice cream cake, but I thought these would be less trouble for you." He grinned shyly. "You know – no dishes?"

"Good move," I said. "And I love Dilly Bars."

Dinner was low-key and fun. Taylor's friend Jess joined us. He and Taylor were doing a school project on wildlife of the prairie, and in a burst of untypical enthusiasm, they'd decided to get started immediately. Hilda, who believed in rewarding zeal, however unlikely the source, had promised to take them to the Museum of Natural History after supper. It was a co-operative meal: I made cornbread; Taylor and Jess sliced up tomatoes and cucumbers from the garden; Hilda made potato salad; Alex barbecued the pickerel; Angus and Eli cleaned up. Afterwards, we ate Dilly Bars on the deck. Life as it is lived in TV commercials.

As soon as we'd finished dessert, Hilda took the little kids to the museum, and the big boys got out the croquet set and had a game with rules so bizarre even they couldn't follow them. Halfway through the game, Eli came running towards us, whirling his croquet mallet above his head. "You can play if you want to, Mrs. Kilbourn, but this is a take-no-prisoners game. Play at your own risk." Then he laughed the way a teenaged boy is supposed to laugh – wildly and uninhibitedly – and ran back to the game. I thought I had never seen him so happy.

Alex waited until the last minute to leave for the airport, and he looked at the yard regretfully before he went into the house. I slid my arm through his. I knew how he felt. After a troubling week, it seemed a shame to put a rent in the seamless perfection of the evening.

Before he picked up his overnight bag in the front hall, Alex pulled a notebook and pen out of his pocket and began to write. "Here's the number of headquarters in Saskatoon, and here's Dan Kasperski's number in case anything comes up."

"Nothing's going to come up," I said.

"Let's hope," Alex said. "Dan Kasperski says he can't figure this one out. Eli's doing a lot better, but he still has no memory of what he did in the time between the football game and his appointment with Kasperski."

"Does Dr. Kasperski think that overhearing what those drunks said caused all of these problems for Eli?"

Alex's jaw tightened. "He doesn't know. His theory is that Eli had been carrying around a lot of unresolved emotions and that asshole's remark just tipped the balance."

"The proverbial straw that broke the camel's back," I said.

"Something like that. Kasperski says it doesn't add up as far as he's concerned, but he's been a shrink long enough to know that there are a lot of times when things don't add up."

Alex held me a long time before he opened the door. "I'm glad Eli's going to be with you tonight."

"It's where he should be," I said.

I watched until Alex's Audi disappeared from my view. As I turned to go into the house, Sylvie O'Keefe drove up. She and I weren't close, but I liked and respected her. She was a photographer whose work had brought her a measure of fame and more than a measure of controversy. Surprisingly, for an artist so provocative, she was a very traditional parent, who was raising her only child with a mix of love, discipline, and routine that appeared to be just the ticket. Jess was a thoroughly pleasant and happy little boy.

"How did Hilda and the kids make out at the museum?" Sylvie asked, as she followed me into the house.

"They're not back yet, but I'm sure they triumphed. Things fall into place when Hilda's around."

She sighed. "I wish Jess and I had a Hilda in our life."

"I'm certainly glad she came into ours."

Sylvie furrowed her brow. "I always assumed you'd known her forever."

We went into the living room and sat down. "No, not forever," I said. "Just seven years. I met her when my friend Andy Boychuk died. She'd been his teacher. She and I became friends, and of course the kids loved her."

Sylvie gazed at me assessingly. "It looks to me as if Hilda's relationship with your family has been a good fit for everyone."

"It has," I said. "For a long time, I worried that it was pretty one-sided. Hilda always seemed to give us so much more of herself than we gave her."

"But something changed?"

"Hilda had a gentleman friend. His name was Frank, and he was the love of her life. When he died last spring, she was heartbroken. We went up for his funeral; then Hilda came down and stayed with us for a couple of weeks. I think she was glad not to be alone, and of course kids are always such a great distraction."

Sylvie grinned at me. "Aren't they just."

Right on cue, the front door opened, and the kids barrelled in, with Hilda behind them.

"How did it go?" Sylvie asked.

Jess went over to his mother. "You know those feathers owls have around their eyes?"

Sylvie nodded.

"They help owls hear," Jess said.

"How do they do that?" Sylvie asked.

Jess tweaked his own ear. "See this?" he said. "It catches the sounds and sends it inside our ears so we can hear. The owls' ears are right behind those feathers."

Taylor came over to me. "Could Jess stay over? It's not for fun," she said earnestly. "We need to work."

"Sorry, T," I said, "the owls will have to wait. We already have an overnight guest. Eli's staying here tonight, and he could use a little peace right now." I put my arm around her shoulder. "It gets pretty noisy around here when you and Jess are working on a project."

Sylvie smiled. "I don't mind a little excitement. If it's all right with you, Joanne, the kids can work at our house tonight."

Taylor's eyes were pleading. "Can I?"

"Sure," I said.

Taylor laid her head against my arm and lowered her voice. "After I go, make sure Eli goes to the studio to see the dragon-boat picture I made for him."

"He's right out back," I said. "Why don't you take him there now?"

She shook her head. "If I'm there, Eli won't be able to really look." She frowned. "Do you know what I mean?"

"Yes," I said, "I know what you mean, and I think you're right. I'll make sure Eli sees the painting."

After Sylvie left with the children, I fixed myself a gin and tonic and went up to my room to read. There was a new biography of the prime minister. The blurb on the jacket promised a Jungian exploration of the dark corners of his psyche. I had just about decided the PM was that rarest of beings, a man without a Shadow, when Hilda knocked on the door. She was wearing her dazzling poppy-red Chinese robe.

"I'm going to make an early night of it, Joanne," she said. "It's been a long day, and Justine's funeral is at ten." She leaned against the doorframe as if she were suddenly weary. "The last funeral I attended was for Frank," she said softly.

"Hilda, would you like me to go with you tomorrow morning?"

"But your Saturday mornings are so busy."

"There's nothing that can't be put off till later except for Taylor's lesson, and Angus can drive her to that."

"It would be good not to have to go alone," she said. "And not just because tomorrow's service will be painful. Joanne, you were right about the currents a murder sets loose. Sometimes this week, I've felt as if I were about to be swept away."

"Then let me be your anchor," I said. "You've been mine often enough."

In all the time I'd known her, Hilda had never made a physical display of affection, but she came over, bent down, and kissed the top of my head. "I hope you know how much I cherish your friendship," she said.

When I went downstairs to say goodnight to the boys, Eli was sitting at the kitchen doing a crossword puzzle. Angus was nowhere in sight.

84

I touched Eli's shoulder. "Where's your goofy friend?" I asked.

Eli gave me a small smile. "He went to Blockbuster to rent a movie."

"You didn't want to go with him?"

"No. I thought I'd just stay here."

I pulled out the chair next to his and sat down. "Feeling a little shaky?"

He gazed at me. His eyes were extraordinary – of a brown so dark they were almost black. "More than a little shaky."

"Taylor left a gift for you that might help," I said. "It's out in her studio."

"What is it?" he asked.

"A surprise," I said, "but in my opinion, a terrific one. Why don't you go out and have a look while I call Mieka and Greg and see if that baby of theirs is any closer to joining the world."

He started towards the door, then he stopped and turned. "Are you looking forward to being a *Kokom*?" he said.

"Yes," I said. "I really am. I like kids. It'll be fun to have a new one around."

"I hope everything works out okay," he said.

"Thanks, Eli, so do I."

My older daughter answered the phone in a voice that was uncharacteristically gloomy.

"I guess I don't need to ask you how it's going," I said.

"It's not going at all," she said. "I followed your advice about the Chinese food, and we've already scarfed our way through the whole menu at the Golden Dragon; I painted the kitchen ceiling; Greg's lost seven pounds from all the long walks we've been taking; and here I sit, still pregnant, barefoot, bored, and in the kitchen."

"Try to enjoy the moment," I said. "When the baby comes, all that peace and quiet is going to look pretty good."

As soon as I replaced the receiver, the day caught up with me. I decided to follow Hilda's lead and turn in early. I had an extra-long shower, dusted myself with last year's birthday bathpowder, put on a fresh nightie, and headed for bed. When I came out of the bathroom, Angus was sitting on my bed.

"Thanks for knocking."

"I did knock. You were in the shower, remember?"

"Sorry. I was just talking to your sister, and I guess I'm a little on edge."

"Still no baby?"

"No. It looks like your niece or nephew has decided to arrive on Mieka time."

My son grinned. "Late. Late for everything." He stood up. "Actually, what I came up for was to find out if you knew where Eli went."

"Isn't he downstairs?"

"Nope. I called and he didn't answer."

"He's probably still out in the studio. Taylor wanted me to give him the dragon-boat picture. She noticed he wasn't having a very easy time lately."

Angus shook his head in amazement. "Most of the time she's such a space-case, but every so often she tunes in."

"When T comes home tomorrow morning, I'll pass along your compliment."

I'd just crawled between the sheets and was reaching to turn out the light when I heard my son racing up the stairs. He burst into the room.

"Mum, something's the matter with Eli."

I sat up. "What do you mean?"

"Just come and see him, please." Angus's voice was tense. I grabbed my robe and followed my son downstairs.

"He's out in Taylor's studio," Angus said.

When I opened the door, the breath caught in my throat. On the easel in front of me was the painting Taylor had made as a gift for Eli. Once every centimetre of that canvas had danced with colour. Eli's painting of the black horse had obscured the brilliance. The lines of the animal's body were graceful, but the place where its head should have been was a jagged edge, clotted and sticky with paint bright as fresh blood. The animal's head was in the right lower quadrant of the canvas. Tongue lolling, eyes bulging, it was obvious the animal had died in terror. Eli himself lay in the far corner of the room; he was curled into the foetal position and moaning.

My son's voice was a whisper. "What's happening, Mum?"

"I don't know," I said. "Go upstairs and get my purse. There's a card inside with Eli's doctor's number on it. Call him and tell him we need to see him. Be sure he understands it's an emergency."

I took Eli in my arms and began to rock him like a baby. When Angus came back after making the call, I was still holding him.

"Dr. Kasperski's coming right over," Angus said. He bent closer to Eli and called his name.

When Eli didn't respond, I saw the panic in my son's eyes. "Why don't you go upstairs so you can watch for the doctor," I said. I tried to make my voice sound reassuring, but I was as scared as Angus was.

Less than ten minutes passed before I heard the doorbell, but it was a long ten minutes. Over the years, my own kids had had their share of broken bones, sprains, crises, and disappointments, and I had cradled them in my arms as I was cradling Eli. But after I had held them for a while, my kids had always responded. I had been able to feel them come back from the place of pain into which accident or misfortune had hurled them. Eli wasn't coming back. He didn't appear to be hurt physically, but his body was rigid. No matter what I did, I couldn't reach him, and I was relieved beyond measure that someone who might be able to was on his way over.

When Angus came through the door, my first thought was that the young man with him was far too young to be a medical doctor. Dan Kasperski's body was as lithe as an adolescent's, and he was wearing the teenaged boy's uniform of choice that summer: cut-off jeans, a rock-and-roll shirt, and sandals. He was deeply tanned, and his hair was black, curly, and shiny. He seemed to radiate energy. Without preamble, he knelt beside me, and reached out and stroked Eli's forehead.

"Eli, it's Dan," he said firmly. "I need you to help me find out what went wrong here."

At the sound of Dan Kasperski's voice, Eli's body relaxed and he opened his eyes. Kasperski slid his arm under Eli's body and raised him to a sitting position. "Let's talk," he said.

"Would you like to go upstairs?" I said. "Eli's bed's already made up for him. He might be more comfortable."

Dan Kasperski leaned close to Eli's face. "What do you say, my friend?"

When Eli nodded, Dan Kasperski helped him to his feet, and I led them upstairs to my older son Peter's room. As I closed the door behind me, I could hear Dan Kasperski's voice, soft and persuasive. "It must have been a terrible thing to have made you so angry. Can you tell me about it?"

I decided not to call Alex until I'd had a chance to hear what Dr. Kasperski had to say. When I went back downstairs, Angus was sitting in the dark in the living room.

As soon as he heard my step, he jumped up. "What happened to him?"

I slid my arm around my son's waist. "That's what Dr. Kasperski's trying to find out."

"Did Eli say anything?"

"Not while I was there."

"Why would he wreck Taylor's painting, Mum? It was a present for him."

"I don't know. I guess he was just angry and confused."

"Is that what we're going to tell Taylor?"

I let my hand fall away from him. "Angus, I don't know what we're going to tell Taylor. And you might as well stop asking me questions because I don't have any answers."

"Mum, I don't mean to keep bugging you, but Eli isn't the only one who's confused."

"Angus, I'm sorry. It's just . . ." My voice broke. "Everything's too much."

For a moment, we stood together miserably. It was my son who broke the silence. "Do you want me to dig out the cards? We could play a game of crib while we're waiting." His voice sounded the way it had when he was little and wanted the reassurance of one more story before lights out.

"You're on," I said. "Loser has to walk Rose on the day of the first blizzard."

We were just starting what looked like the final hand when Dan Kasperski came downstairs. He leaned over and glanced assessingly at Angus's cards. "If your mother's playing for money, she'd better start collecting pop bottles." Then he looked at me. "I gave Eli something to help him sleep. He's down for the count, but you should get in touch with his uncle."

"I will," I said. "There's a flight back from Saskatoon in about half an hour. He can catch that."

"Good. Ask him to have Eli in my office by eight tomorrow morning. We need to get him working on this as soon as possible." For a moment he was silent, then he looked at my son and me. "Do either of you have any idea at all what went wrong here?"

Angus shook his head. "No, I thought everything was great."

"So did I," I said. "We had a pleasant dinner. Eli said he felt a little edgy, but he seemed fine. My daughter's an artist. She'd painted a picture for Eli – as a kind of welcome-home gift for him. She thought it would be easier for him to see the painting for the first time without the rest of us around. Anyway, Angus had gone to rent a movie, so I suggested to Eli that he might want to go out to the studio to have a look at Taylor's gift. When Angus got back, he found Eli the way he was when you saw him."

"Nothing happened . . ."

"Nothing ever *does* happen," I said, and I could hear the frustration in my voice. "At least not anything concrete. He just explodes. Dr. Kasperski, I know there's no magic bullet here, but surely you can do something to get to the source of Eli's problems."

Daniel Kasperski cocked an eyebrow. "Eli and I *are* doing something. We're talking, remembering, reconstructing. It takes time, Mrs. Kilbourn."

"But don't some doctors use sodium pentothol or hypnosis to help them home in on what went wrong in the first place?"

He shrugged. "Some do. I don't. Mrs. Kilbourn, think about it for a moment. Does it make sense to force a person as fragile as Eli to confront memories that are so powerful he's using every ounce of energy he has to suppress them? I know this way takes longer, but when Eli finally does face his demons, I want him to be strong enough to stare them down." He glanced at his watch. "I should be moving along," he said, "but before I go, could I have another look at that painting? When I was in your daughter's studio before, I was pretty much focused on Eli."

Angus shot me an anxious look. "Do I have to go out there again?"

"No," I said. "Why don't you try to grab some sleep?" I turned to Dan Kasperski. "Follow me, but there isn't much left to see."

Dan Kasperski's face was grim as he gazed at the canvas. "What did it used to be?" he asked finally.

"We were at the dragon-boat races Saturday," I said. "That was a picture of Eli and my kids watching the finish line."

"Does Eli like your daughter?"

"I thought he did."

Dan Kasperski continued to stare at the picture. Finally, he turned to me. "Can I take this with me? Signe Rayner might want to use it somehow in her therapy."

I felt a tremendous sense of letdown. "But I thought that you were Eli's doctor now," I said, and I was embarrassed at how forlorn I sounded.

He turned to me. "No matter how much I want to help Eli, Mrs. Kilbourn, he is not my patient. Signe Rayner is treating him. I'm just her surrogate."

I handed him the painting. "From the way Eli reacted to you tonight, I think he sees you as more than a surrogate."

Dan Kasperski frowned and looked away without responding.

"All right," I said, "I understand your position. Since you're not technically Eli's therapist, maybe you could answer a question for me. Is there any reason you know of why a patient who was doing as well as Eli seemed to be doing would suddenly fall apart like this?"

"Sure," he said. "He's a human being."

"Meaning?" I asked.

He laughed. "Meaning, as Albert Ellis once said, that Eli, like every human being who has ever lived, is 'fallible, fucked up and full of frailty.'"

CHAPTER

6

During the next few hours, if I'd been searching for insight into human behaviour, my own and that of those around me, I couldn't have picked a better guide than Albert Ellis. "Fallible, fucked up and full of frailty" pretty well covered it. Alex had taken the late plane back from Saskatoon. He arrived at my place at 10:30, keeping the taxi he'd ridden in from the airport waiting so he could take Eli home. Both of us were edgy with fatigue and fear, and our fight was as stupid as it was inevitable.

When he saw me, Alex didn't make any attempt to embrace me. From the moment he came through the door, his manner was distant and professional. "What happened this time?" he asked.

"I don't know," I said. "Angus and Eli were in the family room. Angus decided to go off to Blockbuster to rent a video . . ."

"Leaving Eli alone," Alex said.

I felt the first stirrings of anger. "Angus asked Eli to go with him. He didn't want to. Eli's sixteen years old, Alex. He doesn't need a babysitter."

"He'd just gotten out of the hospital, Jo. Angus knew that. So did you."

"So did you," I said. "But you weren't around."

"I had a job to do."

"So did I. And I have kids to raise. Alex, I know you're worried about Eli. I'm worried about him too, but your nephew's not the only one who's affected by what happened here tonight. What about my children? Tonight while you were in Saskatoon doing your job, Eli was out in Taylor's studio drawing this grotesque decapitated horse over the painting of the dragon-boat races she gave him."

Pain knifed across Alex's face. "He ruined her painting?"

"Yes, and that was *after* I'd told him Taylor wanted the painting to be a surprise for him. Alex, I'm going to have to explain this to her, but I don't even know where to begin."

I could see the pulse beating in Alex's neck, but his voice was impassive. "He shouldn't have been out there alone, Jo. If you knew he was going through some sort of crisis, you should have called me and stayed with him till I got here."

I took a step towards him. "Alex, there was no crisis. It was a perfectly ordinary Friday evening. As far as I could see, everything was fine."

"Maybe you only saw what you wanted to see, Jo."

"Meaning . . . ?"

"Meaning you might have looked the other way because you wanted a nice peaceful evening. You don't like problems, Jo."

"Alex, that's not fair. If I was afraid of problems, I would have bailed on you months ago. I did everything I could to help Eli. So did my kids. We did our best. It's not fair to blame us because our best wasn't good enough."

"You people are always beyond reproach, aren't you?"

I felt as if I'd been slapped. "'You people' – Alex, you're talking about me and Angus and Taylor. We're not the bad guys." For a tense and miserable moment we faced one another in silence, like strangers whose lives had suddenly collided in some violent and permanent way.

When he finally spoke, Alex's voice was tight. "I'd better get Eli," he said. "Where is he?"

"In Peter's room."

Alex went upstairs. When he came back down, Eli was slumped against him. Dr. Kasperski's injection had relaxed Alex's nephew to the heavy-limbed state of a sleeping child.

Alex didn't stop to talk. When he reached the door, I opened it for him. "Let me know how Eli's doing," I said.

He didn't answer me. I watched as he and Eli made their awkward passage towards the taxi. Till the moment they got into the car, I expected Alex to turn and call out to me. He never did. As the cab pulled away, I felt a rush of pure anger. I slammed the door and started up the stairs. Alex hadn't once asked about Angus, nor had he expressed concern about Taylor. After months of doing everything we could to include Eli in our lives, my children and I had been shut out. We were an abstraction: "you people," an enemy not to be trusted.

Saturday morning, I awoke to the kind of thunderstorm that comes only at the end of a period of suffocating heat: lightning, thunder, and a downpour of rain that pounded the earth so viciously it seemed to assault it. I told Rose she was out of luck. There'd be no walk that morning. When I let her out in the backyard for a pee, I spotted the croquet set near the back gate where the boys had abandoned it after their ferocious game the night before. Eli had been happy that afternoon, grinning, waving the mallet over his head. "You can play if you want to, Mrs. Kilbourn, but this is a take-no-prisoners game." That had been a good time for all of us. As

I ran across the backyard to drag the croquet set under the shelter of the deck, I wondered if we'd ever have a day of such mindless joy together again.

Sylvie dropped Taylor home at a little after 9:00. I didn't say anything about the painting, and miraculously my daughter didn't ask. She was filled with owl news, and as I made pancakes, I was grateful for the soothing rhythms of her prattle. After Angus came downstairs to take her to her lesson, I stood at the kitchen window and watched the rain. If it kept up, my tomato plants would be flattened by noon.

I was dressed and digging through my closet to find a raincoat to wear to the funeral when the phone rang. Certain it was Alex, my heart pounded as I picked up the receiver. But the call was for Angus.

I wrote down the number, hung up, and turned to go back to my closet. Hilda was standing in the door to my bedroom.

She was all in black: patent-leather pumps and handbag, a black suit in the timeless style of Chanel, and a pillbox hat that must have been thirty-five years old. Her outfit was both smart and appropriate, and I glanced assessingly at my black T-shirt and white cotton skirt.

Hilda read my mind. "You look fine, Joanne. This outfit was not of my choosing. I called and asked my next-door neighbour in Saskatoon to select something apropos from my closet. She's a dear soul, but she still lives her life according to *Emily Post's Etiquette*. Now, if I'm not rushing you, I'd like to get there early. Given our cast of characters, I'd like to be around to make certain this goes off without incident. Are you ready?"

I picked up my raincoat. "Ready as I'll ever be," I said.

The funeral was scheduled for 10:00 a.m. at St. Paul's Anglican Cathedral. The cathedral was not my church, but I'd been there on many occasions, happy and sad. One of the best had been the day my daughter Mieka had been married in its chapel.

The rain hadn't let up as we pulled up on McIntyre Street, so I dropped Hilda off and went to find a parking place. By the time I got back to the cathedral, Hilda was in an intense conversation with the Dean. I waved to them and made my way to the chapel. The last time I'd been there had been on Mieka and Greg's wedding day. It had been at 2:00 in the afternoon, and the late summer sun had poured through the stained-glass windows, suffusing my daughter and her new husband in a glow warm as a blessing. As she knelt at the altar, Mieka's profile, under the filmy circle of her bridal hat, had been a cameo. Today the shafts of light that split the chapel's gloom were murky, and as the rain drummed against the windows, I shivered with a nameless apprehension. I slid into a pew, pulled down a kneeler, and prayed that my daughter would come through childbirth safely and that the new baby would be whole and healthy. Then I prayed for my other children, and for Eli and Alex and for all of us.

When Hilda came and knelt beside me, I felt foolishly relieved. I was the mother of four, and soon I would be a grandmother; nonetheless, there were times when I was overwhelmed by the need to hand over all my problems to a grown-up. That morning was one of them.

As we walked back into the church, Hilda touched my arm. "Did you say a prayer for Mieka?" she asked.

"Among others," I said. "How about you?"

She gave me a wry smile. "I prayed for strength."

When the service got under way, I found myself hoping that Hilda's prayers would be answered. Justine Blackwell's funeral was a standing-room-only affair, but despite the crowding, the congregation had divided itself to reflect the two warring halves of Justine's life. On one side of the church sat men and women whose bearing and grooming suggested a privileged past and a promising future; on the other were people with wary eyes and faces which spoke of their hard lives. Hilda and I took our places with those whose cause Justine had championed in the last year of her life. During the wait for the service to begin, the two camps regarded one another with mutual suspicion, but when the first chord of the opening hymn sounded, all eyes followed Justine Blackwell's daughters as Eric Fedoruk led them up the aisle.

The Blackwell women were a striking trio: Lucy, in a black scoop-necked, miniskirted, floral-print dress, seemed more seductress than mourner; Signe, her thick blonde hair braided into a Valkyrie's coronet, looked powerful enough to storm Valhalla; Tina, in black from head to toe, head covered by a lace mantilla, face hidden behind a black veil, suggested minor European royalty. When they took their place in the front pew, the church fell silent. Almost immediately, there was a second stir. Wayne J. Waters may have been wearing a cheap, ill-fitting suit, but he carried himself with the unmistakable air of a man who demanded respect. When he slid into the pew opposite the Blackwell sisters, it was obvious the show was about to begin.

For a while, it seemed Hilda had made all the right choices. The Mozart mass she had selected was pure beauty; the carefully barbered young men who had accompanied Justine's mahogany casket to the altar disappeared on cue; the Dean's prayers were comforting; and the eulogy by Eric Fedoruk was affectionate without being mawkish. He made no reference to the direction Justine's life had taken in the year before she died. When Eric Fedoruk went back to his seat, I glanced down at my program. All that was left was the closing prayer and the recessional. I picked up my purse and let my mind wander to thoughts of curling up on the couch with the Saturday paper and a pot of Earl Grey.

Suddenly, Hilda sat up ramrod straight, cutting short my reverie. Wayne J. Waters had slid out of his seat and started up the aisle towards the casket. As he reached it, he nodded, touched the lid affectionately, then turned to face the congregation. For a moment, I thought he was going to share one of those painful personal memories that have become the vogue at funerals. I was wrong.

"This one's for Justine," he said. "Not the judge Mr. Fedoruk was talking about, but the woman I knew. I learned this for her, because it was her favourite." In a deep and powerful voice he sang Blake's old hymn "Jerusalem," with its thrilling final verses about social justice:

Bring me my Bow of burning gold:
Bring me my Arrows of desire:
Bring me my Spear: O clouds unfold!
Bring me my Chariot of fire!

I will not cease from Mental Fight,
Nor shall my Sword sleep in my hand,
Till we have built Jerusalem
In England's green and pleasant Land.

When he finished, there was a smattering of applause, quickly muffled, from Wayne J.'s side of the church. Then he resumed his seat, and we were back on program. The discreet young men from the funeral home reappeared; the casket came back down the aisle and Eric Fedoruk and the Blackwell sisters followed it. Eric's arm was around Lucy's shoulder; she looked dazed, like the survivor of a disaster. Tina's emotions, hidden behind her black veil, were unreadable, but Signe

Rayner was white with fury. When we came out of the church into the transept she was waiting for us. She grabbed Hilda's arm and took her aside.

"Whose decision was it to let that creature sing?"

Hilda tapped the program. "As you can see, Mr. Waters was not part of the Order of Service. He acted on his own initiative, and I, for one, am glad he did."

Signe's voice was low with fury. "Will you still be glad you let him sing when he's arrested for murdering my mother?" She turned on her heel and strode towards the mourners' limousine. One of the young men from the funeral home helped her in; the door slammed shut, and the car sped off.

"Wait." When I turned, I saw Lucy standing at the entrance to the church. "They left without me," she said. She looked at us beseechingly. "Can I go to the cemetery with you?"

"Of course," I said. "Hop in."

During the ten-minute drive to Crocus Hills Memorial Park, no one said a word. When we drove through the gates, Lucy, who was in the back seat, leaned forward and pointed. "It's just over there," she said. "It's past the place where all the soldiers are buried. You can't miss it. There's this incredible weeping willow."

Hilda turned towards her. "Your mother isn't being buried there, Lucy."

"Why not? That's our family plot. That's where my father is." There was an unsettling edge in Lucy's voice.

Hilda must have heard it too. Her answer was firm and factual. "When I talked to the people from Crocus Hills, they said the family plot was full. We had to purchase a new burial space for your mother. There was no alternative."

Lucy's teeth began to chatter. "That's crazy," she said. "That plot was for all of us." She opened the car door. "I'm going over there."

I glanced at Hilda. She nodded. "Maybe it's best if Lucy sees for herself," she said.

We drove past the area reserved for military burials. Under the gunmetal sky, it was a solemn sight: row upon row of identical grave markers, each with its own small red-and-white Canadian flag.

I pulled up in front of the area Lucy had indicated. Before I turned off the ignition, she was out of the car and running towards the weeping willow. She stopped in front of a low black marble headstone; then she gazed around her, as if she were trying to get her bearings.

Hilda and I walked over to her. The tombstone was engraved simply: RICHARD BLACKWELL: 1902-1967. The grave it marked was surrounded by other graves with small cheap markers. Lucy knelt on the wet grass and read out the names incredulously: WANDA SPETZ (1961-1997); KIM DUCHARME (1970-1997); DANIEL SOKWAYPNACE (1975-1997); MERV GEMMELL (1973-1997). When she looked up at us, her extraordinary turquoise eyes were blank with disbelief. "Who are these people?"

Hilda shook her head. "The man from Crocus Hills told me they're relatives of people your mother met in the last year."

"My mother let strangers be buried in the family plot? Sweet Jesus." Lucy laughed mirthlessly.

I touched her elbow. "Lucy, come back to the car. You can deal with this another time."

She stood up wearily. "Can I? Somehow I doubt that, Music Woman." She started back towards the car, then she turned to face us. "You understand that I don't give a good goddamn about the property. It's just that, after everything else she did to him, my mother shouldn't have done this to my father."

The three of us got back in the car and retraced our route

to the cemetery entrance. Hilda pointed towards the new and treeless area where the limousines and hearse had stopped. A knot of mourners was already standing over the raw wound of a fresh grave, and the men from the funeral home were unloading their cargo.

Lucy put her hands up as if she were warding off a blow. "I'm not going over there," she said. "I want to go home."

I looked at Hilda. Her face was so pale and strained, I didn't even consult her. I just stepped on the gas.

As I started out through the cemetery gates, Eric Fedoruk was driving in. He slowed and rolled down his window.

His eyes were red-rimmed, but his voice was firm. "Is it over already?" he said. "I had an urgent call from a client."

Lucy leaned towards the window on the driver's side. "It isn't over," she said. "Eric, she gave away the burial plots around my father's grave. Did you know about it?"

He winced. "I knew."

"And you didn't tell us. Because you were protecting her. The way you always have."

As I drove down Albert Street, Lucy was silent, sunk into the corner of the back seat.

When I pulled up in front of the house on Leopold Crescent, Lucy mumbled her thanks. Before she went inside, she turned and gave us a small wave. I thought I had never seen anyone so alone.

"I guess if you needed proof that Justine's mind had deteriorated, you have it now," I said.

"I wonder," she said. "I was thinking of another possibility."

"What other possibility?"

Hilda's voice seemed to come from far away. "That Justine found her family so abhorrent that the idea of spending eternity with them was insupportable."

Hilda and I were met by the sounds of the Smashing

Pumpkins when we got home. Normally, the Pumpkins were not my favourite group, but that day the pulsing rhythm of "Bullet with Butterfly Wings" was just the antidote I needed for the misery of our morning. Angus and his girlfriend, Leah, were in the kitchen making grilled cheese sandwiches. Taylor was sitting at the kitchen table, pounding the bottom of the Heinz bottle she was holding over her plate. Just as we walked in, her efforts paid off and she flooded her sandwich with ketchup.

She glanced up at us, triumphant. "I didn't think this was going to work."

Hilda's face regained some of its colour during lunch. It seemed grilled cheese sandwiches and the company of young people was just the tonic she needed. At the end of the summer, Leah's theatre school in Toronto had performed a rock-opera version of Thornton Wilder's *Our Town*, and Hilda appeared genuinely absorbed by Leah's account of how she had played Emily. Hilda had taught high-school English for almost fifty years. *Our Town* couldn't have held many surprises for her; nonetheless, she appeared to find the prospect of an Emily with cropped hair, an eyebrow ring, and a tattoo of foxes chasing a lion around her upper arm as provocative as I did.

After lunch, I tried to get Hilda to take a nap, but she squared her shoulders and insisted on getting to work on Justine's papers.

"I don't mind telling you that business with the family plot has shaken me, Joanne. If there are other surprises, I'd like to know about them before Eric Fedoruk and I discuss the disposition of Justine's estate."

I was surprised. "But I thought Eric Fedoruk was the executor."

Hilda shrugged. "The situation is no longer that clear-cut . . ."

"Why am I not surprised?" I said.

Hilda's smile was wry. "Your point's well taken. For a woman who lived her life with such precision, Justine certainly left her affairs in a troubling state. A second will has just surfaced, Joanne."

"The one that names you executrix," I said.

Hilda nodded. "It was in a safety-deposit box at Justine's bank, and it's going to raise hackles. The original will was drawn up years ago, and it's pretty much what you'd expect of a woman like Justine. She makes contributions to some decent charities and arts organizations, and asks that the major part of the estate be divided equally among her daughters. This new will leaves *everything* to Culhane House, including the home on Leopold Crescent. It was dated three months before Justine's death."

"Then it would take precedence," I said. "Anyone who ever watched Perry Mason reruns knows that, but I wouldn't want to be in the room when Justine's daughters hear the news."

"Nor would I," said Hilda. "And Eric Fedoruk has suggested that we do a little investigating before he brings this explosive information to those most directly involved. He's staved them off until now, a tactic for which he deserves commendation. The Blackwell women have been nipping at his heels. But we were wise to wait. If there is a real possibility that Justine was *non compos mentis*, her daughters are in an excellent position to challenge the second will. You can imagine what the media would make of a legal wrangle between Justine's daughters and Wayne J. Waters and his crew."

I nodded. "That business with the family plot today would certainly make for engrossing reading."

Hilda's eyes were troubled. "Justine put her trust in me. As her friend I have an obligation to protect her reputation, but as her executrix I also have an obligation to see that her estate is settled fairly. I've decided the best route to honouring both obligations is to carry out the task she set me. If Justine was sane, she was entitled to do what she wanted with her money, including give it to Wayne J. Waters. If she was delusional, her money should go where she had intended it to go before her mind became clouded: to her daughters."

"And you have to decide," I said. "Damn it, Hilda, why does it always come back to you?"

Hilda gave me a small smile. "Because much as we wish it were, life isn't all meadows and groves." She stood up. "Now, I really had better get down to business. Luckily for all concerned, until the day she died Justine was a meticulous keeper of records. It's amazing how often one can find an answer to a big question by answering a number of smaller ones."

After Hilda went upstairs, I was restless. I threw a load of laundry in the machine, gave the living room a perfunctory dusting, and flipped through an academic journal that had arrived in Friday's mail. I couldn't shake the image of Lucy Blackwell, standing alone on the doorstep, her dark honey hair sleeked by the rain into the style that evoked the flower child she'd been when she made her first album. Curious, I went back down to the laundry room. The last time we'd cleaned the basement, I'd been merciless. I'd thrown out all our old cassettes. I'd deep-sixed Petula Clark and Jimmy Webb and a score of others, but I'd stashed the cassettes I couldn't part with in my old wicker sewing basket. With its cotton lining patterned in psychedelic swirls of orange, yellow, and red, the basket seemed an appropriate final resting place for old tunes and old memories. Lucy Blackwell's debut album was on the top of the pile. Almost thirty years had passed since she'd posed for the cover photo: a carefree girl on a garden swing, eyes closed in ecstasy, legs bared, shining hair flying. Almost thirty years had passed since Ian and I had embraced in the hush of the university library and whispered our plans for a perfect life.

I took the tape back upstairs, dropped it in the player on my bedside table, and turned down the bedspread. As I slipped between the cool sheets, Lucy was singing "My Daddy's Party." The lyrics were as poignantly beautiful as I had remembered them being, but for the first time I was struck by a curious omission. Lucy Blackwell's account of enchanted evenings in the lives of three little girls, mesmerized by candlelight and grown-up laughter, shimmered with detail, but nowhere in her remembrance of things past had she mentioned her mother's name.

When I woke up, Taylor was standing beside the bed, peering down at me. She was wearing the Testicle Festival T-shirt from Bottlescrew Bill's. "How can you sleep in the middle of the day?" she asked.

"It's easy," I said. "You just have to go to bed too late and get up too early."

She shrugged. "You don't let me do that." She ran her finger along the buttons of my tape player.

"Something on your mind?" I said.

She didn't look up. "You never said whether he liked it." When I looked at her quizzically, she frowned. "You never said whether Eli liked the dragon-boat painting." Her dark eyes were anxious.

"Who wouldn't love that painting?" I said. "Just looking at it made me feel happy."

Amazingly, the diversion worked. "Did you really like it that much?"

"I think it's the best work you've done," I said. "I hated to see it leave the house."

"I could do one for you," Taylor said. "Not the same. Maybe I could paint a dragon boat with all of us in it."

"Sounds good to me," I said.

"Sounds good to me, too," she said. She scrunched her nose. "How come you didn't say anything about my T-shirt?"

"It's Saturday," I said. "This house is a taste-free zone."

The rain had stopped by the time I pulled into the parking lot at NationTV. When I got out of our Volvo, I noticed a spectacular rainbow arching over the east of the city. It seemed like such a good omen that when I got to Jill Osiowy's office I insisted she come to her window to have a look.

"Does this mean all our troubles are over?" asked Jill.

"Every last one," I said. "The rainbow never lies."

Jill had set up the VCR and TV in her office, and as she organized the tapes, I watched the colours of the rainbow fade, then disappear. I was so intent that I didn't notice Jill waiting for me.

She came over and tapped me on the shoulder. "Can we roll now, or do you want to check some pigeon entrails to see if this is an auspicious day for decision-making?

"We can roll," I said.

"Good," she said, then she leaned over and hit *play*.

Our first prospect was an Ottawa academic who was a NationTV regular during federal elections. He was about my age, with a sonorous voice, a fifty-dollar haircut, and the perpetually aggrieved air of an elitist in an imperfect world.

When his commentary was finished, I looked at Jill. "I could never measure up," I said.

Jill ejected the tape. "I know what you mean. He always makes me feel as if I have spinach hanging out of my teeth." She dropped in the next tape.

"Now this one isn't empathy-challenged, but there is another teeny shortcoming," Jill said. The smiling face on the screen belonged to a premier who had been retired by the electorate in his province's last election. In the three minutes during which he spoke about welfare reform, the ex-premier dropped all his final g's and made four factual errors.

"Thick as a two-bob plank," I said.

Jill nodded in agreement. "Wouldn't recognize an intelligent idea if it came with a side order of fries." She brightened. "But you have to admit he is folksy."

"Is that why he made the short list?"

Jill dropped the ex-premier's tape back in its case. "Nope. He made the short list because he's married to my boss's sister." She inserted a third tape. "Let's hope third time's lucky."

Jill's words were light, but I noticed she was watching my face with real interest. My reaction didn't disappoint her. Our third candidate was wearing bluejeans and a T-shirt and he had the kind of energy that made a viewer sit up and listen. He was young, in his late twenties, and as he described the recent convention of our official opposition party, he was smart and irreverent.

"He's good," I said. "What's his name?"

"Ken Leung," Jill said. "He teaches Canada–Pacific Rim Studies at Simon Fraser."

"I like him," I said.

"So do I," Jill said. "What do you think of the shirt?"

"Taylor was wearing one just like it when I left the house," I said.

"Serious?"

"Serious. Bottlescrew Bill's Festival obviously draws a varied clientele."

Jill laughed. "So, is the shirt omen enough for us to offer Ken Leung the job?"

"Sure," I said. "Especially when you factor in his intelligence, his presence on camera, and the fact that he will appeal to a whole new demographic. It'll be good for all of us to have somebody on the show who knows what the world feels like to people born after 1970.

"He speaks Cantonese, too," Jill said. "Do you think Glayne will like him?"

"She'll love him. He's a terrific find. If I were you, I'd offer him the job before somebody else grabs him."

Jill picked up the phone and dialled Ken Leung's home number. The person on the other end of the line said Ken was playing tennis, but he was expected back any moment. Jill said the matter was urgent and left her number. When she hung up, she screwed her face into an expression that was supposed to be beseeching. "Wait with me until he calls? It's so boring here on Saturdays; besides, it will give us a chance to get down and dirty about our lives without Angus flapping around."

"I'll stay," I said. "But at the moment, there's nothing in my life to get down and dirty about."

Jill frowned. "You and Alex *are* still together, aren't you?"

"I guess so, but it doesn't feel like we're together. His nephew's had a lot of problems lately, and Alex and I had a pretty nasty exchange about it last night."

"I didn't think you two ever fought."

"We don't," I said. "Maybe we'd be better off now if we had."

Jill frowned. "Is it that serious?"

"I don't know. There's just so much we never talk about. I think we're both afraid that if we ever really started talking about all the things we were worried about, we'd discover we had too many strikes against us."

"Is there anything I can do to help?"

"No," I said, "but thanks for asking."

Jill glanced at her phone. "Looks like we may be here for a while. Do you want a Coke?"

"Sure," I said.

Jill went to the apartment-sized fridge in the corner of her office. She took out two Cokes, snapped the caps, and handed me one.

I took a sip. "Jill, what do you know about Justine Blackwell and her family?"

Jill's eyes widened. "Where did that come from?"

"From my concern about Hilda," I said.

"I noticed she's become the family spokesperson," Jill said. "It struck me as a little bizarre."

"She's also the executrix of Justine's will," I said. "And I don't like it. I also don't like some of the people who've come with the package. Hilda offered to do an old friend a favour, then all of a sudden she's at the centre of all this hostility."

"Do you want me to do some digging?"

"Yeah," I said, "I do. What's your take on Justine's murder?"

"I haven't got one," Jill said. "If you watch our news or read the paper, you know as much as I know. There's the Wayne J. Waters and Co. angle, and there's the family angle."

"The family angle," I said.

"Surely you've cottoned to the fact that Justine wasn't exactly mother of the year."

"I have," I said. "But Justine's daughters aren't exactly children. They've all accomplished things in their lives. Besides, by the time they hit their forties, most people recognize that there's a statute of limitations on bad parenting."

"Sometimes there are fresh offences," Jill said mildly.

"That sounds as if you know something."

"I know about one specific problem. It was with Tina. About a year ago, Tina decided she needed plastic surgery."

"But she's so attractive."

"She's also forty-four."

"That's not old."

"It's old for television," Jill said. "By the time a woman's forty-four, the camera has stopped being her friend. Tina had been doing the supper-hour news on CJRG for twenty-one years. Anyway, some asshole over in their news division decided to trade her in for a newer model. Tina thought she might be able to hold on to her job if she got one of those bloodless facelifts.

I winced. "What on earth is a bloodless facelift?"

"We did a piece on it last fall. It's the hot new alternative to the surgeon's knife: laser surgery. It zaps wrinkles by literally burning away the skin on the face. Some of the people on the piece we did had great results."

"But Tina didn't."

Jill shook her head. "She tried to do it on the cheap. It's an expensive procedure. Twenty thousand U.S. Tina didn't have that kind of money. Regina's a pretty small market, and those local stations don't pay diddley."

"Why didn't she go to her mother?"

"That's what a lot of people wondered. Rumour had it that Madame Justice Blackwell was too busy dealing with the financial needs of her new friends to spend money on her daughter."

I sipped my Coke. "Do you believe that?"

Jill shrugged. "I don't know. People talk. Anyway, Tina pulled together what she could and went down to the some laser-surgery clinic in Tennessee. They botched it. Her skin looks like she's been burned and she's quite badly scarred. She came to me this summer to ask if we had anything for her in radio. She's good on air and experienced, but we're bringing along our own people. Our own *young* people."

The phone rang. "Speaking of young people," I said. "That must be our Generation X-er."

When Jill picked up the phone, I gathered up our Coke bottles and started out the door towards the recycle box. Jill shouted after me. "Hang on," she said. "It's for you."

Angus's voice was cracking with excitement. "I'm an uncle," he said. "Mieka finally had the baby. I talked to Greg. Everybody's all right. He says the baby weighs – just a minute, I wrote it down – nine pounds, eleven ounces. It could be a linebacker, Mum."

"Nine pounds, eleven ounces. Poor Mieka," I said.

"Greg said she was a little wiped," Angus conceded. "Anyway, I told her we'd come up to Saskatoon tonight. We can go up tonight, can't we?

"We'll leave as soon as I get home," I said. "Wow, I can't believe it! A grandson!"

"Where did you get that? It's a girl, Mum. Her name is – wait a minute, I wrote that down too – the baby's name is Madeleine Kilbourn Harris."

"But you said . . . Never mind. So the linebacker is a girl."

Angus laughed. "Greg said he's signing her up for the Powder Puff League first thing Monday morning."

When I got home, I called Mieka to tell her we were on our way. She sounded tired, but very happy. Then I dialled Alex's number. There was no answer, and he didn't have voice mail. I hung up the phone, reached under the bed, and pulled out the cradle board Alex had made for the new baby. Our relationship had hit a bad patch, but I still wanted him to be part of the next few hours.

I was throwing a nightie into my overnight bag when Hilda came in. Her hot-pink and apple-green outfit was as cheerful as a late summer orchard, and she was beaming. She came over and embraced me.

"Angus told me the good news," she said. "And he told me you're going to Saskatoon tonight. You're welcome to stay at my house, if that would help."

"Thanks," I said. "We'll be all right at Greg and Mieka's. It's only for one night. Hilda, should I call somebody to come in and walk Rose?"

She shook her head. "No need," she said. "I'll welcome the walk before bedtime. I have to finish going through Justine's private financial records, and that's bound to be unpleasant."

"Don't tell me Justine couldn't balance her chequebook," I said.

Hilda didn't smile at my joke. "No, Justine was meticulous. It's just troubling to see how much she gave and how little she seemed to get back." She shook herself. "Not one more word about Justine. This is a day for celebration."

I gave her a hug. "If you change your mind about Rose, there's a list of Angus's buddies by the phone. Any of them will be happy to walk her for the price of a Big Gulp."

Hilda smiled. "A reasonable fee. Now, off with you. Give Mieka and Greg my love, and kiss Madeleine for me." She drew me close. "Take care of yourself, Joanne. You're very dear to me."

"And you are to me," I said. "I'll call you when I get back from the hospital."

"I'll be waiting," Hilda said.

I zipped up my overnight bag, picked up a jacket, and grabbed the tape of Lucy Blackwell I'd been listening to that afternoon. Chances were good that Angus would howl at my choice of travel music, but there was always the possibility that Lucy had been around long enough to be retro.

Before I dropped the tape in my bag, I glanced at the photograph on the cover. Rumour had it that Bob Dylan had taken that photo of Lucy on the swing. Twenty-nine years ago, stuck with the coffee parties and the constituency lists while my new husband made a name for himself in politics, I had, on more than one occasion, envied that lovely girl her life of adventure and freedom. I didn't envy her now. Nothing in Lucy Blackwell's life, past or present, could hold a candle to the prospect of holding Madeleine Kilbourn Harris in my arms.

CHAPTER

7

Royal University Hospital in Saskatoon is a teaching hospital on the west side of the University of Saskatchewan campus. From our spot in the parking lot, I could see the riverbank above the South Saskatchewan River. The leaves of the willows and scrub birch were beginning to change colour. In a week, they'd be saffron; in three weeks, they'd be gone, and the long grey winter would be upon us. But that September evening, as the sun warmed the tindall stone of the campus's oldest buildings, we were in the timeless world of a university at the beginning of term, and the air was fresh with new beginnings.

Mieka's room was on the fourth floor. As Angus, Taylor, and I crowded into the elevator, I found myself hoping her roommates were a tolerant crew. We came bearing gifts. I'd stopped at a stand at the edge of town to buy gladioli, Mieka's favourites, and Taylor had picked out enough spectacular blooms for a Mafia funeral. Angus was carrying the cradle board Alex had made and an industrial-sized bag of Mieka's favourite gumdrops, and I had an armful of gifts from Jill, Hilda, and me, and a weathered package from my older son, Peter, who was working with a veterinarian in Whitehorse. One of Pete's friends from N.W.T. had dropped the parcel at our house the week before with strict instructions that we deliver it when the baby was born.

As soon as the elevator doors opened, Taylor hit the corridor at a dead run. Blinded by the gladioli, she missed by a hairsbreadth colliding with a young woman in a fuzzy pink housecoat who was moving with the painful steps of a patient recovering from a Caesarean section. My younger daughter was headed for trouble, but there was time to nip it in the bud.

"All right, T," I said, "that's enough."

She wheeled around and peered at me through the gladioli.

"Do we need to find a quiet place where we can talk?" I said.

Her lower lip shot out. "No," she said.

"Good," I said, "because you and I have been waiting a long time to meet Madeleine. I don't think either of us wants to waste time cooling our heels out here."

Mieka was in a semi-private room at the end of the hall. Greg met us at the door and, after a flurry of hugs, he ushered us in. Luckily, it appeared that there was no roommate. My daughter was sitting by the window, holding her daughter. I thought I was prepared for the moment, but as soon as I saw mother and child together, my throat closed. I walked over, kissed Mieka, and drew back the receiving blanket so I could see Madeleine. She was a beauty, with a mop of dark hair, a rosebud mouth, and fingers and toes impossibly small and perfect.

"Here," Mieka said, offering the baby to me. I took her. The first time I had held my own daughter, I had been exhausted from a too-long labour and terrified about whether I would be a good mother. The joy I felt when I looked down at my granddaughter that night was unalloyed by memories of past pain or fear of the future. I was simply and overwhelmingly happy.

"Hi, Madeleine," I said. The baby looked up at me intently.

Taylor stood on tiptoe to look into her new niece's face. "She knows who you are," she said softly. "I'm Taylor Love, Madeleine."

Angus leaned over for a closer look. "Pretty nice," he said. He turned to his big sister. "Good job, Mieka."

"Piece of cake," she said. "Now, come on, hand over those gumdrops, and let's open the presents."

The rest of the visit was etched in gold. We found containers for the glads, and I held the baby while Mieka and Greg opened the gifts. Jill had been shooting a series in B.C. over the summer and she'd brought back the tiniest siwash sweater I'd ever seen; Hilda's gift was a Beatrix Potter mug and porringer, and a cheque to start a bank account so the baby could see Beatrix Potter country some day; Peter's unwieldy package contained a handmade quilt in the spectacular colours of a northern sunset. My present was practical: a gift certificate for six months of visits from a cleaning service. We praised all the gifts extravagantly, but it was Alex's present that was the real hit. Greg, who was a weekend carpenter, gazed assessingly at the cradle board Alex had made.

"That's hand-done," he said. "It's a beautiful piece of woodworking."

I felt a rush of pride. "Alex will be glad you appreciated the work he put into it."

There was one final order of business. I called Taylor over. "There's a book in my bag. Could you get it?"

When Taylor pulled out the worn copy of Margaret Wise Brown's *Goodnight Moon*, she eyed it with interest. "You used to read that to me."

I nodded. "And before that, I read it to Angus and before Angus to Peter . . ."

"And before Peter to Mieka," she said. "And now you want to give it to Madeleine."

"I thought you might like to give it to her."

"I'll read it to her," Taylor said. And she did. In the flat cadences of the new reader, Taylor worked her methodical way through the story of the little rabbit saying goodnight to all the ordinary pleasures of his world. It was a stellar performance. Even Angus remained silent. When she'd finished, Taylor handed the book to Mieka.

It was a nice note to leave on. I kissed the baby and, reluctantly, placed her in her father's arms.

"I hate to see you go," Mieka said. "You'll come back first thing tomorrow, won't you?"

"As soon as they let us in," I said.

"Here," she said, handing me a Polaroid picture Greg had snapped of me holding the baby. "The first photograph of you as a grandmother."

Greg walked us to the elevator. It came almost immediately, and Greg surprised me by stepping in with us.

As the elevator doors closed, I turned to him. "Nothing's wrong, is it?"

He shook his head. "Everything's great, especially now that we have a cleaning service. That was an inspiration, Jo. And we'll be okay with Maddy. I've got a month's paternity leave."

"What an enlightened boss you have," I said.

"Actually I have a new boss. That's what I wanted to talk to you about. You know him."

"Who?"

"My Uncle Keith."

The elevator reached the lobby, and the doors opened. "I didn't even know he'd moved back to Saskatchewan," I said.

"It's pretty recent. He's the president of my company now. Started just after Labour Day."

"And the first thing he did was give you a month off?"

"No, the first thing he did was ask about you."

Amazingly, I found myself blushing.

Greg was too diplomatic to comment on my embarrassment. "Jo, I told Keith you were coming up to Saskatoon today. He didn't want to intrude the first night, but he said he hoped you wouldn't leave town without seeing him."

"I'll give him a call before we leave."

My son-in-law pulled out his cellphone. "No time like the present," he said. "You're not supposed to use these things in the hospital, so I'll walk you to your car. You can call Keith from there."

And so, an hour after I had seen my first grandchild, I was standing in the parking lot of the hospital where she'd been born, calling an old lover. It was a scene straight out of a telecommunications ad.

Keith answered on the first ring. Not that long ago, the sound of Keith's voice on the other end of a telephone was enough to make my heart pound. He had been my first lover after my husband's death, and our relationship had been good until geography separated us and Keith found someone else. The situation was hackneyed, but I had been wounded. It had taken Alex and the passage of time to put things in perspective. That day when I heard Keith's voice, I felt the easy uncomplicated pleasure you feel when you're reconnecting with an old friend.

"Jo, is that you? I made Greg promise, but I've been kicking myself ever since. Twenty-four hours isn't much time to discover all the wonders of Madeleine."

"I agree," I said. "Have you seen her?"

"I thought I'd give Mieka a chance to take a deep breath

before she had to put up with the old bachelor uncle, but Greg says Madeleine's a beauty."

"And clever," I said. "Taylor's already read her her first story."

He laughed. "How is Taylor?"

"Thriving," I said. "So's Angus. He's in Grade 12 this year."

"Almost a college man." He paused. "And how is Jo?"

"Happy. Busy."

"Is there any chance we can get together tomorrow?"

"I don't think so," I said. "I want to spend as much time as I can at the hospital."

"Visiting hours don't start till eleven. I could buy you and the kids breakfast. If I remember correctly, you loved that decadent Sunday brunch at the Bessborough."

"You remember correctly," I said.

"Then it's a go?"

I hesitated, but I couldn't think of a single logical reason to refuse. "It's a go," I said. "We'll meet you in the lobby at eight."

I handed the phone back to Greg. "Satisfied?"

He grinned. "Absolutely. The rest of the day will be yours to do with as you please."

When we got to Greg and Mieka's, Taylor began to race up and down the stairs. I knew there would be tears before bedtime if she didn't get rid of some of her energy. As she peeled by me, I grabbed her hand. "Let's go check out the neighbourhood," I said.

In five minutes, we were on our way. My daughter and son-in-law lived in an old two-storey clapboard house in the Nutana section of Saskatoon. It was a neighbourhood that, in the past few years, had surprised itself by becoming trendy. That night, as the kids and I walked along Broadway

Avenue, baskets of geraniums hung from replicas of turn-of-the-century lampposts, and upscale boutiques that sold imported cheese, antique clothing, and pricey toys stood cheek by jowl with shops that still bore the names of original owners and sold homely necessities like hardware and bread. We walked up to the intersection called the Five Corners, and I showed Taylor the school Madeleine would go to. All three of us agreed this was going to be a good neighbourhood for her to grow up in.

Later, as I settled into my unfamiliar bed, a jumble of images crowded my mind. The day just past had been amazing: beginning with a funeral and ending with a birth. I thought of Emily's poignant line from *Our Town* when, on the day of her own funeral, she makes the mistake of revisiting a day in her life. "Do any human beings," she asks, "ever realize life while they live it? – every every minute?" As I looked at the Polaroid photo of my new granddaughter and me, which I'd propped up against the light on the nightstand, I knew that I would hang on to this particular moment for a lifetime.

Keith Harris was waiting just inside the doors of the Bessborough Hotel when we arrived. He was wearing light tan slacks and a sea-green knit shirt that I'd once told him was my favourite. He had the look of well-being golfers have after a pleasant summer: tanned, fit, and at peace with the world. Greg and he shared a family resemblance. They were both men of medium build, with hazel eyes, substantial noses, easy smiles, and faces that were agreeable rather than handsome. Apart from age, the only significant difference between them was their hair. Greg's was dark and thick; Keith's had just about vanished.

When he spotted me, Keith took me in his arms. "It's good to see you, Jo," he said.

"It's good to see you," I said, and I meant it.

We all ate far too much. Once, the Bessborough buffets had featured butter sculptures and chefs in white hats carving hams that glistened with clove-studded fat. The menu had been scaled down and healthied up for the nineties, but the food was still good, and as we walked out of the hotel, Keith offered me his arm. "Care to undo the damage we just did to ourselves?"

It was a perfect early-fall day: cool enough for Angus to run along the jogging path that snakes beside the South Saskatchewan River, but mild enough for Taylor, bright as a butterfly in her red-and-orange sweater, to throw herself on the grass and roll down the hill towards the river. Keith and I sat on a bench near the fountain to watch, and as we watched, we talked about our lives.

Keith's had recently undergone some fairly dramatic changes. After years in Ottawa, he'd come back to Saskatchewan to manage a high-powered investment company. He was a lawyer by profession, but he'd spent much of his working life in the backrooms of Tory politics. I'd spent enough time in the backrooms to know that the political world is parochial, fevered, exhausting, nasty, and addictive. Keith said he was delighted with the change, but I couldn't imagine he would be happy away from the melee, and I said so.

He smiled ruefully. "You're the only who's seen through me. On paper, it's a great decision: it's secure; the money's unbelievable; people won't flee when they see me walk into a cocktail party. And I must admit, it will be nice not to have to listen to some snot-nosed neo-con explain the political process to me. All the same, I'm going to miss it."

"You can still be involved," I said.

"I've got too many enemies to be an *éminence grise*; besides I think my new company would prefer that I keep a low profile." He shrugged. "I'll work it out. One good thing: it's going to be great to be closer to you."

I didn't respond.

Keith touched my elbow. "Are you and Alex still together?"

"I don't know," I said.

"That doesn't sound like you."

"Maybe not," I said. "But it's the truth."

"Want me to change the subject?"

"Yeah," I said, "I do."

For a few minutes we sat in silence, enjoying the sunshine. When Keith turned to me, his smile was rueful. "We must be getting old, Jo: running out of conversational topics."

"I've got one," I said. "Justine Blackwell. Did you know her?"

Keith looked sombre. "That was a terrible thing."

"And close to home for us," I said. "Justine and Hilda McCourt were friends. Hilda was staying at our house the night Justine died. In fact, they were together just before she was killed."

"That must have been a nasty shock for Hilda," Keith said. "Is she handling it all right?"

"You know Hilda," I said. "She's rolled up her shirtsleeves and dug in to help sort out some problems with Justine's estate."

"Good," Keith said. He frowned. "What's that thing about being busy Hilda always says?"

"It's a quotation from Catharine Parr Traill," I said. "In cases of emergency, it's folly to throw your hands in the air and wail in terror – better to be up and doing."

Keith laughed. "Words to live by. Now, to answer your question. Over the years, Justine and I were at a lot of the same functions, but except for the usual pleasantries, I never really talked to her. I did know her husband, though. Dick Blackwell was a big contributor to the party, and he was a great guy – the best. I always thought he deserved a better personal life than the one he ended up with."

"'Personal life' meaning his marriage?"

Keith sighed. "Yeah, 'personal life' meaning his marriage. One should be charitable about the dead, but Justine wasn't much of a wife. She was, however, one hell of a lawyer." He shook his head and smiled. "I saw her in action once. She was amazing. She had exactly the right temperament for criminal law: combative but cool. She was passionate when it suited her purpose, but every display of emotion was calculated: just enough outrage or fervent belief or shining-eyed hope to do the job, and not one iota more." Keith turned his head and glanced at me. "She never broke a sweat."

"Not with her marriage either," I said.

"No, not with her marriage, and not with her children. After Dick died, there was a rumour that Justine had been having an affair. I never believed it – not because she was such a dutiful wife, but because she didn't have that kind of passion."

"You didn't like her much, did you?"

Keith sat up. "Actually, I did like her. She was smart, she was beautiful, and, on the occasions we were together, she was good company. I just think Dick Blackwell would have had a happier life if he'd married someone else. Given the circumstances, that sounds harsh, but it's the truth – at least as I see it. If you want more details, you could talk to Dick's old law partner."

"No," I said, "your opinion's good enough for me."

"Hearing that was worth the price of breakfast."

His gaze was steady, and I was relieved when Taylor came peeling up the hill. She was sweaty and dirty and happy. "Is it time to see Madeleine yet?"

"After we scrub off six layers of dirt, it is. Let's find your brother and go back to Greg and Mieka's and hit the showers."

Angus found us, or rather, he found Keith. They walked ahead of us on the path talking about their common passion, football. By the time we hit the Bessborough parking lot, they had decided to get tickets for the Huskies game that afternoon. After Taylor climbed into the back and Angus slid into the driver's seat, Keith turned to me. "Should I get a ticket for Taylor? I don't think I'll have to twist Greg's arm too hard to get him to come. You and Mieka might enjoy some time alone."

"It's worth a try," I said. I bent down to the car window. "Taylor, Mr. Harris has an invitation for you . . ."

"I heard," she said. "And I want to go."

"Sounds like it's settled," Keith said.

When we said goodbye in the Bessborough parking lot, Keith held my hand a second longer than necessary, then he kissed me on the cheek. "Thanks for the morning, Jo. I hope it's the first of many."

Greg was waiting with the Polaroid when we came into Mieka's room. He wanted some pictures of the kids with Madeleine. Angus went first. He held her in one arm, tight against his body, the way his coach had made him hold a football for an entire weekend after a costly fumble. When he handed the baby off to Taylor, she was wildly enthusiastic. For ten minutes, she sat in the corner with Madeleine, crooning and chatting. When her eyes betrayed her restlessness, Greg said he'd buy the kids a burger before the game, and after a whirl of goodbyes, Mieka and I were left alone.

We pushed Madeleine's bassinet in front of the window, pulled our own chairs close, and gave ourselves over to the singular pleasures of two women wholly absorbed by a new baby. September sunshine pooled in a circle around us; air crisp with the smell of fall leaves and late gardens drifted through the open window, and my daughter and I swapped stories about childbirth and the primal pleasure of holding a child to the breast. In the larger world of the hospital, there was death and fear and pain and suffering, but in the safety of our small circle, there were only dreams and hopes and an unspoken thanksgiving that somehow the two of us had managed to navigate the risky shoals of the mother-daughter relationship and arrive at this moment together.

The drive back to Regina was pleasant and uneventful. All the way home, we saw farmers still out in the fields. It was an excellent crop, and nobody was taking any chances. In a little over a month it would be Thanksgiving. Maybe Greg and Mieka could bring Madeleine down. Keith could come too. If Alex and I could work things out, he and Eli could come. And, of course, Hilda and Leah. It was time for us to reap what we had sown, and it seemed the farmers weren't the only ones who'd be harvesting a bumper crop that year.

It was a little after 9:00 when we pulled up in front of our house. Taylor was sound asleep. As soon as I got out of the car, I could hear Rose barking inside.

Angus got out of the back seat. "What's up with Rose?" he asked.

"She's just glad to see us," I whispered. "Go in and let her out, would you? I'm going to try to carry Taylor up to bed without waking her." I leaned into the back seat and picked up my daughter. When I started up the walk, Angus was still fiddling with the front door.

He turned around and mouthed the words, "It's locked."

"Where's Hilda?"

He looked at me in exasperation. "Mum, I just got here too."

I handed Taylor to Angus, took my key out of my purse, and opened the front door. As soon as I stepped into the hall, I knew something was wrong. The area by the door was covered in dog faeces and urine.

Angus was behind me in the door; Taylor was in his arms, mercifully still sleeping. A wave of panic hit. "Take Taylor down to the family room and put her on the couch," I said.

My son stared at the mess in the front hall, but didn't say a word. He walked towards the family room. I took a deep breath and started up the stairs. My legs were leaden. There wasn't a doubt in my mind that something had happened to Hilda. I felt a dozen emotions, but the overwhelming one was guilt. Hilda was eighty-three years old. Unwilling to face her mortality, I had stood by as she had undertaken a task too onerous for a woman decades younger than she was; then I had left her alone.

The door to her bedroom was shut. My hand was shaking as I turned the knob. The image I'd conjured up of Hilda, dead in her bed, victim of a heart attack that carried her away in the night, was so vivid that, for a beat, I couldn't take in the reality. She wasn't there. Her bed was made up, the sheets and blanket pulled so tight under the chenille spread that a dime would have bounced off them. I ran down the hall to the bathroom. It was pristine: sink shining; towels lined up on the towel rack; fresh roll of toilet paper on the holder. For a foolish and relief-filled moment, I let myself think that everything was all right, that Hilda had just become so absorbed in her delvings into Justine Blackwell's affairs that she had lost track of time. Then, for the second time in forty-eight hours, I turned and saw my son behind me, white-faced and shaking.

"She's in the kitchen, Mum."

"Is she . . . ?"

He shook his head miserably. "I don't know." We started down the hall, but Angus turned into my room.

"Where are you going?" I asked.

"To call 911," said the son whom I'd accused more than once of lacking common sense.

"Good," I said. "After you get them, call Alex."

I ran downstairs. Hilda was sprawled by the back door. She was still in the outfit she'd changed into Saturday night before we left: sandals, apple-green pedal pushers, hot-pink-and-green striped shirt. It was as if the movie I'd been playing in my mind since I heard Rose barking had suddenly become real. There were, however, significant differences between the nightmare and the reality. Even in my worst imaginings, I hadn't seen Hilda's face. She was ashen and, for the first time since I'd known her, expressionless. Her mouth was slack, and her eyes unseeing. The other variation was a critical one. In those first, ghastly moments, I had assumed Hilda had been felled by a stroke or a heart attack, but the blood pooled behind her head, and the blood on the croquet mallet thrown to the floor beside her, told a different story. Hilda's body hadn't failed her; she had been attacked. When I put my fingers to her throat and felt a faint pulse, I thanked God.

Angus came into the kitchen. "They're on their way," he said. "I couldn't get Alex, so I called Jill. I thought I could go to the hospital with you." His voice trailed off. He was staring at Hilda. Suddenly, his face contorted in anger. "What the fuck did they think they were doing with that towel?"

I followed the direction of his gaze. One of our kitchen towels had been folded and placed under Hilda's head.

Angus's voice broke. "What kind of person would do that? Smash someone's skull in, then make a pillow for her head."

The next minutes had the jerky urgency of a movie made with a hand-held camera. As the paramedics fell to their work, they peppered me with questions: What was Hilda's name? Her age? Had I moved her? Had I placed the towel under her head? Did I know what had happened? Had she been conscious at all since I found her? As I answered, my voice was lifeless. I couldn't take my eyes off the activity surrounding my friend. It was purposeful but alien. An oxygen mask had been slapped on Hilda's face, and one of the paramedics, a young man, was kneeling beside her with state-of-the-art equipment that calibrated her pulse, respiration, blood pressure, and temperature. In a careful, calm voice, the young man called out numbers that I knew were related to Hilda's vital signs, but I was too ignorant to interpret them.

Two uniformed policemen arrived. They had their own questions, and I did my best to answer them, but I didn't have much information to give. When they were satisfied that I'd told them all I could, they began to check out my house, looking, they said, for signs of forcible entry or something the attacker might have left behind.

One of the paramedics bent and shone a pencil flashlight into Hilda's eyes, all the while calling her name, trying, I guess, to rouse her to consciousness. A medical collar was fixed around Hilda's neck, and an intravenous was started in her right arm. Finally, the paramedics slid her onto a kind of board. That's when I noticed the dark stain in the crotch of her pedal pushers. It was the final indignity: at some point, my proud friend had wet herself.

"No," I said.

The paramedic closest to me cast me a sidelong glance. "What?"

"She wouldn't want anyone to see her like that." I took off my sweater and placed it carefully so that it covered the stain. By the sink, the younger of the two policeman was wrapping our old croquet mallet in plastic; he, too, carried out his task with exquisite care.

The paramedics began to strap Hilda to the stretcher, and the questions started up again: Did she have any allergies? Any health problems? What medications was she on? Could I check her room and bring any prescription drugs with me to the hospital? When they lifted her and started for the front door, I turned to my son.

"You'll have to stay here," I said. "Jill must have been delayed, but she'll be along. I'll call you as soon as I know anything." I kissed him on the cheek. "I love you," I said.

He nodded numbly.

The paramedics wouldn't let me ride with Hilda. I had to sit in the front seat. The sirens were wailing, and the driver didn't make any attempt to talk. It was a relief not to have to deal with another human being. As we sped across the Albert Street bridge, I was overwhelmed with guilt. I had promised Hilda I'd call from Saskatoon, but I'd forgotten. I had a clutch of good excuses: my excitement about the baby; Taylor's boundless enthusiasm; my reunion with Keith; my need to be with Mieka. All my rationalizations made perfect sense; none changed the fact that I hadn't picked up the phone.

As we pulled into the ambulance bay at Pasqua Hospital, I knew that I would live with that sin of omission for the rest of my life. I followed behind as Hilda was wheeled through the E.R. The medical people exchanged information. Most of it was indecipherable, but the fragments I understood were terrifying: estimated 30 per cent blood loss; thready pulse; pupils sluggish to light; extremities cold.

A nurse stopped me at the double doors that opened into the treatment rooms. Her words were diplomatic, but the message was clear: the experts were taking over; I would just be in the way. I turned back and, for the first time, I took in the scene in the waiting room.

It was Sunday night, and the place was filled with the pain of other people's lives: a filthy, wiry man with the crazed eyes of a prophet or a solvent-drinker; a terrified father with a feverish little boy; two uniformed police officers with a young woman who was very drunk and whose arm hung at an unnatural angle from her shoulder; a teenaged couple with a croupy baby; and a dozen other soldiers in the Army of the Sick and the Unlucky. I found a chair facing the doors behind which Hilda had disappeared. If she needed me, I'd be close at hand.

There was a pile of magazines, soft with age and use, on the table next to me. The magazine on top was titled *Southern Bed and Breakfast*. The prospect of losing myself in a world of magnolias, overhead fans, and silver filigreed holders for iced-tea glasses was seductive, but try as I might, I couldn't close the curtain on the human comedy playing itself out around me. An orderly was leading the wild-eyed man down the hallway; the feverish boy had begun to whimper and cry for his mother. The young woman with the hanging arm had turned against the police who had brought her in. All she was interested in now was getting patched up so she could leave. With her good arm, she was pounding on the chest of the younger of the cops, and saying, "What kind of fuckin' doctor are you, anyway?" He bore the assault with patience and grace.

Time passed at a snail's pace. Whenever the intercom crackled or a man or woman in medical gear appeared in the room, my heart leapt. But the name called was never mine, and as the minutes ticked by, panic threatened to overwhelm me. When Detective Robert Hallam came through the emergency-room door, my first thought was that he had arrived as backup for the police officers with the abusive woman, but although he nodded to them, he kept on coming until he got to me.

In his canary-yellow button-down shirt and Tilley slacks, he seemed an unlikely candidate for knight in shining armour, but, as it turned out, he was able to rescue me. He sat down in the chair next to mine.

"I'm sorry about Miss McCourt," he said.

My words came in a torrent. "Have you heard how she is? No one's said a word to me since I got here, and by now someone should know something."

He sighed heavily. "You're right," he said. "Someone should. Let me go over there and see what I can find out."

Detective Hallam walked over to the desk that separated the ones who feared and hoped from the ones who knew. When he showed the nurse his badge, she picked up the phone and made a call. Almost immediately a young man in surgical greens came through the door behind her. The three of them bent their heads together, then Detective Hallam came back to me.

"It's not good," he said. "They've done a CT scan. She has a bad concussion, but they're waiting for someone who specializes in head injuries to come in to see if she needs surgery. She's also seriously dehydrated, and she's lost a lot of blood. I don't think any of her conditions are life-threatening in themselves, it's the combination, and of course there's her age to consider." Unexpectedly, he smiled. "If you should happen to speak to her, don't tell Miss McCourt I mentioned her age."

"I won't," I said. Then out of nowhere, the tears came.

Robert Hallam waited out the storm. When I was finished, I blew my nose and turned back to him. "I'm sorry," I said.

"It's the not knowing that makes you crazy," he said simply. "But they have promised to let us know as soon as they decide about surgery." He gazed at me assessingly. "Are you up to a few questions?"

I shook my head. "I told the officers who came to the house everything I knew."

His voice was kind. "Well, sometimes people know more than they think they do."

At first, it seemed I was not among them, but when Detective Hallam asked me about the croquet mallet that Hilda's assailant had used, an image, disquieting as a frame in a rock video, flashed through my mind. It was of Eli, whirling his mallet high in the air on the day he and Angus had their crazy game. I didn't tell Detective Hallam about the memory. Stated baldly, it might have evoked a possibility that was unthinkable, and I banished it.

Detective Hallam had a few final questions. He had just snapped his notepad shut when a nurse came out to say that Hilda was being moved to intensive care, and I could see her briefly. I was on my feet in a split second. Finally, I was going to get to pass through the double doors.

Hilda was almost unrecognizable: a prisoner of tubes and of machines calibrating the vital signs of a no-longer-vital life. I bent to kiss her, but I was afraid I'd knock lose some critical piece of the apparatus, so I took her hand in mine. It was icy, and there were pinkish stains on her fingers. Whoever had taken off her favourite Love That Red nail polish had been in a hurry. A doctor came in to examine Hilda. The name on his identification card was Everett Beckles. I stepped back and watched. When he started to leave, I touched his arm. "Is she going to die?" I asked.

"I don't know," he said. "We've done a diagnostic workup, and we've decided against neurosurgical intervention."

"She doesn't need an operation," I said. "That's good news, isn't it?"

Dr. Beckles didn't answer me. He was a black man about my own age, and he looked as exhausted as I felt. "As you can see, we've closed the lacerations on your mother's skull and we're transfusing her. We've given her something to reduce the brain water, and we've started anticonvulsant therapy. In intensive care, they'll monitor her level of consciousness and her vital signs. Everything possible is being done," he said.

"Will it be enough?" I asked.

"We can only hope," he said. "You might as well go home and get some rest. Your mother's going to need you in the next few days."

I started to correct him, but the words died in my throat. My mouth felt rusty, and I ached. I covered Hilda's hand with my own. "I'll be back," I said.

As I waited for my cab, I looked up at the looming bulk of Pasqua Hospital. My second hospital of the day. Two hospitals, two cities: joy, sorrow; hope, fear. Somewhere in the distance, a dog howled. Its cry, feral, heartsick, and lonely, stirred something in me. Only my superior position on the evolutionary scale kept me from howling too.

CHAPTER

8

It was 1:00 a.m. when I got home. Jill had cleaned up the dog mess in the front hall, but Rose lowered her head in shame when she saw me. I bent down and put my arms around her neck. "It wasn't your fault, Rose," I murmured. "Don't blame yourself."

Jill came out to the hall when she heard my voice. She was carrying the Jungian biography of the prime minister I'd been reading. She had her place marked with her finger.

"How's Hilda doing?"

"She still isn't conscious," I said. "They sent me home. She has a concussion; she lost a lot of blood and she was dehydrated. The worst thing is that no one knows how long she was lying here. It could have been twenty-four hours."

Jill caught the edge in my voice. "Don't beat yourself up about this, Jo. Much as we want to, we can't always keep the people we love from harm. Sometimes terrible things just happen." She put her arm around my shoulder and led me into the family room. "Come on. Let's have a drink. One of the delights of this particular B and B is its well-stocked bar."

I sighed. "Scotch, but make it a light one. I have a nine-thirty class."

Jill frowned. "You're not planning to go to the university, are you?"

"I am. First-year students need some sense of continuity; besides, I'm afraid Rosalie will yell at me if I cancel out this early in the semester."

"The only rationalization I would accept," she said.

When Jill came back with our drinks, she handed me mine and took a long pull on hers. "What can I do to help?" she asked.

"You've already done it," I said. "I'm so grateful you could come over and be with the kids tonight. Did Taylor ever wake up?"

Jill shook her head. "Nope. She slept through the whole thing. Cops and all."

I winced. "Do the police have any theories about what happened here tonight?"

"If they do, they weren't telling me." Jill raised an eyebrow. "Of course, they couldn't keep me from listening when they were talking to each other."

"And?"

"And they didn't find any signs of forced entry."

Suddenly I felt cold. "You mean Hilda let her attacker in."

"It looks that way," Jill said grimly. "And it also looks as if this wasn't a robbery. The police asked me to check around and see if anything was missing. I couldn't spot any glaring aberrations. Your desk was a mess, but your desk is always a mess."

"I suppose you shared that little nugget with the police."

Jill nodded. "I did, but they didn't seem very interested. Actually, the one thing they seemed really interested in was some towel. From what they said, I gathered the paramedics must have taken it with them to the hospital."

"They did," I said. "It was one of my kitchen towels. Whoever attacked Hilda had folded it to make a little pillow under her head."

"That's sick." Jill's voice was icy.

"Sick or compassionate. I guess the folded towel could suggest remorse."

"A little late for that, wasn't it?" Jill drained her glass and headed for the liquor cabinet. "Care for a refill?"

"I'm okay," I said. "My stomach's doing nip-ups. Oh, Jill, I'm so glad Taylor didn't see Hilda. She really loves her. So does Angus."

"He gave me a pretty graphic description of the scene you walked into tonight."

"My son has had one hell of a weekend. So have we all, come to think of it." I stood up. "I'm going to grab a shower and get out of this dress. When Angus told me about Mieka, I was so excited, I forgot to pack anything but my toothbrush and a change of underwear. I've been wearing this outfit since Saturday afternoon."

"'Fashion File' says that once you get a look that works for you, you should stay with it."

"I think I've stayed with this one long enough. Jill, I really am grateful that Angus had you to talk to. Do you think he'll be okay?"

"Yeah, beneath all that hip-hop-happenin' attitude, he's a pretty sensible kid. He's worried, of course, but he's handling it." She looked at me hard. "How are you doing?"

"Not great," I said. "But I'm coping, and I'll cope even better when I get some sleep." I finished my drink. A thought hit me. "Jill, is the kitchen . . . ?"

"Taken care of," she said.

"Thanks," I said. "I couldn't have faced that." I stood up. My legs felt rubbery. "Would you mind staying here tonight?

If I have to go back to the hospital, I'd like somebody to be here with the kids."

Jill smiled. "I brought my toothbrush, just in case."

I slept fitfully, listening for the phone that, mercifully, did not ring and trying, without success, to banish the images of the night. The pictures of Hilda's suffering were sharp-edged, but the scene that made my heart pound was one that existed only in my imagination: my old friend, in her cheerful summer outfit, hearing the doorbell, putting down Justine's papers and walking down the hall to admit her attacker. But who had been on the other side of that door? In the week since Justine's murder, Hilda had travelled in circles I could only guess at, among men and women whose characters were a mystery to me. For hours, I moved between sleep and consciousness, trying to conjure up the face of her assailant, but it was a futile exercise. By the time my alarm went off, I knew there was no turning away from the truth: any one of a hundred people could have picked up that croquet mallet and tried to end my old friend's life.

I dialled the number of Pasqua Hospital. Hilda had made it through the night, but there was no change in her condition. For a few minutes I lay in bed, thinking about the day ahead. I wasn't looking forward to it.

Jill was at the sink filling the coffeepot when I got back from the park with Rose. She was wearing the same white shorts and black NationTV sweatshirt she'd had on the night before, but her auburn hair was damp from the shower, and she looked fresh as the proverbial daisy. She glanced at me questioningly.

"No news," I said.

Taylor was sitting at the table with a bowl of cereal in front of her. Her spoon stopped in midair when she saw me.

"Wasn't yesterday the best day? Madeleine is so cute. I can't wait to tell Ms. Anweiler about her. I hope she's wearing her diplodocus earrings."

"Me too," I said. "Now, you'd better finish your breakfast. You don't want to be late. You're an aunt now, so you have to be responsible."

Taylor's eyes grew large. "I'm an aunt . . . really?"

"Sure," I said. "Mieka's your big sister, so that makes Madeleine your niece."

Taylor's spoon hit the bowl. "Now I really can't wait to get to school."

Angus came into the kitchen warily, and I caught his eye. "Come out on the deck for a minute, would you?"

He followed me out to the deck without a word. The air was hazy; the first brittle leaves from our cottonwood tree were floating on the surface of the water in the swimming pool, and the breeze was fresh with the piney coldness of the north.

Angus's voice was a whisper. "Did she die?"

I shook my head. "No, she's still alive but, Angus, I won't to lie to you. She may not make it much longer."

He turned from me. When he spoke, his voice broke. "It doesn't seem right," he said.

"What doesn't?"

He looked around him. "That it can be such a great day when such a lousy thing is happening."

When we went back in, the phone was ringing. Jill gave me a questioning look and then reached for it.

"It's okay," I said. Heart pounding, I picked up the receiver, but it wasn't the hospital calling with news; it was Eric Fedoruk.

"Hilda McCourt, please," he said.

"She's not available right now."

"Is this Mrs. Kilbourn?"

"Yes," I said, "it is."

"Mrs. Kilbourn, could you have Miss McCourt call me as soon as she gets back? She's supposed to come in today to discuss Justine's estate, but she didn't phone my secretary to arrange a time." There was an edge of irritation in his voice.

"She won't be coming in," I said.

"She has to," he said flatly.

"Mr. Fedoruk, Hilda doesn't have to do anything for you. She's in the intensive-care unit at Pasqua Hospital. Someone came into my house and attacked her."

"Is she going to be all right?" The concern in his voice seemed heartfelt, but I was beyond caring about Eric Fedoruk's feelings.

"I don't know if she's going to be all right," I snapped. "All I know is that I want you and everybody else connected with Justine Blackwell to stay away from Hilda. Leave her alone. No more making her the final arbiter; no more signing off on responsibilities; no more sending the press to my house. It's time everyone took responsibility for their own lives. Got it?"

Eric Fedoruk was stammering out his apology when I hung up. His words cut no ice with me. I was sick of justifications and explanations.

Jill made a face when I hung up. "Glad I wasn't on the other end of that," she said. "Jo, what's going on here?"

I gave her the bare bones: Justine's transformation in the past year; the request she'd made of Hilda; the will which named Hilda as executrix; the warring factions in Justine's life; the tensions that existed between Justine and all the people she was closest to.

"And you think what happened to Hilda is connected to Justine's death?"

"I don't know," I said. "Ever since you told me the police

think Hilda must have known her attacker, I've been reeling. But, Jill, there has to be a connection. It's just too much of a stretch to believe that seven days after Justine's murder, somebody would take it into their head to try to kill Hilda."

Suddenly, Jill frowned. "Jo, is there some sort of guard on Hilda's hospital room?"

"I don't know." The penny dropped. "Oh God, what if . . . ?" I jumped up, went to the phone, and dialled police headquarters. Detective Hallam was way ahead of me. In the early hours of the morning, he had sent a constable to Pasqua Hospital to monitor everyone who went in or out of Hilda's room.

I could feel the relief wash over me. I hung up and turned to Jill. "It's taken care of," I said.

Jill looked thoughtful. "Let's hope it is. Jo, I don't like any of this. I especially don't like the fact that we don't know who we're dealing with here." She picked up her coffee mug, walked to the sink, and rinsed it. Then she turned to face me. "When I get to the office, I'm going to see what I can pull together on the people in Justine's circle."

"You mean biographical stuff?"

"That and gossip. It's amazing how few secrets there are in a town this size. I'll call you tonight, and let you know what I come up with."

"Why don't you come for dinner? I'm going to have to tell Taylor about Hilda, and it would be good if she knew that some things in her world are still the same."

She gave me a weary smile. "That's my role in life," she said, "the permanent fixture. Six o'clock, okay?"

"Six o'clock's perfect," I said.

Before I left for the university, I made one more call. I hadn't left my office number at the hospital. I gave it to the nurse in intensive care and told her I'd come by later in the afternoon. She said to make sure I had some identification; there was a young constable outside Hilda's door, and she was a tiger.

The lecture I gave to my first-year students wasn't the best I'd ever given, but it wasn't the worst either. When I finished, I went down to the Political Science office to pick up my mail. I was in luck. Rosalie was on the phone. I dropped a note on her desk, saying I could be reached at home for the rest of the day, and made my escape.

I stopped at the IGA and picked up a roasting chicken and some new potatoes. I was putting away groceries when my neighbour came over with two deliveries from the florist. One was addressed to Hilda, the other to me. I opened mine: an arrangement of bronze and yellow mums in an earthenware pitcher. The card read: "With the hope that you'll accept my most sincere apologies, Eric Fedoruk." I took the phone off the hook, set the alarm for 2:30 p.m., and went upstairs to bed. I was asleep before my head hit the pillow.

It was five to three when I drove into the parking lot at Pasqua Hospital. Angus had a football practice, so he wouldn't be back till supper time, but Taylor would be home at 3:30. My visit to Hilda would have to be a quick one. To the right of the glass doors of the main entrance, the usual contingent of smokers in blue hospital robes huddled, their intravenous poles looming over them like spectral chaperones. In the lobby, a gaunt young woman with a frighteningly yellow pallor looked on as a little boy showed her an apple he had cut out of red construction paper. The elevator was empty, and there was no one in the corridor as I walked into the intensive-care unit.

A fine-featured blond man, about the age of my daughter Mieka, sat at a desk in the centre of the nursing area. A small bank of TV monitors was suspended above the desk, and as he made notes on the chart in front of him, the young man kept glancing up to check the screens. The patients' rooms radiated in a semicircle off the area in which he was sitting. In one of those rooms, a radio was playing country music. The sound was incongruous but oddly reassuring. There was another reassuring note: in front of the room I presumed to be Hilda's, a uniformed police constable gazed out at the world, alert and ready.

I waited till the young man at the desk finished with his chart. "I'm here to see Hilda McCourt," I said.

"I'll have to ask for some identification," he said.

I took out my driver's licence and handed it to him. He glanced at it and handed back. "You can go in, Mrs. Kilbourn. Detective Hallam okayed you." He picked up another chart.

"Wait," I said. I leaned forward so I could read the name on his picture ID. "Mr. Wolfe, I wonder if you could tell me how Miss McCourt is doing?"

He shook his head. "No change. She's still scoring low on the Glasgow Coma Scale. That's the way we measure responses to things like light and speech and pain. The higher the score, the better the prognosis."

"And her prognosis isn't good?"

"You'll have to talk to her doctor about that." Nathan Wolfe flipped to Hilda's chart. "Miss McCourt's doctor is Everett Beckles. He'll be making his rounds in about an hour. You can talk to him then."

"I can't stay," I said. "Could you ask him to call me?"

Nathan Wolfe slid a notepad towards me. "Leave your number, but don't count on a call. Dr. Beckles is really busy."

"Thanks," I said. "Is there anything I should know before I go in there?"

"Nothing special. Just be sure to talk to her. Sometimes just hearing a human voice helps."

"Is that why the radio's on over there?"

Nathan nodded. "The guy in that room was in a motorcycle accident. His wife says he's a big Garth Brooks fan, so she brought the radio so he'd hear some familiar voices when she couldn't be here."

When I started into Hilda's room, I remembered that I was carrying the flowers my neighbour had brought over. I handed them to Nathan. "These were sent to Miss McCourt. I know she can't have them in her room, but maybe you'd like them for the desk out here."

"This place could use some brightening," he agreed. He opened the floral paper carefully. Inside were at least three dozen creamy long-stem roses. Nathan whistled appreciatively. Then he reached into the folds of paper, took out the card, and handed it to me. "You'll want this," he said. "Whoever's paying the bill for those roses deserves a thank-you."

I glanced at the card. "For Hilda, with our love and best wishes, Signe, Tina, and Lucy." I ripped the card in two and handed the pieces back to Nathan. "Put this in the trash, would you? The people who are paying for those roses don't deserve diddley."

The constable who was on duty outside Hilda's room was a young woman I'd met before. Alex had introduced us at a dinner honouring outstanding police work. Her name was Linda Nilson, and she'd won an award for community service. She was coolly attractive: tall, slim, with a nicely chiselled profile, and dark hair cut in the kind of pixie style Audrey Hepburn made famous in *Roman Holiday*.

She smiled in recognition when she saw me, but still insisted on seeing a piece of ID, and I was relieved at her thoroughness.

Intubated and wired, Hilda looked impossibly small, but she'd lost the ashen look that had frightened me so much when I found her in the kitchen the night before. I bent to kiss her forehead, then opened my purse and took out a photograph I'd taken of her at the lake. She was sitting in our canoe, paddle poised. As always, she was dressed for the occasion, this time in white shorts, a navy-and-white striped gondolier's shirt, a bright orange lifejacket, and a straw boater to keep the sun off her extravagant red curls.

I taped the picture to the head of her bed. "This is so everyone will know what a knockout you are," I said. Then, heeding Nathan's advice, I began to talk. At first, I was self-conscious, then, despite the grim surroundings, I found myself relaxing into the easiness I always felt when I was with Hilda. I talked about everything that was on my mind: Mieka's baby; seeing Keith Harris again; my fears about the deterioration in my relationship with Alex; the dinner I was planning with Jill. I was careful to avoid any mention of Justine and her troubled family in my monologue. I was amazed when I looked at my watch and saw it was already 3:20. I kissed her forehead again. "I'll be back after supper," I said. "And this time I'll bring a book to read to you."

Taylor and I arrived at the house together. "Perfect timing," I said.

She beamed. She followed me into the kitchen and, as I prepared the chicken, she told me her about her day. It had been a good one. Ms. Anweiler had picked her to be the class monitor for the week ahead. Taylor was going to have a chance to show how responsible she was. I asked if she wanted a dress rehearsal in responsibility, and she agreed to set the table and wash the potatoes while I went out to the garden.

The herbs in our clay pots were flagging, but there was still tarragon, and the parsley was plentiful if drooping.

Whatever the state of our parsley crop, my late husband, Ian, had always revelled in quoting his mother's aphorism: "Parsley thrives in a house where the wife dominates." As I snipped herbs for the chicken, I thought, not for the first time, how good it would be to have a husband to laugh with and to lean against. I was tired of dealing with problems alone, tired of having no one to pick up the baton when I dropped it, tired, to use an old friend's telling image, of being "always a driver, never a passenger."

Keith Harris and I had talked vaguely of marriage when we were together, and I think at some level I believed it was a likelihood. There were no impediments. He had never married. My kids liked him, and the fact that he was Greg's uncle was icing on the cake. We were the same age; in fact, we shared a birthday. Other people approved of us as a couple; I approved of us as a couple. Then he found someone else, and my fantasy that Keith and I would walk hand in hand through the golden years faded.

Alex and I had never talked of marriage. We had been content to enjoy the here and now, but lately even the here and now had been riddled with tensions. That day, as I bent to pick tomatoes for dinner, I wondered whether what we had had ever really been enough for either of us.

When the chicken was in the oven, I walked out to Taylor's studio and told her about Hilda. I was honest, but I didn't dwell on the worst possibilities. We would jump off that particular bridge when and if we came to it. Taylor's reaction surprised me. She loved Hilda, and she was a child whose emotions were close to the surface, but that afternoon she took the news calmly.

When I finished she said, "Is Hilda going to die?"

I shook my head. "I don't know."

Taylor looked at me steadily. "She talked to me about this."

"When?" I asked.

"At the cottage. I told her that next summer I'd be able to swim right across the lake, the way Eli's mum did. And I said, 'Promise you'll be there,' and she said she couldn't promise, because a promise was a serious thing and she might not be able to keep it because she was old and nobody lives forever."

"Did she say anything else?"

Taylor nodded. "She said she'd had more fun than anybody."

I touched my daughter's cheek. "Let's hope there's more fun ahead," I said. I left Taylor painting and went back in the house. The next day in my senior class, we were dealing with federal–provincial relations during the eighties. I'd lived it, but I didn't remember it, so I had some serious boning up to do.

The small room I used for an office was down the hall from the kitchen. As soon as I saw my desk, I knew that Jill's assessment had been right. It was a mess, but it wasn't a mess I'd made. I started sifting through the chaos. Nothing appeared to have been taken. Whoever had ransacked my desk obviously had concerns larger than unmarked freshman papers and academic articles. Before I'd left for Saskatoon, Hilda had told me she was planning to spend Saturday night working on Justine's personal financial records. But I hadn't noticed any papers that might have belonged to Justine in our house. I went upstairs to Hilda's room. It was pristine. The only evidence that Hilda had stayed there was her library books, which were neatly stacked on Mieka's old desk by the window. There were no papers. I checked the family room, and the dining room. There was nothing. I called Jill, but she was gone for the day. Then I called the police. The officer I spoke to took my information without comment, but she seemed interested, and she made certain she got a number where I could be reached that evening if the investigating officers had further questions.

Perplexed, I went back to my office and picked up an article on the Romanow–Chrétien constitutional tour of 1981. The press had dubbed it the Uke and Tuque show; reading about it, even in the dry language of academe, brought back a lot of memories. I became so absorbed I almost forgot to get the squash ready. It was only after I'd prepared it with butter, brown sugar, and nutmeg, the way Hilda liked it, that I remembered Hilda wouldn't be at the dinner table to enjoy it.

By the time Jill arrived, the chicken and squash were ready, a casserole of new potatoes was waiting to be micro-waved, and I was slicing tomatoes to sauté with zucchini and onion and garlic. Jill was carrying a bottle of Chablis in one hand and a file folder in the other.

She handed me the folder. "Some interesting stuff in there, but it can wait." She waved the Chablis. "This, on the other hand, won't keep for a minute."

I poured us each a glass of wine.

Jill took hers and raised her glass. "To absent friends," she said solemnly.

"To absent friends," I said.

She pulled out one of the kitchen chairs and sat down. "So," she said, "what's shaking around here?"

"A mystery," I said. "That mess you saw on my desk wasn't of my making."

She narrowed her eyes. "You mean somebody tossed it?"

"Hilda was working on some financial records that belonged to Justine Blackwell. I think they must have been looking for those. Judging from the fact that the papers are nowhere in evidence, I'm guessing that whoever attacked Hilda found what they were looking for."

Jill sipped her wine thoughtfully. "This is beyond us, Nancy Drew."

"I know," I said. "I've already called the police. I've done everything I can. So have you. Let's take the night off."

"Good plan," she said. "We can start by refilling our glasses."

Dinner was less boisterous than usual, but we tried. Angus gave us a rundown on his team's chances for the coming season; Taylor talked about the trip to the Legislature Ms. Anweiler was taking her class on the next day. Jill had some funny behind-the-scenes stories about NationTV. I recounted Ian's mother's parsley story. We all missed Hilda.

After supper, Jill and the kids drove to the Milky Way for ice cream and I went back to the hospital. It had taken a while to decide which book to bring to read to Hilda. There were three on her bedside table: Justine's *Geriatric Psychiatry: A Handbook*, A. S. Byatt's *Still Life*, and a translation of Bede's *Ecclesiastical History*. In my opinion, none quite fit the bill. I was casting about for something when I remembered Hilda's passion for L.M. Montgomery. So as I stepped into the elevator of the Pasqua Hospital, there was a copy of *Anne of Green Gables* in my hand.

I waved it at Nathan as I walked by the desk. "Ever read this?" I asked.

He looked up from his charts, "No, but I saw the TV series when I was fourteen, and I was hot for Megan Follows till I hit Grade 11."

There was a new police officer outside Hilda's door. He looked tougher than Mark Messier, and I didn't stop to chat. I showed him my driver's licence, went inside, pulled up my chair, and began to read: "Mrs. Rachel Lynde lived just where the Avonlea main road dipped down into a little hollow, fringed with alders and ladies' eardrops . . ." As the tubes attached to Hilda delivered their elixirs of antibiotics and nutrients and carried away her body's waste, and the machines recorded heartbeats and blood pressure, I kept on reading. I read until the intercom announced that all visitors must leave and Anne, holding the carpet-bag that contained all her worldly goods, entered Green Gables for the first time. When I bent to kiss my friend goodnight, I thought I detected a flicker in her eyelids. As I passed Hilda's police guard, he looked up at me. "Sorry to see you go," he said. "I was just getting interested."

Jill was still there when I got home. Angus and Leah were in the family room studying, and Taylor was in bed, but not asleep.

When she heard me come into her room, she propped herself up on one elbow. "How's Hilda?" she asked.

"The same," I said. "But no worse."

"Is that okay?"

"Yeah," I said, "that's okay, at least for now."

Taylor spotted the copy of *Anne of Green Gables* in the outside pocket of my bag. She leaned over and took it out. "Hilda told me a story from this," she said. "It was about this girl who dyes her hair green. Hilda said she'd read the whole thing to me at Christmas if I learned to sit still for a book with no pictures."

When I stood up after kissing my younger daughter goodnight, I was dizzy with exhaustion. The day had finally caught up with me. It took an act of will to force myself to go back downstairs. Jill was sitting at the kitchen table poring over the folder of information on Justine and her circle that she'd brought with her.

"Good stuff in here," she said. Then she caught sight of my face and frowned. "You look lousy, Jo."

"That only seems fitting," I said, "because I feel lousy. Jill, stay as long as you like, but I'm heading for bed."

Jill pushed her chair back and stretched lazily. "Nope,

I'm out of here. I've had enough fun for one day too. But let's get together after you've had a chance to look through that folder. For a figure of judicial rectitude, Justine Blackwell certainly surrounded herself with a compelling cast of characters."

"More compelling than the characters in *Anne of Green Gables*?"

Jill made a face. "Where did that come from?"

"It's a long story."

"Well," said Jill, "considering your state of mind, I won't press for the particulars. And, to answer your question, Justine's cast of characters may not be as compelling as Lucy Maud's, but they're a hell of a lot more dangerous."

CHAPTER

9

When I looked at the photo that dominated the front page of our local paper Tuesday morning, my heart began to pound. For a paralysing moment, I was certain that the young aboriginal man being pushed into the police squad car was Eli Kequahtooway. The man's face was half-turned from the camera, but his dark hair, worn loose except for a single traditional braid, was like Eli's, and his slender, long-legged body was the same.

Rose and I had just come back from our run around the lake, so I wasn't wearing my reading glasses. When I finally found them and looked at the picture more closely, I was relieved to see that the man being arrested was older than Eli, perhaps in his early twenties, and that his features were coarser. Still shaken, I glanced up at the headline. The man in the photograph had been charged with Justine Blackwell's murder.

The accompanying story was short on facts. The man's name was Terrence Ducharme. He was twenty-three years old, lived in the downtown core, and was employed as a busboy at the Hotel Saskatchewan, the hotel where Justine had celebrated her thirty years on the bench the night of her murder. I poured myself a cup of coffee, sat down at the kitchen table, and read through the item again. The journalist who had written it treated Ducharme's arrest as the end of the story, but to my mind there were still too many loose ends. It was entirely plausible that, given her activities in the last year of her life, Justine had encountered Terrence Ducharme. It was even conceivable that she and Ducharme had quarrelled. But where did Hilda fit in? What possible motive could Terrence Ducharme have had for assaulting her? The missing financial papers had to be the link, but what interest could a busboy at the Hotel Saskatchewan have in Justine Blackwell's banking?

I looked up at the kitchen clock. It was 6:45, not too early for a phone call, especially when I had a credible excuse like needing further information. Alex wasn't assigned to the case, but he might have facts that weren't in the papers. I poured myself another cup of coffee, picked up the phone, and dialled Alex's number.

Eli answered on the first ring. I tried to be matter-of-fact. "Eli, it's Joanne. How are you doing?"

"I'm okay," he said.

He didn't sound okay. His voice was dull, as if he'd been awakened from a deep sleep.

"Are you back at school yet?" I asked.

"No," he said. "I couldn't hack it. Dr. Rayner said I didn't have to."

"What happened to Dr. Kasperski?"

"I don't know," Eli said in his new dead voice. "I guess he quit."

He fell silent. It was apparent that holding up his end of a conversation, even a bare-bones one like ours, was painful for him. I didn't want to add to his misery. "Is your uncle there?" I asked.

"I'll get him," he said.

"Eli, wait. If you need me, you know how to get in touch with me."

"Yeah," he said, "I do." He paused. "Thanks."

Alex's greeting was terse. "Kequahtooway."

"Alex, it's Jo."

"Sorry, I thought it was headquarters." He paused. "How are you?"

"I'm okay," I said. I waited for him to ask about Hilda. I was certain that, by this point, he would have heard that she'd been assaulted, but he either hadn't heard or didn't want to bring up the subject. The dead air between us became awkward.

"Did Mieka have her baby?" he asked finally.

"She and Greg had a little girl. They're calling her Madeleine."

"Everybody okay?"

"Everybody's fine. Alex, I took the cradle board up to Saskatoon. Greg and Mieka thought it was terrific."

He didn't respond. This time it was my turn to pick up the conversational ball.

"Eli says he's back with Signe Rayner. Is he doing all right with her?"

"She started hypnosis with him yesterday. She's hoping to get to the source of whatever it is that's eating at him."

"But Dan Kasperski was so opposed to hypnosis. He said that forcing Eli to confront his memories before he's ready to deal with them could be devastating."

"Signe Rayner is his doctor, Joanne."

There was a warning in Alex's voice. I didn't heed it. Instead, I blundered on. "I just wonder if she has the feeling for Eli that Dan Kasperski has. For one thing, I thought it would be good for Eli to get back to school."

This time, there was no mistaking Alex's anger. "Drop it, Jo. Whether Eli goes to school or not isn't your concern any more. Friday night you made it pretty clear that you didn't give a damn about Eli's problems."

"I never said that."

"That's what I heard."

"I'm not responsible for what you think you heard." Suddenly, I felt an overwhelming sadness. "This is exactly what I didn't want to happen."

"Then unless you had a specific reason for calling, maybe we'd better just hang up. Take care of yourself, Jo."

"You too," I said, but he didn't hear me because the line had already gone dead.

Miserable, I walked into the bathroom. I hadn't learned a thing about Terrence Ducharme, and I had widened the breach between Alex and me. I stepped into the tub, adjusted the shower to its pounding cycle, and tried to wash away the last five minutes of my life.

It didn't work. As I towelled off, I knew that Alex and I had begun the ugly cycle of wounding each other with every word we spoke. Even the ordinary conversations we'd had in the past suddenly seemed heavy with meaning. I thought of an exchange we'd had the previous spring when we'd been in his office at the police station. Except for a medicine wheel, a CD player, and his collection of classical CDs, Alex's office was spartan and impersonal, and I'd paid him a half-rueful compliment about his ability to hang on to what mattered and leave the rest behind. His reply had been far from light-hearted. He said that he never left anything behind and that the only way he could function was to keep the externals of his life uncomplicated.

I flattened my hand against the bathroom mirror, cleaned

a circle in the shower fog, and stared at my reflection. I didn't like what I saw: an almost fifty-one-year-old woman who had become extraneous, a complication in the life of the man she loved, or thought she loved.

When I walked into my bedroom to get dressed, Taylor was lying on my bed in her nightie, kicking her feet in the air and talking on the phone in the declamatory tones she reserved for adults.

"She's the same," my younger daughter said, "but Jo says that's okay for now. Jo says as soon as Hilda can have visitors, Angus and me can go see her." Taylor spotted me, jack-knifed her legs in and swung her body around so she was sitting on the side of the bed. "Jo's finally out of the bathroom," she announced to the person on the telephone. "Do you want to talk to her? It's Mr. Harris," she said, handing me the phone. She gave me a little wave and skipped out of the room.

Keith's voice was warm and concerned. "I had no idea about Hilda. You should have called me, Jo."

"There was nothing you could do."

"I could have been there."

The simple logic unnerved me; my words tumbled out. "I'm so scared," I said. "I'm trying to keep a brave front up for the kids, but Hilda looks so frail, Keith, and there are all these tubes. The medical people try to be helpful, but half the time I don't understand what they're talking about. They have this chart called the Glasgow Coma Scale; it's supposed to measure Hilda's level of functioning. I try to take it all in, but I'm just too tired and too afraid of what's going to happen."

"I'll come down there," he said.

"No," I said. "I'm all right. You just got me at a bad moment. If I need anything, I've got Jill and the kids.'

"And Alex?"

"No," I said, "I don't think Alex and I will be seeing each other for a while." I took a deep breath. "I really am handling this, Keith. Don't worry about me."

"Easier said than done," he said, "but I'll give it my best shot. Now, are you ready for some good news?"

"The novelty might do me in."

Keith laughed. "I'll start small. I saw Madeleine last night."

"Tell me more," I said.

"Well, she is intelligent, charming, and very lovely – obviously a testament to the excellence of the Kilbourn–Harris genes."

"You're talking to Madeleine's grandmother," I said. "None of what you just said is news to me. All the same, it's nice to hear you say it."

"Any time," he said. "I'm always available, Jo."

When we hung up, it was together.

Keith's call buoyed me. By the time I got to the university, I thought it was possible that I might get through the day after all. The first omens at school were positive. When I got to the Political Science office, Detective Robert Hallam was inside chatting with Rosalie Norman. Even a fleeting look revealed that Rosalie had broken with tradition in two ways: she had replaced her inevitable twin sweater set with a smart black turtleneck, and for the first time in human memory, she was laughing.

The laughter died when I walked in, but Rosalie did manage to retain a smile. "Detective Hallam's here to see you," she said. "Why don't you have your calls forwarded to me, so that you can chat without being interrupted." Rosalie presented her offer as if mutual accommodation was an everyday occurrence for us; in fact, I couldn't have been more surprised if she'd proposed that we throw off our shackles and lead the people of the university in a revolution.

Nonetheless, it was a sensible suggestion, and I accepted it. As soon as Detective Hallam and I were settled in my office, I hit call-forwarding on my telephone and turned to my guest. "What's up?" I asked.

He shrugged. "More questions – what else? Did you see the morning paper?"

"Yes," I said. "I'm glad you made an arrest in the Justine Blackwell case."

"So are we," he said mildly, "but I thought this particular arrest might present you and me both with some questions."

"Such as . . . ?"

"Such as, who attacked Miss McCourt? We're back to square one there, Mrs. Kilbourn."

"You thought the incidents were connected?"

"That's why we put the guard outside her room."

"And now you're taking the guard off?"

"No way we can justify tying an officer up now," Detective Hallam said. "It looks like we're dealing with a routine break-and-enter that went sour. Miss McCourt was just in the wrong place at the wrong time."

"I don't believe that, Detective Hallam."

"I'm afraid you're going to have to," he said. "Terrence Ducharme was nowhere near your house last Saturday night. He was at his anger-management meeting from seven till ten; then he had one of the counsellors from Culhane House over to his place for a sleepover. Except for when Terry went to the can, he wasn't alone for a minute."

"So he's in the clear."

"Looks like . . ."

"But Justine Blackwell's death *was* connected with Culhane House."

Robert Hallam frowned. "You sound as if you're sorry to hear that."

"I *am* sorry to hear that," I said. "Culhane House is just the kind of project that appeals to bleeding-heart liberals like me."

"Pick your causes carefully, Mrs. Kilbourn. Justine Blackwell made a pet of Terrence Ducharme and lived to regret it."

"Did she meet him through Wayne J. Waters?"

"No, the judge and our boy, Terry, share some history. He appeared in her court after he had a nasty run-in with an old woman who hired him to paint her garage. Apparently, Terrence wasn't much of a lad with a paintbrush, so the old lady refused to pay him. Terry retaliated by burning her garage down. He had priors, so Justine gave him the maximum sentence. By the time their paths crossed again, Terrence was a proud graduate of every twelve-step program the correctional system has to offer, and he was Wayne J.'s protégé. Of course, the new and improved Justice Blackwell thought Terrence Ducharme was the greatest thing since suspended sentences. She got him enrolled in educational upgrading, arranged for him to do some casual work, and paid a year's rent for him at a rooming house on Winnipeg Street."

"That's not all she did," I said.

Detective Hallam shot me a questioning look.

"There's a Ducharme buried in Justine Blackwell's family plot," I said.

"In the *family* plot? Why the hell would she do that?" He shrugged. "Why the hell did she do anything? Anyway, I'll bet there was one thing she had second thoughts about."

With the timing of the born storyteller, Robert Hallam waited for me to prompt him. I complied. "What was that?"

"Getting Terrence Ducharme that job at the Hotel Saskatchewan. He was working the night she died. Apparently, he did his usual bang-up job. At one point in the evening, he dropped a plate of those fancy little whatchamacallits."

"*Canapés,*" I said.

Detective Hallam gave me a mock bow. "Thank you. Justine caught him picking up the *canapés* and shoving them back on the plate. I guess she went ballistic. Apparently, she was quite fussy."

"*Fastidious* was the word Hilda always used."

"Whatever. Anyway, the judge tore a strip off Terry, and he followed her when she left. He told one of his buddies he was going to make her apologize."

"Justine's been dead for over a week. Why didn't all this surface before?"

"Terry's buddy ran afoul of the law yesterday and decided the story Terry had told him about the judge was a good bargaining chip."

"And your whole case rests on his story."

"Are you telling me how to do my job, Mrs. Kilbourn?"

"No," I said. "I just want to be sure you got the right person. Detective Hallam, I'm not trying to second-guess you. My only interest in any of this mess is Hilda. I want to be sure she's safe."

"None of us are safe, Mrs. Kilbourn. You should know that by now."

"Detective Hallam, I can't believe that what happened to Hilda was just bad luck. The night she was attacked, she was working on Justine Blackwell's financial papers. Doesn't that point to a connection?"

"Did you see the papers, Mrs. Kilbourn?"

"No, but Hilda told me she was going to work on them. My desk was ransacked, and now the papers are missing."

His face reddened with the effort to keep his temper in check. "Something you never saw is missing. You're a smart woman, Mrs. Kilbourn. You know that's not enough."

"Then what about the towel?" I asked. "If the person who attacked Hilda wasn't someone who knew her – even casually – why would they put that towel under her head?"

He flipped his notepad shut. "Just a sicko," he said. "I've seen worse things put in worse places."

There was a discreet knock, then Rosalie peeked around the door. "Just a friendly reminder," she said. "Ten minutes to class." Her radiant smile would have melted a harder heart than mine.

"Thank you," I said. It was an inadequate response to Rosalie's once-in-a-lifetime performance, but it was all I could muster. Detective Hallam pushed back his chair. I scooped up my books. "You'll keep in touch," I said.

"Count on it," he said.

As I left, Rosalie was dimpling at Robert Hallam. "I've just made some fresh coffee. It's a new blend. It'll put a spring in your step, I guarantee."

Class went well. It was early in the term, but my Political Science 110 class already showed signs of being an exceptional group: interested, talkative, and pleasant. Nevertheless, by the time I'd erased the boards, and reassured the last student, I had a knot of tension in my neck and a rawness in my nerves. I couldn't stop thinking about my conversation with Detective Hallam, and I couldn't shake the image of Hilda lying on our kitchen floor, white-faced on the blood-soaked towel.

As I walked out of the education building, the sun was full in my face. It was the second week in September, but students were lying on the grass, reading, tanning, smoking, and watching the scurrying of the colony of gophers that lived out their existence beneath the academic green. I gazed towards the concrete bulk of the classroom building. In my office on the third floor, there were a half-dozen tasks that could use my attention; all of them could wait. I turned right and followed the sidewalk that took me away from my office and towards the end of the lake that was set aside for birds who were nesting, migrating, or just hanging out. Most of the time, the birds at the sanctuary were familiar species: pelicans, mallards, Canada geese, ducks, pintails, snowgeese, loons, mudhens, grebes. But sometimes, during migration, amazing visitors presented themselves.

Often, when the weather was good, Alex and I met here at lunchtime to eat our sandwiches and split a Thermos of tea. One fall day, we came upon an explosion of gulls. The water was white with them. We sat at the water's edge and watched, and then we lay on the bank, hand in hand, looking up at the sky and listening.

Remembering that day, I felt a tug. I wanted Alex. All I had to do was dial his number and say . . . Say what? Say I remembered another September day? Say I wanted him back? Say I didn't care about the wall that seemed to spring up between us whenever the subject of race came up or about the way people looked at us when we walked into a room together? Say I was ready to try again with Eli, the child of glass, and with the shards that pierced all our lives every time his fragile psyche shattered? As I picked up my books and started back towards my office, I knew I wouldn't make the call. I was fifty-one years old, and, at the moment, I was shouldering all the burdens I could carry.

There were no messages on my voice mail; my e-mail was clear; my desk was empty. It wasn't quite noon. I stuck my head into the Political Science office to tell Rosalie I was leaving. She was arranging rusty-gold marigolds in an old-fashioned glass milk bottle. She looked up expectantly.

"I love marigolds," I said. "They always make me think

of the September when my older daughter started school. Every morning she'd take her safety scissors out to the garden and snip a bouquet. She always cut the stems too short. I often wondered what her teacher did with all those stubby little flowers."

Rosalie laughed softly. "And marigolds last forever," she said.

"One of their charms," I said. "Anyway, there's nothing I need to stick around here for, and I have a friend in the hospital, so I'm off."

"Just a minute." Rosalie took a handful of the flowers, folded a piece of waxed paper expertly over the stems and handed the bouquet to me. "For your friend," she said.

As I walked along the hall towards Hilda's room, I had my copy of *Anne of Green Gables* in my bag and Rosalie's marigolds in my hand, prepared for anything. In the room where the young man was recovering from his motorcycle accident, Garth Brooks was singing "Ain't Going Down ('Til the Sun Comes Up)." Earlier in the week, I had brought in a radio for Hilda, and there was music in her room too. It was Callas singing "In questa reggia" from *Turandot*. Garth and Maria seemed like a compelling duet to me, yet the nursing station was empty. When I saw Nathan Wolfe leaning over Hilda's bed, I panicked, but as he turned to greet me, he was smiling. "Good news," he said. "She's coming out of it."

I looked at Hilda. Much as I longed to, I couldn't detect any sign of change. "Did she regain consciousness?" I asked.

"No," he said. "But remember me telling you about the Glasgow Coma Scale?"

"Yes, but I was so scared, I couldn't seem to take anything in."

"Got time for a quick lesson now?"

"Of course."

"Let's go out to the desk."

I followed Nathan to the nursing station. He picked up a pencil and a pad of paper. "Okay, this is how we monitor changes in the patient's level of consciousness. We look at three aspects of behaviour; the first is –" he printed the words "Eyes Open." "If the patient's eyes open spontaneously, that's a 4; if they open when you speak to them, that's a 3; if they open to a pinprick, a 2; not at all is a 1." As he spoke he wrote the numbers in a column opposite the responses. "The second is Motor Responses. If a patient can move what you ask them to move, that's a 6; if they respond to localized pain, that's a 5; if they withdraw, that's a 4; abnormal flexion – that's this," he said, demonstrating – "is a 3; extends is a 2; and nothing is a 1. The third thing we look at is Verbal Response. If a patient's conversation is oriented, they get a 5; if their conversation is confused, they get a 4; if they use inappropriate words, that's a 3; incomprehensible sounds get a 2; and nothing gets a 1." He added up the best responses in each category. "Highest possible score is 15; the lowest is 3. A score of 7 or less is generally accepted as coma. Miss McCourt's been scoring pretty low, but today when I pricked her arm, she opened her eyes and withdrew her arm."

I looked over Nathan's shoulder at the column of figures. "So those responses score 2 and 4," I said. "That's a 6."

"And," said Nathan in the tones of an enthusiastic nursery teacher, "she made some incomprehensible sounds. So 8 in total. She's moving up."

I stared at the column of figures. "What can I do to keep her moving up?" I asked.

Nathan smiled. "The problem with these figures is that they make recovery look like a neat and orderly process, and it isn't. A lot of what happens we can't explain."

"Then what should I do."

He shrugged. "If you're comfortable with it, just keep on doing what you've been doing."

I handed Nathan the marigolds. "Thanks," I said. I took *Anne of Green Gables* out of my bag and waved it. "If you need us, Hilda and I will be in Avonlea."

I read until Matthew and Marilla decided to let Anne stay, at least provisionally. Every time I turned a page, I glanced over at Hilda, watching for a sign of response. She seemed more restless than she had been, but she did nothing that would have counted on Nathan's Glasgow Coma Scale. When I finally closed the book, I was discouraged. "I'll be back tomorrow," I said. "Rest well."

As I opened our front door, I realized how much I was looking forward to an afternoon alone. I took a package of pork chops out of the freezer, set them on a plate on the counter to thaw, then picked up the phone and checked my messages. Eric Fedoruk had called twice; so had Wayne J. Waters. Signe Rayner, announcing that she was spokesperson for her sisters, expressed her deepest concern. All of my callers left numbers where they could be reached and implored me to get back to them. I deleted the messages without writing down a single phone number. Hilda and I were simplifying our lives.

I decided to begin my simplification by logging some pool time. The sun was high as I walked through the leaves to the swimming pool. The water was warm, and I didn't hesitate before I dove in and gave myself over to the mindless pleasure of swimming laps. If I'm lucky, I can lose myself in swimming, and that day I was lucky. When I finally noticed Keith standing by the edge of the pool, he was laughing.

"I was beginning to think I was going to have to jump in there to get your attention."

"What are you doing in Regina?"

"I came down to see you. Is this a private pool party, or can anybody join?"

"Got your suit?"

"As a matter of fact, I do," he said. "Now that I'm out of politics, I'm turning over a new leaf. This morning I bought the first bathing suit I've owned in twenty-five years. And I brought it with me, because I heard the weather in Regina was unbelievable, and I thought you and I might find time to do this very thing."

"I don't believe it."

"Believe it," he said. "Now, if you'll excuse me, I'm going to go in the house and jump into my new Speedo."

"The Speedo I don't believe."

"And you're wise not to. The only suits left on the clearance table were depressingly sombre and modest, but they *were* cheap."

For half an hour, Keith and I swam laps, silently and companionably. Then we collapsed on the lounge chairs and soaked up the sun. For the first time in days, I felt my nerves unknot completely. It was a nice sensation. Keith was telling me some unrepeatable gossip about our ex-premier, and we were both roaring with laughter when I glanced over and saw Alex standing by the side of the house.

"I rang the doorbell," he said. "I thought you might be back here."

I jumped up and started towards him. "Alex, I'm so glad to see you. Come in and sit down." My voice was all wrong – falsely hearty. "Keith just got here," I finished weakly.

Alex looked over at Keith, then back at me. "Then I won't intrude."

Keith was on his feet. "Why don't I go inside and give you two a chance to talk."

Alex's eyes never left my face. "Thanks," he said, "but I just came by to ask about Hilda. Bob Hallam mentioned her case today. I guess he assumed I knew about it. You should have said something, Jo."

"You never gave me a chance," I said.

For a beat, we gazed at each other in silence. I could see the anger in Alex's eyes, but when he spoke, his voice was steady. "It's pretty obvious you're moving along with your life. I'll let you get back to it." He nodded in Keith's direction, then disappeared through the side gate.

I didn't go after him. I stood frozen, listening till I heard the car door shut and the motor roar. Finally, Keith came over and put his arm around my shoulder. "I'm not making a pass," he said. "The sun's gone in. You've got goosebumps."

I leaned into him. "I'm glad you're here," I said.

"So am I."

He took my hand, and we walked into the house. As soon as we were inside, Keith took me in his arms and kissed me: a lover's kiss, not a friend's. It wouldn't have ended there, except that just as his hand slid over my breast, the front door slammed. Taylor was home. Keith smoothed my hair and smiled. "Does anyone on earth have lousier timing than me?" he asked.

"I don't think so," I said.

He shrugged. "Well, be warned. I'm going to keep trying till I get the timing right."

That night after dinner, Keith flew back to Saskatoon. Still shaken by the afternoon's events, I grabbed my bathing suit off the clothesline, changed into it, and headed for the pool again. As I knifed through the quiet water, I tried to focus on my grandmother's axiom for troubled times: forget the experience, remember the lesson. Lap after lap, I worked at bringing perspective to the day, but it was no use. Try as I might, I could neither forget nor remember. When I finally gave up and went to the house, I had found neither peace nor insight. The best I could hope for was distraction. I changed into my sweats, opened a bottle of Great Western beer, picked up the folder of material Jill had brought, and started reading.

I began with the guest list of Justine's last party. Jill had thoughtfully provided the rap sheets for a number of the merrymakers. The list of their offences against the Crown was impressive: break-and-enter, forgery, hit-and-run, counterfeiting, vehicular homicide, fraud, armed robbery, manslaughter, and assaults of every possible kind with every conceivable weapon.

Angus would have characterized the men and women among whom Justine Blackwell elected to spend the last hours of her life as a bad-ass group, but bad-ass or not, Justine had believed she owed them reparation. Much of the information Jill submitted was photocopied, but she had handwritten the notes from her phone calls and interviews, and the picture of Justine that emerged from these notes was of a woman prepared to use every resource she had to make amends.

According to Jill's sources, Justine had supplied the down payment for the building on Rose Street that became Culhane House, and she was making the mortgage payments. She'd promised a substantial renovation of the building to make it suitable as a kind of residential halfway house; she had guaranteed that any contractor who did the work would have to use ex-prisoners as part of their labour force. There had been more personal philanthropies: she had signed herself on as a guarantor of loans; she had paid instalments of tuition; she had written cheques to dentists and clothing stores and used-car rental agencies. But from Jill's information, one thing was clear. Justine might have been atoning, but she was atoning with a tight hand on the pursestrings. Except for small gifts, all Justine's bequests were

167

conditional. With just a few well-placed calls, Justine could have put an end to Operation Reparation.

Wayne J. Waters' empire was a shaky one. And according to Jill's notes, Wayne J. was not a man to handle stress or reversal of fortune equably. He had started out as a kid doing break-and-enter, moved up through the ranks to robbery and armed robbery, and finished as a generalist, a jack of all illicit trades. He prided himself on never becoming involved with drugs or prostitution, but those seemed to be the only lines he refused to cross. He was immensely strong and enormously glib. No one Jill had talked to could say with any certainty whether Culhane House was a genuine attempt at altruism or just another scam. On one point, all Jill's sources were in agreement: despite his seeming conversion, Wayne J. Waters was a very dangerous man.

I was relieved to put his file aside and pick up Eric Fedoruk's. There was nothing in it to make the pulse race. An illustrated magazine article chronicled his smooth transition from hockey player to successful lawyer. There was a nice photo of him with Justine, whom the caption characterized as his childhood neighbour and enduring mentor. From Jill's notes, it appeared Eric Fedoruk was one of those lucky people who move from accomplishment to accomplishment. His two passions were the law and his Ducati Mostro, which Jill pointed out helpfully was a motorcycle. He had never married. "A possibility for me here," Jill had written in her large looping hand. "I've always longed to hop on one of those Eurobrutes and ride off into the sunset at 160 kph."

There wasn't much in the photocopied material about Lucy Blackwell's life that I didn't already know, but Jill's notes contained a surprise. After her father's death, Lucy had attempted suicide. She had been hospitalized briefly, and when she was released, she headed for San Francisco. Within months, she had a song on the charts and, apparently, she'd never looked back. Jill said her source was utterly reliable, but to my mind the story raised a number of questions, not the least of which was why Justine would allow a vulnerable sixteen-year-old to strike out on her own. It was puzzling, but when it came to Justine's life, it seemed there were many puzzles. I tried to remember if there were any suicide references in Lucy's famously autobiographical songs, but I came up blank. Like Wayne J. Waters, Lucy Blackwell had apparently decided there were areas where it was wise to draw the line.

There were other troubling revelations in Lucy's file. For one thing, Jill's source said that Lucy had been forced to finance *The Sorcerer's Smile* herself. The movers and shakers in the music industry had made it known that they saw Lucy as yesterday's singer, and that they had no interest in backing a CD boxed set that encapsulated her personal history in music. The rejection must have bruised Lucy's ego, but her decision to go ahead with the project had hit her in the pocketbook.

During the heady years of the eighties, Lucy had built a home in Nova Scotia. Jill had included a photo spread from *InStyle* magazine on Lucy at home in the oceanfront hideaway she had designed herself. The house was fanciful, idiosyncratic, and, to my mind, beautiful. In the article, Lucy had been lyrical about what her home on the ocean meant to her, but last year she had sold it, a sacrifice to her determination that her musical legacy would be preserved. The final photograph in the article was a close-up of Lucy exultant as the waves crashed behind her on the beach. Her smile was dazzling, but as I closed the folder, I found myself wondering about the pain behind the smile.

On the Post-it note she had stuck to the eight-by-ten glossy of Tina Blackwell, Jill had scrawled a three-word

169

question: "See the problem?" I could. On the few occasions I'd caught Tina on TV, she'd struck me as the epitome of glazed perfection: flawless makeup, hair teased and sprayed to look casual, classic jewellery, sleekly fitted jackets. In the photograph in front of me, Tina Blackwell was still an attractive woman, but even the benevolent hand of the retoucher hadn't been able to erase the inevitable signs of aging: the softening of the jawline, the droop of the eyelid, the tiny lines around the corners of her eyes, the feathering of her lips. The printed material on Tina was minimal. Jill had included three items: a copy of the announcement CJRG had made when they fired Tina, or in their sly corporate-speak, "freed her to pursue other opportunities"; a copy of the c.v. Tina had submitted to NationTV, and her cover letter to Jill offering to take "even a very junior position if one is available." CJRG had referred to Tina as "a longtime employee." In fact, she had been there for more than twenty years, her entire working life. With her surgically scarred face and her one-line résumé, it was hard to imagine what was ahead for her.

I almost put the material on Signe Rayner aside without reading it. So far, when it came to lousy lives, Justine Blackwell's daughters were two for two, and I wasn't eager for more sad revelations. But if I was going to resolve Hilda's unfinished business with Justine Blackwell, I had to be resolute. I opened the file, and as soon as I saw the first newspaper clipping, I was riveted. Dr. Signe Rayner was a woman with a past. The clippings were three years old, and they were from the Chicago papers. The parents of an adolescent boy Signe had been treating sued her after the boy committed suicide. According to trial transcripts, while the young man was under hypnosis Signe had returned him to an infantile state, and encouraged him to see her as his mother.

Signe's lawyers had earned their fees. They established that the dead boy's father, an architect, had recently declared bankruptcy, and that the mother had her own lengthy history of psychiatric problems. A clutch of Signe's professional colleagues had testified that, while her approach was unorthodox, it was not unethical. They supported Signe's contention that she was attempting to help the boy return to the genesis of his problems and that, in urging him to consider her as his mother, she was simply offering herself as an ally in his battle against his demons. The boy's parents lost their case. Signe Rayner was cleared of wrongdoing.

Despite her exoneration, she left Chicago, moved back to Regina, and began again. It was a puzzling coda to a court victory. A suspicious mind might have theorized that there had been some sort of prior agreement between Signe and her professional colleagues in Chicago, a kind of *quid pro quo* in which they agreed to support her in court if she agreed to remove herself from their jurisdiction.

I reread the account of Signe's bizarre relationship with the dead boy, then I picked up the telephone and dialled Alex's number. If Shakespeare was right about past being prologue, Alex needed to take another look at the doctor he was trusting to take his nephew to the brink and back again.

CHAPTER

10

I tried Alex's number until 11:00, when, exhausted, anxious, and furious at his refusal to have an answering machine, I turned out the lights and went to bed. Twice during the night, I woke up, rolled over, and dialled again. There was still no answer. The next morning I made a pact with myself; I wouldn't even attempt to call until after Rose and I had our walk and I'd showered and dressed for the day. Like most bargains with a fool, my compact got me nowhere. When Rose and I got back, I dialled Alex's apartment, and there was still no answer. Undeterred, I made another pact. The kids loved James Beard's pecan coffee cake, and I hadn't made one since the beginning of summer. I'd stay away from the phone until I'd made a coffee cake and put it in the oven.

My homage to James Beard paid off, but not with the dividend I'd expected. By the time Taylor and Angus straggled down to breakfast, the kitchen smelled the way a kitchen in a well-run home is supposed to smell in the morning, and I'd decided that calling Alex was a dumb idea. He was a man who operated on fact, not theory, and my concerns about Signe Rayner were based on conjecture. Calling him would make me look hysterical. More seriously, it would make me look desperate. Whatever lay ahead for Alex and me, I didn't want him to remember me as a woman who grasped at any excuse to ring up her ex-lover.

After we'd eaten, I felt better. I'd made a world-class coffee cake, and I hadn't made a fool of myself. Not a bad record to rack up before 7:30 a.m. But praiseworthy as my restraint might be, it didn't change the fact that I still needed answers, not just about Signe Rayner, but about other members of Justine's circle of family, friends, and acquaintances. Detective Hallam might not have believed that Hilda had been attacked because someone Justine knew was desperate to get at her financial papers, but I did.

I was certain that Hilda's assailant was connected somehow to Justine, but most of the people in Justine's life were unknown quantities to me. Fortunately, as I'd been measuring out the cinnamon and butter for the coffee cake, I'd come up with a candidate who might be able to help me fill in the blanks. Eric Fedoruk had grown up next door to the Blackwells; he had considered Justine his mentor, and he had been her lawyer. If I was going to unearth the truth about Justine's life, he might just be my man.

For a successful lawyer, Eric Fedoruk was surprisingly accommodating. When I called his home number, he didn't miss a beat before offering to meet me at his office within the hour. The address he gave me was on the top floor of one of the twin towers at the end of Scarth Street Mall. I was early enough to get a parking spot a block away, but as I walked towards his building, the morning sun bounced off its glass face, blinding me. I hoped it wasn't an omen. There had been few occasions in my life when I'd been more aware of the need to see clearly.

Eric Fedoruk was waiting for me when I stepped off the elevator. His black motorcycle boots had been replaced by nutmeg calfskin loafers, his fawn suit looked like Armani, and his buttercup-yellow tie demanded attention. When he offered his hand, I was glad I wasn't being billed by the hour.

"I was relieved to get your call," he said, as he steered me smoothly past the firm's receptionist into his office. It was spacious and airy, filled with natural light from two walls of floor-to-ceiling windows. The other two walls were filled with photographs and hockey memorabilia. Eric Fedoruk led me past his desk and the client chairs which faced it to a trio of easy chairs that had been arranged around a low circular table in the corner of the room. He held out a chair for me.

"Can I get you anything before we begin?" he asked.

"Thanks," I said, "I'm fine." I leaned towards the window. "What a spectacular view of the city."

"It is, isn't it?" he said. "And it's beautiful in every season." He made a face. "I sound like I'm running for President of the Chamber of Commerce."

"You've got my vote," I said. "I think Regina's a great place to live."

He grinned. "It's nice to be having a civil conversation. You know, we *are* on the same side in this."

"Whose side is that?"

He didn't hesitate. "Justine's. In your case, Miss McCourt's, but she was on Justine's side. Now, since we are allies, can we graduate to first names?"

"That's fine with me, Eric," I said.

"Good." His eyes, the grey of an autumn sky before a storm, met mine. "Now, why don't you tell me what brought you here this morning."

"The attack on Hilda," I said. "I think the police are on the wrong track. Eric, I'm certain Hilda knew her assailant. Before I left the house that night, she told me she was going to spend the evening working on Justine's financial records. I think she was searching for something that would help her resolve the question of Justine's mental competence once and for all."

"And you believe she found it."

I nodded. "I do. I think that there was something in Justine's personal papers that tipped the scales, and that whoever came to my house that night knew it was there. That's why they tried to kill Hilda, and that's why they ransacked the house until they found what they were looking for."

Eric Fedoruk looked hard at me. "Where do I fit in?"

"I'm hoping you can help me understand some of the people in Justine's life. The problem is I don't know enough about any of them to ask the right questions." I leaned towards him. "I guess all I can do is ask you to tell me about Justine."

Pain crossed his face. "I don't know where to begin."

I gave him what I hoped was an encouraging smile.

He returned it; then he shrugged and glanced around his handsome office. "Well, for starters, I wouldn't have any of this if it hadn't been for her."

"She opened the right doors for you."

He shook his head. "She changed the course of my life," he said softly. "If it hadn't been for her, I never would have been a lawyer. Which means that, at this point, I would have been an aging jock, trying to get by with a smile, a handshake, and a basement full of game tapes nobody gave a damn about." He shuddered. "It's scary to look back and think how close I came. Anyway, thanks to Justine, it didn't happen."

"She was your mentor."

"She was more than that," he said. "When I was fifteen, all anybody saw when they looked at me was a kid with a great slapshot. My dad died a month after I was born, and I guess my mother was sort of overwhelmed by all the scouts knocking on her door telling her that, as soon as I turned sixteen, I should be in junior A. Of course, that was what I wanted too. My mother was just about to cave in, when – he smiled at the memory – "Justine took me out to dinner."

"Because she saw you as somebody who had more going for him than a slapshot."

"Right," he said. "She took me to the old Assiniboia Club, and she laid out a plan for my life. Get serious about my studies. Go to university. Play hockey for a while. Then go to law school. As we were talking, all these big-shot lawyers kept dropping by our table 'just to chat.'"

"Justine had invited them?"

"She never left anything to chance. Anyway, it was heady stuff for a fifteen-year-old: a glamorous successful older woman taking his life seriously, treating him like an adult."

"And you followed the plan?"

"To the letter. I finished high school, got a hockey scholarship to the University of Denver, graduated *cum laude;* went straight to the Maple Leafs, where, for six years, I had more fun than most people have in a lifetime, then came back to Saskatchewan and enrolled in law school."

"Right on track," I said.

"Yeah," he agreed. "But it was a good track to be on."

"Justine must have been an amazing woman."

"She was that," he agreed.

"All the same, what she did for you surprises me. It was so parental, and I got the impression she wasn't much of a mother."

"Given the daughters she had, Justine was as good a mother as she could be," he said tightly.

"Her children do seem to have had troubled lives," I agreed. "But, Eric, surely some of their troubles have to be rooted in their relationship with her. You may have every reason to be grateful to Justine, but from what I've heard she didn't find family life very congenial."

"If you got your information from her children, you should remember that there are two sides to every story."

"I know that," I said. "And I know that Justine's daughters aren't exactly poster girls for filial devotion, but they weren't my only source. Hilda got so involved with Justine and her circle that I had a friend do a little checking around. Some of what she came up with puts Justine in a pretty negative light."

"Such as?"

"Such as the fact that Lucy tried to kill herself after her father died. As soon as she recovered, she ran away and, apparently, Justine just let her go."

"There were reasons," he said coldly.

"What possible reason could any mother have for letting a distraught sixteen-year-old just take off?"

Eric Fedoruk's face was stony. "It was a complex situation, and Justine was the injured party." He got up, walked to the window and stood with his back to me.

"I take it the subject is closed," I said.

"It is," he said wearily. He turned to face me. "I want to co-operate with you, believe me. I want the truth to come out. Justine had nothing to hide, but that particular time in the family's life was painful for so many people. Can't we just drop it?"

"All right," I said. "We'll drop the subject of Lucy's running away. But, Eric, if Justine is the woman you say she is, wouldn't putting some of the other rumours to rest be the best way to honour her memory?"

"I was her lawyer, Joanne. There are matters I'm just not free to discuss."

"But there must be things you can talk about. Wayne J. Waters, for example. You and Justine must have discussed him."

"We *argued* about him. I don't think Justine and I were together once over the past year when his name didn't come up. I thought that he was pond-scum and that Culhane House was a scam." He looked away. "Justine didn't share my feelings about his character or his project."

"But Hilda told me Wayne J. and Justine quarrelled about money the night she died."

"I guess he was afraid she was reconsidering her commitment to Culhane House. She wasn't, of course. She'd just put her financial support on hold, the way she'd put everything else on hold until she'd found an answer to the question that was consuming her."

"Whether she was in full possession of her faculties."

Eric winced. "Exactly. By the night of her party, Justine had been so badly shaken by all the people, including me, who were questioning her behaviour that she did a very lawyerly thing: she decided to hold all her affairs in abeyance until she was certain she was sane."

"Then she hadn't rejected Wayne J."

"No. I wish she had. But on the night she died, Justine was still passionate about Culhane House, and she still trusted Wayne J. It makes me faintly queasy to say this, but in the last year of her life, Justine was closer to him than she was to anyone. She just wanted to make certain that when she signed a cheque, she was making a rational decision about the use of her money."

"Is that why she didn't loan Tina the money for the plastic surgery she needed?"

Eric Fedoruk looked genuinely puzzled. "Is that the story you heard? Because whoever told you that doesn't have the facts. Justine gave Tina the money she asked for. If we had the financial records, I'd be able to show you the cancelled cheque." He shrugged. "Unfortunately, we don't, so you'll just have to take my word for it."

"Eric, if Justine gave her the money, why did Tina get the surgery done on the cheap?"

"That's a question for Tina to answer, but if you want my opinion, somebody gave her a hard-luck story. Tina tries, but she's easily led."

"By men?"

"By everybody. But Tina's not the issue here; Justine is. And no matter what you hear, Justine was never selfish and she was never vindictive. At the end, she was just very confused." His voice was close to breaking.

I leaned towards him. "Eric, why didn't she get help? Her own daughter is a psychiatrist. She could have recommended someone."

"Signe was hardly a disinterested party."

"Because Justine was her mother?"

"No, because in the last year, there was a lot of tension there. Justine was doing everything in her power to get Signe to stop practising psychiatry."

I felt a chill. "Because of what she'd done to that boy in Chicago."

"Who told you about that?" Eric's tone was edgy.

"The news clippings were in my friend's research. But the papers said Signe was exonerated. Was she guilty? Is that why her mother didn't want her practising any more?"

Eric's eyes met mine. "I can't talk about this, Joanne."

"Were you involved in Signe's defence? I know you couldn't act for her in the States, but did you advise her? Is that why you can't talk about the case?"

Eric looked at his watch. "I have a nine o'clock appointment. I've already kept him waiting too long."

I stood up. "Thanks for seeing me," I said. "You've been a help."

"Have I? Maybe the more helpful thing would have been to tell you to get out while the getting's good."

"Meaning?"

He shrugged. "Nothing. Just be careful, Joanne. Now, if you'll excuse me, I really do have to see my client."

Waiting client or no, Eric Fedoruk was a gentleman. He walked me to the elevator and pressed the call button. As we listened to the elevator make its smooth ascent, I knew I was looking at my last chance. "I know you can't discuss what happened in Chicago," I said, "but can you answer a hypothetical question?"

He raised an eyebrow. "Depends on the question."

"Eric, if you had an adolescent child, would you let Signe treat him?"

For a beat, he didn't answer, and I thought I'd pushed too hard. But as the elevator doors opened, his eyes met mine. "I would move heaven and earth to keep Signe Rayner from getting anywhere near a child of mine." he said. Then he smiled. "Of course, that's just hypothetical."

As soon as I got to the university, I called Alex at the police station. He was in a meeting, but I gave the woman on the other end my name and told her it was an emergency. As I waited for Alex to come to the phone, my heart was pounding.

At first, he sounded like himself, warm and concerned. "Hilda's not worse, is she?"

"No," I said. "This isn't about Hilda. Alex, I have more information about Signe Rayner."

He made no attempt to conceal his irritation. "I thought we'd agreed Eli's treatment was no longer your concern."

"We didn't agree," I said. "You decided, but, Alex, you were wrong. You've got to hear me out. Even her own mother didn't think Signe should be practising medicine, and Eric Fedoruk says he wouldn't let her treat a child of his."

Alex's voice was coldly furious. "A woman who hangs out with felons and allows strangers to be buried in her family plot isn't exactly what I would consider a credible arbiter of someone else's competence. Damn it, Jo, are you so determined to prove that you're right that you've lost sight of the facts? At the end, Justine Blackwell's life had become so bizarre that even she wasn't sure of her sanity."

"Then what about Eric Fedoruk?"

"I couldn't care less what some lawyer with a six-figure income would do with his child. My only concern is Eli, and, Joanne, whether you like it or not, Dr. Rayner is giving my nephew something he hasn't had a lot of in his life: consistency. She's there, Jo. Every appointment, she's there waiting. She never decides Eli's too much trouble. She never abandons him. She never . . ."

I cut him off. "Sorry I bothered you," I said, and I slammed down the receiver. I was still shaking with anger when the phone rang. When I picked up the receiver and heard Keith Harris's voice, it seemed as if providence was taking a hand in the sorry mess of my life.

"Are you okay, Jo?" he asked. "You sound a little down."

"Nothing a few kind words won't fix."

"My pleasure," he said. "Now, listen. I have news."

As Keith gave me an account of the latest episode in his fortunate life, I felt my pulse slow and my spirits rise. The tenant who had sublet his father's Regina apartment was moving out at the end of September, and Keith saw the freeing up of the apartment as significant. "Everything's working out just the way it's supposed to," he said. "Part of a larger cosmic plan." As I hung up, I decided that maybe it was time to step aside and let the universe unfold as it should.

The rhythms of everyday life pushed us ahead. I talked to Mieka and Greg every night and we e-mailed each other every day. Their news was as miraculous as it was commonplace. Madeleine was eating and growing and discovering. When I told them about the attack on Hilda, I tried to minimize her injuries, but as my daughter continued to press me about coming up to Saskatoon again, I was forced to tell her the truth. Mieka had always loved Hilda, and the anxiety in her voice when she asked for details saddened me. Those first days with Madeleine should have been a time of cloudless joy, but it seemed that days of cloudless joy were in short supply that September.

I taught Taylor how to send messages to Madeleine on e-mail, and she and Jesse got an A for their project on owls. Even these accomplishments weren't enough to offset my daughter's awareness that all was not right in her world. My daily reports on Hilda's progress appeared to reassure her, but Taylor continued to be perplexed about Alex and Eli's absence from our lives. My explanation that Alex and I had just decided to spend some time apart didn't satisfy her. It didn't satisfy me either, but as unsatisfactory as the story was, I didn't have a better one. Alex didn't call, and after a few days I stopped expecting him to. As the third week of school started, Anita Greyeyes, the woman who would have been Eli's teacher, phoned to ask me what arrangements had been made about Eli's schooling. I gave her Alex's work and home numbers and told her that she should deal with him directly. Another link had been severed.

My professional life was moving into high gear. My classes were taking shape, the inevitable academic committee meetings had begun, and Jill and I had started to mull over topics that might work on our first political panel of the new season.

I visited Hilda at least once every day, and here the news was good. Even my untutored eye could discern cause for hope. Increasingly, as I read to her or as we listened to the radio together, she became restless, as if she were wearying of her long sleep. Even her stillness seemed closer to healthy consciousness. Nathan Wolfe was encouraged too. Hilda's numbers on the Glasgow Coma Scale were rising, and Nathan and I fussed over each incremental gain like new parents. Despite our hovering and hoping, when the breakthrough finally came it had the force of a surprise.

It was on a Friday afternoon, thirteen days after Hilda had been assaulted. I'd come to the hospital just after lunch. My morning had been busy, and Hilda's room was warm. From the moment I started to read, I could feel my eyelids grow heavy. After five minutes, I closed my book, turned up the radio, leaned back in my chair, and gave myself over to the considerable pleasures of Henry Purcell. When I woke up, "Rejoice in the Lord Alway" had been replaced by the news, and, for once, there was news worth noting.

Boys playing along the shoreline of Wascana Lake had discovered the marble-based scales that had been used to bludgeon Justine Blackwell to death. The scales, which had been presented to Justine with such fanfare at the dinner were half-buried in the gumbo of the lake bed. It was a case of *sic transit gloria mundi*, but it was also a piece of real evidence in an investigation which, if the media could be believed, was woefully short of concrete proof that Terrence Ducharme had murdered Justine. Reflexively, I glanced over at Hilda.

What I saw made my pulse race. She was conscious, but the woman before me was not the Hilda I knew. This woman's eyes were wild, and her mouth was contorted with rage and effort. She was trying to speak, but the sounds that came out of her mouth were guttural and unintelligible. When her eyes met mine, I almost wept. In that moment, I knew that she understood her circumstances and grasped the fact that we were both powerless to change them.

"It's all right," I said. "It's going to be all right."

She shook her head furiously and made a growling sound.

"What is it?" I asked. "Is there something you want me to get?"

For a beat, she stared at me. Then she lifted her head, and, in a voice rusty with disuse and hoarse with effort, she pronounced a single recognizable word. "Maisie," she said. "Maisie."

"She has to build new pathways," Nathan Wolfe said. It was mid-afternoon, and Nathan and I were sitting in the cafeteria of Pasqua Hospital. Twenty-four hours earlier, Hilda had entered a brief period of consciousness, and I had felt the darkness lift, but soon after she had articulated the single word "Maisie," my friend had lapsed back into her silent private world. Now Nathan and I were splitting a plate of fries, drinking Coke, and talking about what came next.

"She's almost there," Nathan said. "The restlessness and the fact that she actually talked are great signs, but it's going to take time. And learning how to say what she wants to say is going to take *a lot* of time. The communication pathways she used before are blocked, and until she builds some new ones, Miss McCourt has to use whatever's handy to get her message across.

"She could find the name 'Maisie,' but not 'Justine,'" I said.

Nathan speared a fry and dipped it in gravy. "She was lucky she made a connection you could understand," he said. "'Maisie' is at least in the ballpark. A lot of recovering coma patients come out with stuff like 'potato' when they mean 'water.'" He chewed his fry reflectively. "Makes it tough to meet their needs when they're thirsty."

"So how do I meet Hilda's needs?" I asked.

"Do anything you can to keep her from getting frustrated," Nathan said. "Listen hard to what she's trying to say, and translate. Play it by ear. You'll get the hang of it."

My chance came sooner than either Nathan or I anticipated. When we went upstairs to intensive care, Hilda was lying on her back. Her eyes were open, but she didn't appear to be seeing anything. Nathan was quick to spot my fear, and he did his best to be reassuring. "Lethargy and stupor are part of the package, Mrs. K. Just do what you usually do, and don't panic if she gets agitated. That's part of the package too. In fact, a little flailing around is good exercise for the patient's arms and legs." He smiled.

I didn't smile back. "I hate this," I said. "I hate standing in this room, talking about Hilda as if she were a piece of wood."

Nathan pulled back Hilda's sheet, poured some skin-care lotion into his hand and began to rub it into her legs. "I know how you feel," he said, "but in these cases, there's a lot of behaviour that seems scary if you're not prepared for it."

I watched as Nathan massaged Hilda's legs and arms. As he rubbed her muscles, he talked to Hilda in a voice that was as soothing as his hands must have been.

"You're so good with her," I said.

"I like the work," he said. "Every so often, these patients come back. It's a real rush when you've got to know the physical part of a person so well, and all of a sudden the rest of them's there."

After Nathan left, I picked up *Anne of Green Gables* and began to read. As soon as she heard my voice, Hilda became uneasy. She shifted position, then drew her legs up.

"It's okay," I said. "I won't read any more. We can talk. Let's see . . . It's the third week in September, and it's Saturday – a real fall day. This morning, before her art lesson, Taylor and Jess decided they were going to earn money raking lawns. Taylor thought they'd get more people to sign on if we bought some of those Hallowe'en leaf bags. She and Jess have about ten customers lined up. I hope this doesn't end up like Angus's pet-walking service. Remember that time we spent the whole weekend walking dogs and cats because he'd overbooked?"

Hilda's eyes were closed, but she seemed to be listening, so I rambled on about the latest batch of baby photos Keith had brought down from Saskatoon and about Angus's disgust at his football team's 0–2 record. I had just started describing the cormorants I had seen that morning in the park when Hilda's eyes flew open. "Maisie," she said, and her tone was pleading.

Remembering Nathan's advice, I translated and played it by ear. "I'm not sure how much you've been able to pick up about Justine's case from the radio," I said, "but there isn't much to report. Twelve days ago, the police arrested a man named Terrence Ducharme. He was one of the ex-convicts Justine got involved with in the last year. I'm sure the police are hoping they can connect him to those scales they found in the lake yesterday, but I haven't heard anything."

Hilda's eyes opened. As she took in her situation, there was the same bleak shock of recognition I'd seen the day before. I grasped her hand and leaned closer to her. "You're in the hospital here in Regina," I said. "You've had an accident, but you're going to be all right."

My explanation seemed to satisfy her. She squeezed my hand, then closed her eyes again. I leaned over and kissed her forehead. "I missed you," I said. "Don't leave me yet."

Anxiously, I searched her face for a hint of response. There was none. I sat with her, listening to the opera on the radio until 3:00, when the shift changed, and a nurse I hadn't seen before came in to record Hilda's vital signs. I was in the way, and I knew it.

I kissed Hilda's forehead and promised to come back.

That night was our first political panel of the new season. Keith had come down the night before to lend moral support, but it was going to be a short weekend for us. He had business in Toronto, and he was taking the early flight out Sunday morning. When I got back from the hospital, he was in the backyard with Taylor and Jess, throwing around the yellow plastic football Eli had given me for safekeeping at the Labour Day game. Remembering, I felt a stab of guilt. Then I swallowed hard and tossed off the feeling. The football was, after all, only a cheap toy, and Alex had made it clear that Eli was no longer my concern.

Taylor threw me the ball. I had to dive, but I caught it.

"Good hands," Jess said appreciatively.

"Go deep." I threw him a pass and he made an effortless catch. "You're looking pretty sharp there yourself," I said. The four of us threw the ball around for a while, then Taylor and Jess went off to their lawn work.

Keith and I watched the kids until they had dragged their leaf bags and rakes around the corner onto Rae Street and disappeared from sight. "I envy them," I said. "I can't even remember when the biggest worry I had was filling a leaf bag."

Keith looked at me hard. "Let's grab Rose and take a walk. There won't be many more days like this."

"I should look at my notes for the show."

"I'll buy you an ice cream cone."

"Sold," I said. "These days, I come cheap."

We walked along the levee on the north side of Wascana Creek. It was an amazing day, and it seemed that literally everyone and his dog was out. Rose was a gregarious creature and as she greeted dog after dog, she seemed like her old self again. Keith and I bought cones and took them back to a quiet spot on the levee where we sat down, with Rose between us, and watched life in the creek.

When we'd finished eating, Keith leaned towards me. "You're looking a lot better. When you came back from the hospital, you looked pretty wiped. It worried me."

"Sorry," I said. "It's just that I'm so scared. And I feel so impotent. I just don't know what to do for Hilda. She asked about Maisie again today. Keith, I don't understand why she keeps going back to Justine's death. It has to be so upsetting for her."

"It's unfinished business, and you know as well as I do that once Hilda starts a job, she sees it through." He pointed towards the opposite shore. "Look," he said, "there's an otter over there on the bank."

"But not for long," I said, as the otter slipped into the creek and disappeared. "You're right, you know. Hilda prides herself on honouring her obligations. It must be so frustrating for her knowing that she never came to a final judgement about Justine." I stood up and brushed the dust off my slacks. "At one point, I thought I could finish the job, but as Hilda said, there are so many cross-currents in Justine's life. I didn't know who to believe, and I guess I just gave up trying."

"Want some help?"

"From you?"

"From me and from somebody with a little perspective. Jo, from what you've told me, everyone you've talked to has a vested interest in how that decision about Justine's sanity comes down. Maybe I can flush out a couple of impartial observers for you."

"Do you have anyone in mind?"

"I may," he said. "Dick Blackstone's old law partner is in a seniors' home down here. His daughter lives in town, and I ran into her last weekend. She said her dad's getting bored playing pinochle, and I should go see him. Let me give Garnet Dishaw a call and see if he's up for a visit."

"Do you think he'll be able to help?"

Keith shrugged. "I don't know, but at least we'll be a diversion from pinochle." He grabbed Rose's leash and stood up. "Ready to go?"

"You bet." I put my arm through his. "It's good to have somebody ready to share the load."

"Anything else I can do?"

I smiled up at him. "Sure. You can fill me in on all those provocative rumours I hear about dark plans to unseat your federal leader."

"I thought you hated backroom gossip."

"Not when it's about you guys," I said. "I love it, and the more stilettos the better."

By the time I walked into the TV studio that night, Keith had arranged for us to meet Garnet Dishaw at Palliser Place, the seniors' home in which he lived, as soon as the show was over. I'd been less successful with my second request. Despite my encouragement, Keith hadn't volunteered a single indiscreet insight into the machinations of his party. Luckily, the show that night didn't need inside information about dirty deeds.

Our topic was the proliferation of conservative parties in Canada. It was a red-meat topic, and Ken Leung made it sizzle. Glayne Axtell and I rose to the occasion. It was fun, and it was good television, but the real payoff came in the call-in segments. For the first time I could remember, we had callers who said they were under thirty years old. They were informed, witty, and iconoclastic; by the time the show ended, we all knew that it had generated more light than heat. It was a good feeling.

The glow endured. When I slid into the passenger seat of Keith's Mercedes, I was still buoyant.

"Ready to meet the prototypical curmudgeon?" Keith asked.

"Bring him on," I said. "Tonight I'm a match for anybody."

Palliser Place was a low-slung modern building with large windows and an air of being well kept. Its flower beds were already cleaned out for winter, and there wasn't an errant leaf on its spacious front lawns.

The young woman at the reception desk was reed-slim and carefully made-up. When we asked to see Garnet Dishaw, she rolled her eyes.

"He's in the hall outside his room, practising his golf shot," she said. She pointed with a well-shaped, French-manicured nail. "West wing."

Garnet Dishaw had set up a portable tee halfway up the hall. And he was indeed practising. The deep green broadloom of the hall was littered with balls from the shots he had missed. As we started down the hall, he was just getting into his swing. He connected with the ball, but he had an ugly slice and the ball ricocheted off a door a couple of metres away from us and bounced along until it came to rest at my feet. Keith bent down and picked it up.

"Good to see you again, Garnet," he said, extending the ball in his hand like a peace offering.

Garnet Dishaw had the patrician, silver-haired good looks of a lawyer in an old movie. He was dressed in the same casual manner as Keith: a golf shirt and casual slacks, but

Garnet's clothes hung on him. It was obvious that not long before he had been a much larger man.

"Come inside, Keith," he said. "No use letting these senile old fools hear your business. Although your secrets would be safe enough; there isn't a person on this wing who's had a coherent thought since 1957."

When he bent to pick up the golf ball nearest him, I noticed he had trouble straightening. "Let me get those," I said. "Why don't you two go on in. I'll be along."

Garnet Dishaw and Keith disappeared into the last room in the hall. When I'd made the floor safe again, I joined them, or attempted to. Floor-to-ceiling bookshelves were pressed against every wall, and they were filled with books. In the corner, there was a single bed, covered with a piece of brightly patterned madras; next to it was a single chair and a TV table crowded with glasses and spoons and bottles of medications.

"You'll have to sit on the bed," Garnet Dishaw said. His voice was deep and assured, the voice of a man who, whatever his current circumstances, was accustomed to being listened to. "These residential rooms were designed for people who've decided to leave the past behind, but I am not among them. We inmates of Palliser Place are not allowed to screw anything into the walls without the written consent of the board of governors and of all the cherubim and seraphim, so we must make do with freestanding shelves." He squared his shoulders. "Now," he said, "may I offer you a drink? This institution subscribes to the principle of teetotalism, but most regulations can be subverted." He walked into the bathroom and returned with a bottle of Johnny Walker. "An old college trick," he said. "Not many people risk foraging through a man's laundry hamper, and even fewer sign on when the man is in his eighties. An old man's dirty laundry is not a pleasant thing," he said. Then he bowed to me. "I apologize for speaking of such matters before we've been formally introduced. May I offer you a drink, Ms. . . . ?"

"Kilbourn," I said. "And I'd love a drink. It's been a long day."

"Sensible woman," he said, approvingly. He poured whisky, no ice, no water, into glasses and handed them around. "All right," he said. "What's up?"

"Justine Blackwell," Keith said.

Garnet's shoulders sagged. "An awful thing," he said. "Death doesn't hold quite the terror for me that it does for you. Nonetheless, Justine deserved better; no one should die unprepared."

"Had you kept up with her at all?" Keith asked.

Garnet sipped his drink and settled back in his chair contentedly. "Good stuff. Something to be said for limiting one's intake. And yes, we had kept up, although I can take no credit for our association. *Palman qui meruit qui ferat.* Honour to whom honour is due. The praise goes to Justine, the Ice Queen, as she was known many years ago. She wasn't icy at all, of course. Just focused. That's never regarded as an admirable trait in a woman. I digress, a foible to be avoided at all costs when one is old. If I'm not careful, I could end up in a place even less forgiving than this.

"At any rate, Justine did keep in touch. And it surprised me. Before I retired, she was always good about Christmas gifts: the perfect cheese from Quebec or the best pecan fruitcake from Texas. I knew I was merely a name on a list; nonetheless, it was a good list to be on. But when I was . . ." His face clouded. The pain of his memory was apparent, but he forced himself to go on. "When I was compelled to move down here, to my daughter's house, Justine stayed in touch. She was very faithful about visiting. I'll give her that . . ."

Keith leaned forward in his chair. "Somehow that surprises me."

Garnet Dishaw's bright eyes were piercing: "You thought she'd no longer have use for someone who was no longer of use to her?"

Keith's gaze didn't waver. "Something like that."

"To be honest, you weren't the only one who was surprised. The first time she came into my daughter's house, you could have blown me over with a fairy's fart, but she was sincere. And she didn't treat me like . . . Never mind. she treated me the way she always had. Even when my daughter moved me in here, Justine came."

"When did you move in here?" I asked.

He scowled in annoyance. "I don't know," he said, "last year sometime."

"Did you notice a change in Justine in the last year?"

"I'm not blind," he snapped. "When Justine visited me at my daughter's house, she looked the way she always looked, like she'd just stepped off a bandbox. In the last year, she looked like a goddamn tree-hugger."

I leaned forward in my chair. "But she was still Justine."

"Of course. She was trying to find answers to some big questions. That's what you do when you're old. I thought the answers she'd come up with were arrant nonsense, but they made sense for her."

"So you didn't think she'd lost her mind."

Garnet Dishaw sat back in his chair. "Why would I think that?"

"I'm not trying to meddle in Justine's personal affairs. These questions have to do with her estate."

"Are those girls of hers fighting over the lolly? Her death was a stroke of luck for them, no doubt about it." He drained his drink. "Poor Dick. Seeing his daughters like that would have been painful for him." Garnet Dishaw's voice took on a faraway quality. "Still, it wouldn't have been the first pain they caused him, nor would it have been the worst. He died of a broken heart, you know."

"Of a broken heart," I repeated.

Garnet Dishaw heard the doubt in my voice, and he turned on me angrily. "You heard me. If the great Howie Morenz could die of a broken heart because his leg shattered and ended his career, Richard Blackwell could certainly die of a broken heart after his whole life was shattered. I don't want to talk about this any more." Garnet pushed himself up from his chair and extended his hand to Keith. "It was good to see you again, my friend."

Keith took his hand and shook it. "Garnet, what the hell are you doing in a place like this?"

Garnet Dishaw made a moue of disgust. "I had a couple of falls," he said. "The first one was in the courthouse in Saskatoon. My feet got tangled up in my robe – a boffo Marx Brothers moment for my colleagues, but I ended up in hospital. My daughter brought me down here to recuperate and I slipped on the goddamn bathroom floor at her state-of-the-art house. We weren't getting along, and the fall gave her the chance she needed to get rid of me." His voice became a stage falsetto. "'With my job and the children and all, I can't give you the care you need, Dad. You'll be better off where there's someone there to look after you twenty-four hours a day.'" When he spoke again, his voice had regained its normal tone. "It's not an easy thing to face the fact that you're extraneous."

Our eyes locked, and for a beat there was a powerful and wordless communication between us. "No," I said. "It's not easy at all."

"Will you come to see me again?"

I nodded. "I'll come again."

"Good." He looked puckish. "And bring something for the laundry hamper."

The drive home was a short one, and Keith and I were silent, absorbed in our own thoughts. When we pulled up in front of my house, I turned to him. "What did you make of Garnet's comment about Justine's death being a stroke of luck for her daughters?"

"That thought's never occurred to you?"

"I guess it has, but it just seemed too terrible to consider."

"That's where you and Garnet part company then, because I don't imagine there's much about human behaviour that he classifies as being 'too terrible to consider.'"

"I liked him," I said.

"I like him too." Keith touched my cheek. "It's not easy, is it?"

"You mean what's waiting for us in the years ahead?"

"That's exactly what I mean," he said. "It would be nice not to be alone."

"Yeah," I said. "It would be nice not to be alone."

He kissed me. "I'll phone you from Toronto."

It was a little after 9:00 when I walked through the front door. When I called hello, only Rose responded, but she led me to the others. Angus and Leah were on the back deck, curled up together in one of the lazy lounges.

"You two look cosy," I said.

"We are," Angus agreed. "But we're ready to move along, and a little coin for coffee at Roca Jack's would be appreciated."

"Is everything okay with Taylor?"

Leah stood up and stretched. "She's out in her studio painting. Mrs. Kilbourn, that new picture of hers is sensational."

"You're just saying that because you're in it," Angus said. My son gave my shoulder an avuncular squeeze. "Now, Mum, about that cash infusion."

I opened my bag and gave him a bill.

He waved it appreciatively. "Feeling generous tonight?"

"I'm investing in my old age," I said. "I want to make you so indebted to me that you wouldn't even consider making me spend my sunset years in Palliser Place."

CHAPTER

11

The first voice I heard Sunday morning was Detective Robert Hallam's. His gravelly baritone was uncharacteristically tentative. "I'm glad you're up and about, Mrs. Kilbourn. You are an early bird, aren't you?"

"It appears you are too."

"They say the early bird gets the worm."

"Exactly what worm are you after, Detective Hallam?"

He cleared his throat. "Actually, I'm after Rosalie Norman's telephone number." He coughed again. "It's not in the book, and I thought perhaps you might have it. You wouldn't be violating any privacy rights. Rosalie and I are planning to meet for lunch tomorrow."

"Couldn't wait, huh?"

"It's not that. It's . . ." He lowered his voice. "I thought Rosalie might like to go to the matinee of that play at the Globe."

"They're doing *Romeo and Juliet*, aren't they? I hear it's a very passionate production."

"Do you think Rosalie will feel I'm coming on too strong?"

I thought of the new kittenish Rosalie with her black turtleneck and laughter in her voice. "She'll love it," I said. "Hang on. I've got last year's university directory here. Her number will be in it."

After I gave him the number, he repeated it twice, then lowered his voice to a whisper. "Thank you, Mrs. Kilbourn. I appreciate your help."

"Any time. Detective Hallam, while I've got you on the line, have you made any progress on finding out who attacked Hilda McCourt?"

"No. We're back to interviewing people in your area about whether they spotted anyone suspicious that evening."

"Didn't you already do that?"

He sighed. "You bet we did. Twice. We're not exactly popular with your neighbours. But Inspector Kequahtooway is pretty determined about this one."

"I didn't think he was part of the investigation."

"He wasn't. But he followed up some leads on his own time, then asked to be assigned officially."

I remembered how I'd slammed the phone down the last time Alex and I spoke. More coals heaped upon my head. I took a deep breath. "Could you transfer me to Inspector Kequahtooway?" I said. "I'd like to let him know how grateful I am that he's involving himself in Hilda's case."

"No problem, and thanks again, Mrs. Kilbourn. I know I got off to a lousy start with you, but you're a peach."

"At the moment I'm feeling a little bruised."

"What?" he barked.

"It's a joke."

"I don't get it," he said. "Hang on, I'll transfer you."

For a few minutes, I languished in the silent land of *on hold*. Finally, Detective Hallam was back on the line, and his gravelly baritone was back to full volume. "Not on duty," he said. "Inspector Kequahtooway has booked off on personal business. One of the other aboriginal guys said he thought Inspector K. said something about going out to his reserve with his nephew."

"Thanks for trying," I said. "I hope you and Rosalie enjoy the play."

I took my coffee out to the backyard. It was another five-star day, perfect weather to be out at Standing Buffalo. The hills would be warm with the colours of autumn: silver sage, burnt umber, goldenrod. Echo Lake, free at last of its summer burden of Jet Skis and motorboats, would be serene. Karen Kequahtooway had loved those hills, that lake. I sipped my coffee and tried to imagine this woman I'd never met. As a child, she had, Alex said, been surefooted, confident, filled with life; as a mother, her love for her son had made her vulnerable. Her hopes and her fears for him ended in a twisted mass of glass and metal when the brakes on her car failed and she missed a hairpin turn on the road that winds through the Qu'Appelle Valley. Eli had been with her on that lonely road; he had seen everything, and now Signe Rayner was forcing him to unearth all the pain he had buried beneath his memory's surface.

When I spotted Eli's plastic football abandoned in our fading flower garden, the symbolism overwhelmed me. I didn't even try to hold back the tears. Eli was worth crying over; it had been a lousy month, and I was tired of being brave. After a few minutes of noisy crying, I felt better. I found a tissue in my jeans pocket that didn't look too disreputable, blew my nose, and walked down to the garden to pick up the football. When I turned to go back to the house, Taylor was running towards me. She was still wearing her nightie, her face was swollen with sleep, and her hair was a tangle. At that moment, I couldn't have conjured up a more beautiful sight.

I bent down and hugged her. "So," I said, "what's the plan for the day?"

"Come and see my new painting," she said. "Then we can decide."

I followed her out to her studio. One glance at the canvas on the easel and I knew Leah Drache had been right: the new picture was sensational. It was a fantasy, a picture of Taylor's dream dragon-boat team. The boat was pulled up on the shore, and the members of the crew were getting ready for the race. Taylor, wearing her orange lifejacket over her green Bottlescrew Bill T-shirt, was already seated in the prow, beating her drum. Mieka and Greg and Madeleine were in place behind her. Hilda was helping Leah climb into the seat behind them. Angus and Eli were still on the shore, handing out paddles. I was sitting at the back of the boat, alone.

I pointed to the empty place beside me. "Who's going to sit there?" I asked.

Taylor shrugged. "I don't know. Maybe just a made-up person."

"I'm glad you put Eli in," I said.

"I miss him," Taylor said.

"I miss him too," I said.

"I don't get it," my younger daughter said.

"What don't you get?"

"Why just because we lose Alex, we have to lose Eli too."

As I scrambled the eggs for breakfast, I thought about what Taylor had said. She was right. The fact that Alex and I hadn't been able to work things out didn't end my family's commitment to Eli. Whether Alex wanted me to be involved or not, Eli could use an advocate. I popped two English muffins into the toaster and poured the juice. Church was in an hour, and I had to get cracking because suddenly I had plans for the day.

During the service, I couldn't keep my mind from wandering. Twice, Angus had to turn the page in our shared prayer book; each time, he favoured me with the chilly raised eyebrow of the pious. But even my son's theatrical opprobrium couldn't prevent me from thinking of Eli and of Signe Rayner. By the time the choir and congregation had sung the recessional, I'd made up my mind. In the past month, Justine's daughters had burned up the wires calling to express their concern about Hilda; an impromptu visit would simply be a charitable way of responding to their interest, and if I had a chance to ask Signe Rayner one or two pointed questions, so much the better.

Taylor and I dropped Angus off at Leah's, grabbed a quick sandwich at home, then walked across the creek bridge to The Crescents. I'd considered calling Jess's mother to ask if I could leave Taylor with her, but my daughter loved to visit. There was a less altruistic reason to take Taylor along. She was an exuberant little girl, and I was counting on her enthusiasm to smooth over any uneasiness the Blackwell sisters might have about an unannounced social call.

As soon as we hit Leopold Crescent, Taylor found something worth looking at. A man at the house across the street from Justine's was out with his leaf-blower. Taylor watched with professional interest until he was finished, then she went over and asked him how his machine worked. He was an amiable, unhurried man who looked like the adviser in an ad for prudent long-term investments, and he explained the intricacies of his leaf-blower with the kind of loving attention to detail that characterizes the born teacher. Taylor was in luck. So was I. After he'd finished explaining, I held my hand out to him.

"Thanks," I said. "That was great. My daughter's just started a leaf-raking business, so you've given her something to aspire to."

"It was my pleasure, Mrs. . . . ?"

"Kilbourn," I said, "Joanne Kilbourn."

"Darryl Hovanak," he said. "And if your daughter wants a job working with me next fall, I might just take her on. These old trees are one of the beauties of this neighbourhood, but they do create work."

"This is such a beautiful street," I said. "Have you lived here long?"

"Twenty-eight years."

"Then you knew Justine Blackwell," I said.

His face clouded. "I did," he said. "Her death was a loss to us all. She was a good neighbour, and –" he gave me a small self-deprecating smile – "she was almost as house-proud as I am. Her place was always shipshape."

"Even with all her houseguests?" I said.

He frowned. "Did she have houseguests? I never saw anybody. Justine kept pretty much to herself."

"Even in the last year?"

Darryl Hovanak eyed me warily. "Mrs. Kilbourn, I hope you're not from the media."

"No," I said. "I teach at the university, but a close friend of mine is also an old friend of Justine's. My friend was concerned about . . ." I let the sentence drift.

Darryl Hovanak completed it for me. "About wild parties, that sort of thing? Tell your friend to put her mind at ease. From the day I moved in here till the day she died, Justine Blackwell was the best neighbour a man could ask for."

Taylor and I rang the doorbell of Justine's house, but there was no answer. I was just about to give up when Lucy Blackwell came around from the side of the house. She was wearing a flowing ankle-length skirt in swirls of russet and deep green, a loose-fitting deep-green blouse, and, wound around her neck, a scarf of the same flowing material as her skirt. With her tanned bare feet and her dark honey hair, she looked gypsyish. The effect was dazzling.

"This is a surprise," she said with a smile that was a beat too slow in coming.

"Surprises are good," Taylor said agreeably.

"Some are," Lucy said. She turned to me. "What can I do for you, Music Woman?"

"I need to talk to you," I said. "All of you. It won't take long."

She frowned and took a step towards me. "I don't think now's a good time to talk."

"It's as good a time as any," I said. "Are your sisters in the backyard too?" Then, without waiting for an answer, I pushed past her and headed for the garden.

It was obvious from the scene that greeted us that Taylor and I had interrupted a very elegant alfresco luncheon. On the fieldstone patio, three wrought-iron chairs had been arranged around a circular table covered by a snowy linen cloth so full it edges touched the ground. A graceful vase of yellow anemone was in the centre of the table, and at every place setting crystal glasses for water and wine blazed.

A woman carrying a tray came through the French doors that opened onto the patio. I had never met her, but there was no doubt about her identity. Tina Blackwell's hair was different than it had been in her TV days: the shellacked, platinum, anchorwoman 'do had been replaced by *faux sauvage* spikes in a becoming ash blonde, and her outfit was decidedly youthful: a tiny black mini, black lace-up boots, and retro op-art tights. It was a great look, but it was hard to get past the ruin of Tina Blackwell's face. The skin around her eyes was ridged with scar tissue and her cheeks looked as if they had been scraped raw. As soon as I saw her, I flashed a glance at Taylor, but she neither stared nor looked away. She kept walking until she was beside Tina.

"This is so pretty," she said, looking at the table appreciatively. "Is it somebody's birthday?"

"No, just a fancy lunch," Tina said, turning her face away in a gesture that seemed poignantly instinctive.

I walked over to her. "I'm Joanne Kilbourn, Hilda McCourt's friend. This is my daughter, Taylor."

Tina acknowledged Taylor's presence with a nod and a small smile. She raised her hand to her ravaged cheek. "I was sorry to hear about Miss McCourt's accident."

"It wasn't an accident," I said. "It was an assault, a vicious assault."

Tina Blackwell looked towards her sister. "I thought you said she had a fall."

Lucy shook her head. "Too much Prozac, Tina. You're going to have to cut back." She took a step towards me. "How's Hilda doing? We've called you, but you never return our calls, and that policewoman outside her door at the hospital is a dragon."

"You went to the hospital?" I said.

"You're not the only one who cares about Hilda."

"Sorry," I said. "To answer your question, she seems to be improving."

Signe Rayner came out through the French doors. She was wearing her signature muumuu-caftan; this one was magenta, and with her blonde hair swept into its Valkyrie braided coronet, she was a figure of such obvious rectitude that it seemed impossible to imagine her guilty of professional misconduct. But if I had mastered one lesson in my life, it was that appearances can be deceiving. Signe nodded to me. "Is Miss McCourt coherent?" she asked.

"She's improving," I said. There was an awkward pause.

Lucy and Signe exchanged glances. Suddenly, Lucy was all hostess. "We were just about to open a bottle of wine. Will you have a glass? Toast Hilda's recovery?"

"There's nothing I'd rather drink to," I said. As Lucy poured the wine, Tina disappeared into the house. When she came back, she was carrying a bottle of Snapple. She handed it to Taylor. "I hope this is all right," she said.

"I love Snapple," Taylor said. "Thank you." She pointed to a small pool at the bottom of the garden. "Is that a fishpond?"

Tina nodded. "And the fish are still in it. Do you want to go down and have a closer look?"

"Could we?"

Tina looked surprised. "You want me to come?" She picked up her glass of wine and shrugged. "Why not?" she said.

Lucy watched as her sister and my daughter walked to the end of the garden, then she turned to me and lifted her glass. "To Hilda."

"To Hilda," I said.

The wine was an excellent Liebfraumilch, but it was the glass that drew my attention. When I held it up to the light, the sun bounced off its beautifully cut surface and turned it to fire. I looked towards Signe Rayner. "And to Eli. Let's hope they're both back with us soon."

Signe Rayner flushed, but she didn't duck. "You were saying that Miss McCourt is improving. What's her prognosis?"

"Guarded," I said. "It's not easy to recover from the kind of blow Hilda sustained. Eli seems to be taking time to recover too. Dr. Rayner, I'm just a layperson and I know you can't talk about the specifics of Eli's case, but I wonder if you could explain to me why a psychiatrist would use hypnosis with a boy like Eli. It's obvious, even to me, that he hasn't got the strength to deal with his memories."

Signe Rayner looked at me coldly. "I couldn't explain Eli's treatment in terms that would make sense to you."

I leaned forward. "Fair enough," I said. "Then tell me if there are risks involved. Could a sensitive boy, like Eli, who was pushed too hard, get to the point where he might harm himself?"

Signe Rayner's eyes, the same extraordinary turquoise as her sister's, bored into me. "Mrs. Kilbourn, what's your agenda here?" she asked.

"I have no agenda," I said. "I'm on a fact-finding mission."

"Then may I suggest you use the university library. They have an adequate section on psychiatric practices."

"Thank you," I said, "I might just do that." I put down my glass and turned to Lucy. "You were lucky to find replacements for your mother's Waterford," I said. "This is an old pattern. I would have thought it would be impossible to match."

Lucy had the good grace to avert her eyes. I called Taylor, and she and Tina Blackwell came back. They had obviously enjoyed their time together and Tina looked stricken, when I said we had to leave. "So soon?" she said.

"You're just about to have lunch," I said.

Tina Blackwell looked quickly at Signe. Whatever she saw in her sister's face obviously made her decide not to press the invitation. "I'll walk you out," she said.

"Thanks," I said. "I wonder if I could use your bathroom before we leave."

"Of course," she said. This time Tina didn't seek her sister's approval. "Follow me," she said.

I held my hand out to Taylor. "Come on," I said. "You might as well go, too."

We walked in through the French doors. They opened into the living room, a coolly beautiful room with dove-grey walls, exquisite lace curtains that pooled on the floor, and furniture with the gleaming wood inlays and fine upholstery of the Queen Anne period. A rosewood pier table between the two floor-to-ceiling windows at the far side of the room was covered in photographs. Taylor, who loved pictures, ran over for a look. "Are these your kids?" she asked.

Tina smiled. "No, those photographs are of my sisters and me."

They had been lovely girls, and the photographs of them chronicled a happy life of Christmas stockings, Easter-egg hunts, summers at the lake, and birthday parties. "My father took all those," Tina said softly. "We stopped taking pictures after he died." She took a deep breath. "Now, you wanted to powder your nose. I'm afraid all the bathrooms are upstairs. They're in the usual places. Just keep opening doors till you find one."

"Thanks," I said. Walking up the curving staircase was a sensual pleasure. The bisque-coloured carpeting under our feet was deep, and the art on the walls was eye-catching. The works were disparate in period and technique, but all the pieces were linked by subject matter: justice and those who dispensed it. There was a reproduction of a Ben Shahn painting of Sacco and Venzetti, a wonderful contemporary painting of Portia by an artist named Kate Rafter, whom I'd never heard of, but whom I was willing to bet my bottom dollar I'd be hearing about again. There was also a striking black-and-white photograph of LeCorbusier's High Court Building in Chandigarh, and a kind of mosaic depicting Solomon's encounter with the two mothers. Interspersed with the art were formal photographs of actual judges in full judicial rig-out.

I could have taken Tina at her word and opened every door on the second floor, but by the time I got to the top of the stairs, I didn't need further proof to validate the theory I'd been forming since I talked to Justine's neighbour. Epiphanies be damned: there was no way in the world the woman who had assembled this house would have exposed its treasures to people who had the rap sheets I'd seen in Jill's report. I was now ready to bet the farm that the scene Hilda and I had walked in on the Monday after Justine's murder had been carefully arranged. The odour of garbage, the sticky floors, the desecration of the wallpaper in the dining room had all been part of an elaborate hoax. Clearly, the game had been to make us believe Justine's mind had disintegrated, but her daughters had lacked the time and the stomach to finish the job. I remembered how carefully we had been shepherded into the dining room, and led out again. Given the time constraints, the Blackwell sisters had put on the best show they could.

At least, two of the sisters had. Tina seemed to be in the clear. She hadn't been around the day Hilda and I had visited, and today she hadn't hesitated when I asked if we could use the bathroom. Nothing seemed certain in this house, but given her openness, it seemed reasonable that Tina Blackwell hadn't been part of the farce that had been prepared for Hilda and me.

I looked at the emblems of justice that decorated the wall beside Justine's staircase. Suddenly, all I wanted to do was get away from Leopold Crescent. I turned to Taylor. "Come on T, let's blow this pop stand."

"We didn't pee."

"Do you have to?"

"No, but you said . . ."

"I made a mistake. Let's go."

Tina looked wistful as she let us out the front door. "Thanks for coming over, Mrs. Kilbourn, and thank you, Taylor. It was good to forget for a while."

"It was fun," Taylor said.

"Maybe someday I could visit you," Tina said.

"Any time," I said. "By the way, I forgot to mention that

I'm a friend of Jill Osiowy's. She tells me she admires your work."

For the first time that afternoon, Tina turned her face fully towards me. "Does she admire my work enough to ignore this?" she asked bleakly.

As we walked home, I tried to sort out the information I'd gleaned from our visit to the Blackwell sisters. It seemed that, like characters in a Pinter play, Justine's daughters' most significant communications were carried out through silence and subtext. While I puzzled over the line between illusion and reality, Taylor performed the useful work of planning the rest of our afternoon. As always, she proposed enough projects to fill a thirty-six-hour day, but we settled on a more modest agenda. We'd get the car, drive to the hospital to see Hilda, then take in the new show at the Mackenzie Gallery.

Our stay at the Pasqua was short. Hilda appeared to be sleeping comfortably, and we didn't want to disturb her. Taylor left her a drawing she'd made, then slipped away to sit with Nathan. When Taylor was out of earshot, I leaned over and kissed Hilda's forehead. "Justine's daughters lied to us, Hilda, but it won't happen again. Now that I know what we're dealing with, I won't be so gullible. We'll get to the bottom of this. I promise."

The new show at the Mackenzie was too cutting edge for Taylor and me. We hurried through, then headed outside to visit the Fafard cows; half-sized bronze sculptures of a bull, cow, and calf in front of the gallery. The animals' names were Potter, Valadon, and Teevo, and for me, the time we spent admiring their perfect lines and the gentleness of their expression had the restorative power of a romp in a meadow.

My sense of renewal was short-lived. When we got home,

I could hear the phone ringing before I unlocked the front door. I raced to pick it up, heard the husky music of Lucy Blackwell's voice, and felt my spirits plummet.

"Music Woman, you've got to give me a chance to explain."

"Go for it."

"Not on the phone. Can we meet for a drink somewhere?"

"I have a family, Lucy. I have to make supper."

"I'll take you to a restaurant – all of you. Please, you have to listen to what really happened."

I almost hung up on her, then I remembered Signe Rayner. There was a chance that if I heard Lucy out, she might answer some of my questions about her sister. I took a deep breath. "Forget the restaurant," I said. "You can come over. But it's going to have to be a quick visit."

Lucy Blackwell was at our front door in ten minutes. She was still wearing the gypsy outfit, but there was nothing carefree in her manner. As she looked around the living room, she seemed both tense and unfocused. "This is so homey. That rocking chair is perfect."

"It was my grandmother's," I said.

Lucy laughed softly. "Somehow that doesn't surprise me. Can I sit in it?"

"Of course," I said. "Would you like a drink?"

She shook her head. "I had too much at lunch. After you left I was feeling a bit shaky."

"Because I'd caught you in a lie."

She flushed. "Yes. What Signe and I did was stupid, and childish, but it wasn't malicious. It was," she shrugged helplessly, "make-believe. We were just using make-believe to show you the truth. In the last year, my mother had fooled so many people." Lucy leapt to her feet and came over to where I was sitting. In a swift and graceful movement, she knelt on the rug in front of me. "Mrs. Kilbourn, you saw

Tina's face today. That abomination was a direct result of my mother's enlightenment."

I almost cut her off. I had believed Eric Fedoruk when he told me that Justine had given Tina the money she asked for, and I'd had my fill of make-believe. But there was a real possibility that, as she spun her latest fiction, Lucy would reveal a truth that I needed to know. I sat back in my chair. "Go on," I said.

Lucy's gaze was mesmerizing. "Tina was in a business where you can't get old. When she asked for help to get the surgery that might have saved her career, my mother didn't even hear her out. Instead of cutting her a cheque, Justine gave her a speech about how *privileged* we all were, and how it was time we stopped taking and started giving. That job of Tina's might not have looked like much to you or me, Joanne, but it was her life. You should see her apartment. It's *filled* with pictures of her doing all this demeaning public-relations stuff for CJRG: riding the float in the Santa Claus parade, flipping pancakes at the Buffalo Days breakfast, running in the three-legged race with the sports guy on her show. Total fluff, but it was her *identity*." Lucy raked her fingers through her hair. "Tina's always been fragile, emotionally. My mother knew that. She knew terrible things might happen if Tina was hurt again."

"What kind of terrible things?"

Lucy looked away. "Forget I said that. I didn't come here to talk about Tina."

"That's right," I said. "You came to explain why you and Signe decided to produce that little vignette for Hilda and me."

She winced, but she soldiered on. "I told you, it was just a way of getting you to see the truth."

"How many lies do you think it's going to take before I see the truth, Lucy?"

Her body tensed. "What do you mean?"

I moved closer to her. "I know Tina got that money from your mother."

"How do you know?"

I remembered Eric Fedoruk's certainty. "There's a cancelled cheque," I said. It was a bluff, but it did the trick.

In a flash, Lucy was on her feet. "Tina must have lied to me," she said weakly and she started for the door.

"Wait," I said. I got up and followed her. "My turn now, and I haven't got time to figure out which of you is lying about what. Lucy, I have one question for you, and the answer you give me had better be truthful because I'm running out of patience."

Lucy gazed at me intently. "What's your question, Music Woman?"

"What happened between Signe and the boy in Chicago?"

Her face registered nothing. "I have to be going," she said.

"No, you don't," I said. "Not until you tell me if the story is true."

"Signe was found innocent."

"That wasn't what I asked."

Lucy walked to the window. "Is that your Volvo out there?"

"Yes."

"I've always wanted a Volvo wagon." Her back was to me, and her tone was flat. It was impossible to tell if her words were derisive or heartfelt.

"Lucy, you're running out of time here."

"Okay, I'll tell you the truth. I don't know what Signe did in Chicago, but she isn't using that treatment on Eli Kequahtooway. My sister doesn't make the same mistake twice."

"She talked to you about how she's treating Eli?"

Lucy shrugged. "She may have mentioned it." She whirled

around and gave me her dazzling smile. "So, that's it, Music Woman. You've shaken out all the skeletons in our closet." She adjusted her scarf. "Now, I'd better be on my way, let you get on with making supper for your kids." Lucy Blackwell looked at me wistfully. "It must be nice to lead such an ordinary life."

As I stood in my garden in the late-afternoon sunshine, picking the last of the summer's tomatoes, I thought about Lucy. If the purpose of her visit had been to clear the air, she hadn't succeeded. As far as I was concerned, the Blackwell sisters were still, in Winston Churchill's famous phrase, "a riddle wrapped in a mystery inside an enigma."

All during dinner, I pondered the problem of where to find the pieces that would make sense of the puzzle. The possibility I came up with was born of desperation. After supper, I got Taylor bathed and in bed, pointed Angus towards his books, and drove downtown to Culhane House and the person who, according to Eric Fedoruk, had been Justine's closest companion in the final year of her life.

When I got out of my car on Rose Street, the chill of apprehension I felt wasn't wholly attributable to the fact that I was walking in an unfamiliar area on a moonless Sunday night. Detective Robert Hallam had characterized Wayne J. Waters as "lightning in a bottle"; it was impossible to predict how he'd react to an unexpected encounter. I checked the address I'd written down. Culhane House was only half a block away. I was almost there; it would be foolish to turn back now.

The building was an old three-storey house on a corner lot. In the first half of the century, this had been a fashionable downtown address, but the people who were on their way up in the world had long since abandoned the neighbourhood to those who were going nowhere. From the outside, Culhane House looked solid and serviceable. In selecting it as the site of an organization that would serve as both hostel and headquarters for ex-cons, someone had chosen wisely. The location was central; the upper storeys could be used as temporary living quarters, and the bottom floor appeared to be spacious.

The hand-lettered sign on the front door said "Enter," so I did. The room into which I walked was dark, acrid with cigarette smoke, and, except for the sounds coming from the television, silent. On the TV screen, the Sultan was plotting vengeance against Aladdin and Princess Jasmine; none of the half-dozen or so people watching his treachery even glanced my way.

"Do any of you know where I can find Wayne J. Waters?" I asked.

The blonde in leopardskin spandex draped over the chair closest to me gave me the once-over. "He's in the office," she said, "right through them double doors. But hang on to your pompoms, girlie, he's in a lousy mood."

The room in which I found Wayne J. appeared to have been the dining room in the house's earliest incarnation. The chandelier he was sitting under had long since shed its crystal teardrops, but the long oak table in front of him and the sideboard in the corner were battered beauties. When he saw me, Wayne J. jumped to his feet and surprised me with a smile. "I'd given you up for dead," he said. "How's Hilda?"

"Coming along," I said.

He made the thumbs-up sign. "Good, she's a classy broad."

"She is," I agreed.

"You got time for a coffee?" he asked.

"Sure," I said. "It's been a long day. Coffee sounds great."

When he went off to get the coffee, I looked around the office. There wasn't much to see: an old Tandy computer; a battered filing cabinet; a poster of a kittens rollicking with a roll of toilet paper under the words ". . . been up to any mischief lately?"; and a wall calendar for the month of September. The calendar had the kind of surface that can be written on with markers, and it was a crazy quilt of colour. When I examined the entries more closely, I saw that they were a record of appointments, colour-coded to match the various names in the legend printed at the bottom of the calendar. Terrence Ducharme's name was in red marker, and his list of meetings would have kept him busier than most middle-class children: Anger Management; A.A.; Substance Abusers Anonymous; Interpersonal Skills. I was checking the entry for the night Hilda had been attacked when Wayne J. came back with the coffee.

"Terry didn't do her, you know." His tone was conversational.

I turned to face him. "I know," I said. "The police told me he had an alibi for the night Hilda was attacked."

"I'm not talking about Hilda," he said. "I'm talking about Justine."

"But he didn't have an alibi," I said.

"Maybe he lacked an alibi," Wayne J. said judiciously, "but he did have a disincentive."

"You're going to have to explain that."

"There's nothing to explain," Wayne J. said, setting our mugs of coffee carefully on the table. "Terry knew the same thing everybody here knew."

I slid into the chair nearest me and picked up my mug. "Which was?"

Wayne J. blew on top of his coffee to cool it. "Which was that I would have considered it my personal duty to kill anybody who touched a hair on Justine Blackwell's head."

Whatever his intention, Wayne J.'s words were a conversation-stopper. For a beat, we sipped our coffee, alone in our private thoughts. Wayne J. seemed content to be silent, but I wasn't. I hadn't come to Culhane House to reflect; I'd come to get answers.

"How are things going for you now?" I asked.

Wayne J. gave me a sardonic smile. "Fuckin' A." The table in front of him was littered with bills. He scooped up a stack in one of his meaty hands. "As you can see, our creditors grow impatient. Unfortunately, Culhane House lacks the wherewithal to meet their demands."

"And no prospects?" I asked.

He laughed his reassuring rumble. "None that are legally acceptable. And believe me I've explored my options. I even bit the bullet and went to Danger Boy's office."

I must have looked puzzled.

"Eric Fedoruk," he said. "Owner of one of the sweetest machines money can buy, and I'll bet he never takes it past 160 kph. What a waste! Anyway, Mr. Fedoruk gave me a rundown of the situation with Justine's money. He used a bunch of legal mumbo-jumbo, but I've spent enough time in courtrooms to cut through that crap. The bottom line is that I'm going to have fight like hell to get any of Justine's money."

"Are you going to do it?"

"No."

"That surprises me," I said.

Wayne J. leaned towards me; he was so close I could smell the Old Spice. "Why? Because I'm broke and because everything I care about is going down the toilet?"

"Something like that."

"Some things are worth more than money, Joanne."

I sipped my coffee. "What is it that's worth more than money to you, Wayne J.?"

"Not dragging Justine's name through the mud. If I got myself a lawyer and went to court about this, those daughters of hers would haul out all the dirty laundry. They don't have much regard for their mother."

Here was my opening. "What went wrong between Justine and her children?" I asked.

"They're losers, and Justine was a winner," he said judiciously. "And losers always hate winners. It's human nature. And you know what else is human nature? No matter what a winner does for a loser, it's never enough." Suddenly Wayne J. clenched his hands, raised his fists, and brought them down on the table so hard, I thought the wood might crack. "She fucking did everything for them," he said. "She gave Tina a bundle for that facelift or whatever the hell it was she wanted. And the singer was always there with her hand out too."

"Lucy asked Justine for money?"

Wayne J.'s tone was mocking. "It costs money to make records. Haven't you heard?" He was warming to his narrative now. "And the shrink had her own monetary needs – major ones. I know because I was involved in that one."

"What?"

He shook himself. "Look, I shouldn't be talking about any of this. It's violating a confidence."

"Justine's dead," I said. "Nothing she told you can hurt her any more."

Wayne J. furrowed his brow in contemplation. "What the hell," he said. "The good doctor never even thanked me. This couple in Chicago was shaking her down. Justine didn't want her daughter involved, so she asked me to deliver the money to them. It was the only time she ever asked me to do her a favour. I was proud to do it." Remembering, he looked away. "I was glad Justine didn't have to deal with those people. They were garbage. The architect was a peckerhead – totally pussy-whipped. His wife was crazy and mean as hell. She had this little dog, and she made it wear boots when it went outside. To keep it from tracking in mud, get it? No wonder her kid needed a shrink."

"Did you ever find out why these people were blackmailing Signe Rayner?"

"I never asked," he said. "I just delivered the money, and told them it was a one-shot deal. If they got greedy, they'd get sorry." His eyes bored into me. "Mrs. Kilbourn, I'd appreciate it if you kept this little story to yourself. I don't want anything floating around that will make Justine look bad."

"Then help me out with something else because, in my opinion, this *does* make Justine look bad."

He laughed mirthlessly. "That screw-up about the burial plots at the cemetery," he said. "I noticed you and Hilda didn't stick around."

"We had Lucy Blackwell with us," I said. "When she saw there were strangers buried in the family plot, she was devastated."

Something hard came into Wayne J.'s eyes. "Lucy's mother had her reasons for doing what she did."

"What possible reason *could* she have had? I know Justine had undergone some profound philosophical changes in the past year, and I know she wasn't close to her daughters, but didn't she have any feelings at all for her husband?"

"She respected him," Wayne J. said. "That's why she did what she did. She said he'd be better off spending eternity surrounded by the kind of people he'd spent a lifetime defending than with Goneril and Regan, whoever they are. I figured that was some kind of family joke, but Justine wasn't laughing when she said it. She was dead serious." He reached for my empty coffee cup. "Refill?"

"No thanks," I said. "I'd better be getting home."

He stood up. "Come on," he said, offering me his arm. "I'll walk you to your car. After dark, this neighbourhood is no place for a lady."

CHAPTER

12

I woke up the next morning with a sore throat, itchy eyes, and sniffles. By the time I'd showered, taken some echinacea, told Rose our walk was cancelled, and hustled the kids down for breakfast, I was ready to go back to bed. But the day ahead was mercifully short of demands: my first-year students had a quiz, and Howard Dowhanuik, our ex-premier and my friend since Ian's early days in politics, was coming in to talk to my senior class in the afternoon. It was a day to limit my aspirations and take comfort in Woody Allen's dictum that 99 per cent of life is just a matter of showing up. If I played my cards right, I could be home, curled up in bed with a hot toddy and a good novel, by 3:30 p.m.

When I walked into the Political Science offices, Rosalie was on the telephone. As soon as she heard my step, she blushed, whispered something into the receiver, and hung up.

"How was *Romeo and Juliet*?" I asked.

"Transcendent," she said. "Robert said he'd never realized Shakespeare was so s–e–x–y."

"I'm glad you had fun," I said, as I started towards the door.

"Wait," she said. She handed me a pink telephone-message slip. "Your calls are still getting transferred out here."

I glanced at the name. The message was from Alex.

Rosalie smiled shyly. "Maybe we'll both be lucky in love today," she said.

"Maybe," I said, but my voice lacked conviction.

Alex sounded as if he had a cold too, but even making allowances for the fact that he was unwell, his tone was more encouraging than it had been in days.

"Bob Hallam said you were looking for me," he said.

"I just wanted to thank you for getting involved in Hilda's case."

"Actually, Jo, I wonder if we could get together and talk about that."

"Has something happened?"

"Yes, but I'd rather talk to you about in person. Are you free for lunch?"

"Yes."

"It's raining, so I guess the bird sanctuary's out," he said.

His reference to our shared past touched me, but I was too taken aback to pick up on it. "There's a new restaurant in the University Centre," I said. "It's called Common Ground. If you can get past the symbolism, there's homemade soup and a piece of fresh bread for $2.49."

"Twelve o'clock okay?"

"Twelve o'clock's fine. Alex, I'm looking forward to see you again."

"Same here, Jo."

When I hung up, my heart was pounding. Alex had sounded like himself again. I had no idea what had brought about the change, and I didn't care. For the first time in days, we were talking, and in three and a half hours, we'd be talking face to face.

Garnet Dishaw's call came just as I was about to leave for class. Even over the phone, his voice seemed to fill the room. "I wondered if you could find a few moments this evening to come by and talk about Justine," he said.

I thought about the warm bed and the good novel I'd promised myself. "Of course, but could we make it earlier?"

"Later suits me better," he said. There was a silence. "Evenings are long around here."

"May I bring something for the laundry hamper?"

"I knew you were a perceptive woman?"

I laughed. "What's your preference?"

"Surprise me," he said. "But when you go to the liquor store, remember that extravagance is not numbered among the seven deadly sins."

The morning crawled by. For once, no students straggled behind after class to talk. Back in my office, there was a stack of papers to mark and a pile of minutes to read from a committee I'd agreed to join. But I knew my limits. Until I met Alex for lunch, any activity I undertook would get short shrift. Angus had been hinting at his desperate need for a new fall jacket, and the morning paper had announced a sale at Work Warehouse. The liquor store wasn't far from the Golden Mile shopping mall. If I took care of my errands in the morning, I could still grab some recuperative time in the afternoon.

Angus's jacket didn't cost me substantially more than the bottle of Johnny Walker Black I picked up for Garnet Dishaw. When I went into the mall bathroom to check my makeup before I drove back to the university, I knew how to spend the money I'd saved on the jacket. The clear lip gloss I'd chosen in June because it looked so great with a tan made me look sepulchral now that my tan had faded, and the circles under my eyes and the redness under my nose were not flattering. The cosmetics counter at Shoppers Drug Mart was beckoning, and I purchased with abandon: a new blush, a deeper lipstick, and a small tube of concealer. By the time I headed back to the university for lunch with Alex, I looked not great but better.

I was five minutes late getting to the University Centre. The noon-hour crush was on, and I had to battle my way through kids with wet slickers and sodden backpacks. Somehow, Alex had managed to find a table. It was in the corner, and as I pushed my way towards him, the opening notes of a Mozart horn concerto came over the sound system. Mozart was one of our mutual passions, and while I knew that the playing of classical music in the U.C. was a device to keep students who ached for heavy metal or grunge on the move, the fact that Dennis Brain began playing just as Alex and I were about to meet seemed like a good omen.

I slid into the chair opposite him. "I had some shopping to do. I hope you haven't been waiting long."

He shook his head and smiled. "I never minded waiting for you, Jo."

"Good," I said. "Shall we get our soup? I saw the sign. It's Louisiana gumbo, the real thing; they even use filé."

He frowned. "Sounds like you're getting the same cold I've got."

"I'm counting on the gumbo to be a pre-emptive strike."

We lined up with the students, ordered our soup and slices of dark pumpernickel, and went back to our table.

Alex sipped his soup gratefully. "I'm glad you suggested this place."

"Me too. So, what's up?"

He shrugged. "All hell's breaking loose. Terrence Ducharme's alibi turned out to be true. He's admitted all along that he jumped into the car with Justine Blackwell when she drove away from the hotel. But his story was that, after they drove to the park, Justine pulled into that little turnoff near the information centre and they talked until they made their peace with one another. According to Ducharme, she offered to drive him home, but he decided to walk because he was still pretty churned up."

I thought of the X's marking Terrence Ducharme's anger-management classes on the calendar in Culhane House. Seemingly, his efforts at behaviour modification were paying off. "Somebody's come forth who saw him walking home?" I asked.

"No, somebody's come forth who saw him back at his rooming house," Alex said. "Ducharme has always sworn that when he got back home, the old lady across the hall heard him, stuck her head out, recognized him, and went back into her room. Unfortunately for him and for us, by the time we started questioning Ducharme, the old lady had taken off. We did some checking, but the woman, whose name is Leota Trumble, hadn't told anyone in the building where she was going. Apparently, she's an odd bird, doesn't trust anybody to know her business." Alex buttered his bread and took a bite. "To be frank, we didn't exactly pursue the matter with vigour. The feeling was that Miss Trumble's absence was just something Ducharme had latched onto as an alibi."

"But he was telling the truth," I said.

Alex nodded. "Miss Trumble and a friend were on what she calls 'a musical motor tour of the American South.' They finished up at Graceland and came home."

"I guess after you see Graceland, everything else is anti-climactic."

Alex smiled. "Anyway, Miss Trumble corroborates Terrence Ducharme's story. He came home exactly when he said he did. More to the point, he was clean as a whistle. No blood on him, and whoever bludgeoned Justine Blackwell to death would have looked like they'd been in a bloodbath."

Instinctively, I winced at the ugliness of the image. Alex leaned towards me and covered my hand with his. "I'm sorry. That detail wasn't necessary."

"I'm all right," I said.

Alex left his hand on mine, and his dark eyes searched my face. "Are you really, Jo?"

I shook my head. "No," I said. "I'm confused and mad and hurt. How about you."

"The same," he said.

"Alex, what happened to us? I know we had more against us than most couples – the fact that I'm older and the difference in race – but I always thought the things we shared mattered more to us both than the things that divided us."

"I used to think that too."

A trio of students with baggy pants and sports caps turned backwards approached our table. They were laughing and horsing around, and as they started past us, one of them fell against me with enough force to tip my chair halfway over. His friends dragged him back quickly, but all three were full of apologies, and none of them would budge until I assured them no harm had been done.

When they'd finally moved along, I put my hand back in Alex's. "I guess when soup's only $2.49 a bowl, you have to accept the floor show."

"I can put up with the floor show as long as we're talking."

"So can I," I said. "Alex, why did you change your mind about us?"

"I didn't change my mind. Look, I won't explain this well, but I'm just starting to understand some things." He fell silent.

"What kinds of things?" I asked.

"Well, for starters, why I was such a jerk with you. After Eli came, all these problems I thought I'd dealt with began to surface again. I told you about how wild I was when I was a kid."

"I always found it hard to believe," I said. "You're so controlled now."

"Maybe that's part of the problem, because, when I look back, I honestly can't remember a day when I didn't wake up angry. If you're an aboriginal kid with a chip on your shoulder, there's always somebody willing to give you a reason to keep it there. My mother was a great woman, but even she couldn't seem to reach all that rage."

"But *you* found a way to reach it."

"I thought I had. Police work was a good fit for me. Part of being a cop is learning to depersonalize, tune out the insults, focus on the task at hand. By the time you and I met, I really believed I'd found the right formula: work, music, and no complications."

"And I was a complication."

He smiled. "You were. So were your kids."

"That's why you resisted so long."

Alex looked at me hard. "Resisting was a mistake, Jo. That was the best time of my life. I felt as if – this sounds like such a cliché – but I felt as if I'd found my place. Then Eli came. When I saw how angry he was and how much he was suffering, it was as if someone ripped my skin off. I was right back there. And I couldn't do anything to help him. I couldn't change anything. I just had to stand by and watch."

"Alex, why didn't you tell me all this before?"

"I don't know. At the time, you were part of the problem, and so were Angus and Taylor. They're great kids, Jo, and they brought me so much joy, but after Eli came, all I could see when I looked at them was how easy their lives were." He swallowed hard. "They're so confident, Jo. On his worst days, Angus has more confidence that life's going to work out than Eli will ever have – than *I* will ever have. And

Angus has reason to feel good about himself. Doors open when he knocks; people welcome him; he gets chosen for the ball team; he doesn't hear slurs every time he walks down the street. When I saw what Eli was going through, all the old wounds just opened again."

"I wish I'd known, Alex."

"I did everything I could to keep you from knowing, then I was furious when you didn't see that everything was going wrong. I felt the same way about the situation with Eli. I didn't want you to see all of his problems, then I was angry when you didn't understand what he was going through."

"At least I understand now," I said.

"When it's too late."

"Why is it too late?"

"Because you, very sensibly, have found someone else."

"But I haven't," I said. As soon as I said the words, I knew they were true. "Keith and I are just friends. Even if you and I can't work things out, my relationship with Keith isn't going to change." A student walking by looked at us curiously. I leaned across the table and lowered my voice. "Alex, I've had two loves in my life: the first one was my husband, and the other one is you. Neither relationship was very easy, but that doesn't mean I'm ready to settle for less."

I could see the tension leave his face. "Is there any place around here we can be alone?"

I shook my head. "Just my office, and Rosalie will be hovering. I'll walk you to your car." Alex's Audi was in the visitors' lot behind the University Centre. As soon as we got into the front seat, we were in each other's arms. Necking in a car parked in a public place was as awkward and as wonderful as it had been in high school. When Alex's cell-phone rang, it seemed like an intrusion from another world.

Unfortunately, it was an intrusion that demanded action. When he ended the call, Alex reached over and smoothed my hair. "Time to go," he said. "I'll come by the house tonight, but it'll probably be late. Is that okay?"

"It's more than okay. But if you can make it earlier, why don't you bring Eli?"

"I'll ask him, but I don't think he'll come. He doesn't like leaving the apartment." Alex sighed heavily. "Damn it, our first good moment in weeks, and we're already back talking about Eli."

"Eli's what we should be talking about," I said. "How bad are things there?"

"He seems to get worse every day, Jo. He's tight as a drum and he's started having these night terrors. He says they're like movies. Part of what he's seeing is Karen's death, but there's a lot of stuff that doesn't fit in. He says it's dark in his dream, and Karen was killed in the late afternoon. She'd just picked Eli up from school. And he keeps talking about all the blood. Jo, I saw Karen's body after the accident. There were all these internal injuries, but she just looked like she was sleeping. That's what made it so hard . . ." His voice broke. "Anyway, Dr. Rayner says I shouldn't talk to Eli about the night terrors, that the only one who can help him deal with what he's seeing is a professional."

"Meaning Dr. Rayner," I said.

"Yeah," Alex said wearily, "meaning Dr. Rayner. I'm beginning to think you're right about her."

"Then let's dump her," I said. "Alex, there are a number of very disturbing things in her history. I have news clippings about a case in Chicago. A boy's parents sued Signe Rayner because her therapy drove their son to suicide. They lost their lawsuit, but there's not much doubt in my mind that Signe Rayner was guilty."

I told him what I knew. When I finished, Alex shook his head. "That's good enough for me," he said. "I'll phone Signe as soon as I get back to the office. And I'll call Dan Kasperski to see if he can take Eli as a patient."

I sighed with relief. "Good," I said. "It's time Eli did better. It's time we all did better."

I got out of the car and started towards the University Centre. When Alex came after me, I thought that he just wanted to seize the moment to say something fond and foolish, but his words weren't about love; they were about danger. "Promise me you'll be careful," he said. "There's going to be a press conference this afternoon to announce that Ducharme's out of the picture, so all bets are off. We've got an officer outside Hilda's room again, so we're covered there. But until we make an arrest, don't rule anybody out, and don't take any chances."

"That's an easy promise to make," I said. "I've got a lot to stay safe for."

As soon as I got back to my office, I called the hospital. Nathan reassured me that indeed Constable Nilson was back in front of Hilda's door. Then in a voice edgy with excitement, he said, "I was going to call you. I wanted to be sure you came by when I was on duty. We've waited so long for good news about Miss McCourt."

"And there is good news?"

"The best."

I still had my coat on. I looked at my watch. Bang on 1:00. If I hit the lights right, I could see Hilda and be back in time to walk with Howard Dowhanuik to my senior class. "I'll be right over," I said.

As I drove down the freeway, I tested the rawness in my throat. It was still there, but it wasn't worse. Maybe the echinacea and the gumbo had lived up to their billing, and my cold had been vanquished. It was a comforting thought, because the day that had started out so free of demands was getting complicated. Sick or well, I had a dance card that was rapidly filling up.

Nathan was in his place at the nursing station. When I called out to him, he picked up Hilda's chart from the desk. "Look at that," he said, pointing to the latest figures on the Glasgow Coma Scale. "If she keeps progressing at this rate, we'll be able to move her out of intensive care."

"She's doing that well?"

Nathan gave me the thumbs-up sign. "The numbers never lie."

As soon as I saw Hilda, I knew I didn't need the Glasgow Coma Scale to tell me that she was better. The signs were imperceptible but real. Everything about my old friend suggested that, sometime in the hours since I'd last seen her, she had crossed the divide that separates the sick from the well. I walked over to her bed, but, worried about germs, I didn't bend to kiss her. It was enough just to know that she'd decided to rejoin us.

I glanced at the photograph that I had taped to her bed when she'd first been brought to intensive care. For the first time, the picture of Hilda sitting in our canoe didn't make my eyes sting. The day I'd snapped that picture, Hilda had taken Taylor up to the top of a hill to pick wild strawberries. They had returned with sun-pink cheeks, mosquito bites, and mouths stained with fruit. Seeing them coming triumphantly towards me with an ice cream pail half-full of berries had been one of the best memories of the summer. Now it seemed possible there would be other sun-filled days, other memories.

"I knew you were indestructible," I said.

Hilda didn't open her eyes but she turned at the sound of

my voice. "For a while, I had my doubts," she whispered. Then she smiled and went back to sleep.

My banner day continued. Howard Dowhanuik was a major hit with my senior class. Freed by retirement of the politician's need to weigh his words, our ex-premier was profane, indiscreet, knowledgeable, and funny, and the kids loved him.

When the last admiring student had wandered off, he turned to me. "I believe it's payback time. Does the Faculty Club still have that excellent bottle of fifteen-year-old Dalwhinnie tucked away?"

"They do, but, Howard, will you take a rain check? I've been promising myself a nap all day."

He was a big man, and he had the habit some big men in politics have of using their size as a tool to cajole. He draped an arm around my shoulders, dwarfing me. "Scotch would do you more good. Now that you're over fifty, why don't you let go of some of that caution? Open up a little. Embrace life."

I removed his arm from my shoulder. "I am planning to embrace life," I said. "That's why I need a nap."

As soon as I got home, I took some more echinacea and wrote the kids a note saying I was upstairs in bed. I slept for an hour and, when I woke up, I felt better. After I'd showered, I started to change into my sweats; when I remembered that Alex was coming over, I replaced the sweats with my new silk blouse and a pair of slacks. I was burrowing through my jewellery drawer for the mate to my best gold hoop earring when I thought about my meeting with Garnet Dishaw. I picked up the phone and dialled Alex's number to make sure he wouldn't come by while I was gone. Eli answered on the first ring. He sounded keyed-up and anxious.

"Who is it?" he asked.

"It's Jo, Eli. How are you doing?"

"I'm okay. Do you want my uncle? Because he's not here."

"Will you get him to call me when he comes in?"

"Is that all?"

"No," I said. "Your uncle and I had a long talk today. We're back together again, Eli, at least we're going to try to be, and we want you to be part of the picture. I've missed you – so have Angus and Taylor."

"They're not mad at me?"

"No."

"And they're not scared of me?

"Why would they be scared of you?"

He didn't answer. As the silence between us lengthened, I gave up. "If you ever want to talk, I'm a pretty good listener."

"Okay," he said.

"Eli, I mean it. Any time you need me, I'm here."

"I'll remember that," he said, then he hung up.

I was sitting at the kitchen table shuffling through take-out menus when Angus came downstairs. He'd obviously squeezed in a visit to the barber after school, and he was dressed for success: shined loafers; pressed slacks, and the jacket, shirt, and tie we'd bought for Madeleine's upcoming baptism.

"You're looking pretty *GQ* for dinner from Pizza Hut," I said.

He frowned at a piece of lint on his jacket sleeve. "Mum, I'm eating at the Draches tonight, remember? Mrs. Drache's brother is here from Toronto. He's a rabbi. Leah's even taking out all the rings from her body piercings."

"Talk about formal," I said. "What's Leah doing about that tattoo of the foxes chasing the lion?"

"Her mother bought her a long-sleeved dress. You should see it, Mum. She looks great, but she doesn't look like Leah. Anyway, I won't be late. Mrs. Drache says her brother needs his sleep."

"A man after my own heart," I said.

Angus looked quizzical. "What?"

"Nothing," I said. "Have fun, and say hi to the Draches for me."

Taylor and I passed up pizza in favour of won-ton soup, Chinese vegetables, and a double order of her favourite almond prawns from Kowloon Kitchen. As we ate, I filled her in on the visit we were going to pay Garnet Dishaw. As always, she was keen to extend the circle of her acquaintance, but when I mentioned that Garnet and I would need some time alone to talk, she looked thoughtful.

"I'll need some fresh books from the library to take with me," she said.

"Taylor, the library's downtown, and Mr. Dishaw lives out by the airport."

"I've already read the books I've got a hundred times."

Most of the time, Taylor was an accommodating child, but when she dug her heels in, there was no budging her. "Okay," I said, "we'll go to the library, but you'll have to promise me you'll tread easy with Mr. Dishaw. I'm not sure he's used to kids. Now come on, let's fill up the bookbag. The library's waiting."

As I walked by Hilda's room, I stopped and looked in. Everything was just as she'd left it, shining and ordered. Her bed was neatly made; her makeup kit, hairbrush, and comb were carefully arranged on the guest towel she always placed on the vanity to protect the finish; the books she had been reading the night before the attack were centred on her nightstand. Even the library books she had taken out when she'd been in search of an appropriate quote for Justine's funeral were still on Mieka's old desk, neatly aligned, and, it suddenly occurred to me, overdue.

The books were on my card, and Hilda would be mortified if she knew they hadn't been returned promptly. She had, I noticed, made quite a selection: Francis Bacon; Thomas Aquinas; Plutarch; and, the winner, Montaigne. I picked up the *Essays*. The envelope containing Justine's authorization was still where Hilda had slipped it to mark her place the morning before Justine's funeral. Events since then had given a painful resonance to the words Hilda had finally chosen: "What? Have you not lived? That is not only the fundamental but the most illustrious of your occupations. . . . To compose our character is our duty. . . . Our great and glorious masterpiece is to live appropriately."

I closed the book, but not before I'd removed the envelope. As far as I was concerned, if Hilda was going to live appropriately from now on, she had to be as far as possible from Justine and her troubled life. It would be a distinct pleasure to put a match to this document that had caused my old friend so much grief. I started to put the envelope in my pocket, but curiosity drove me to read Justine's final written instructions one last time.

When I took out Justine's letter, there was a surprise. Enclosed in the single folded sheet of expensive letterhead were two items that hadn't been there the morning Hilda and I had discussed Justine's life. The first was a slip of paper upon which were written two names, a Chicago address, and a telephone number with a 312 area code; the second was a cancelled cheque for thirty thousand dollars made out to Tina Blackwell and signed by Justine. The cheque was almost a year old. I turned it over. On the back were Tina's endorsement and the stamp of the branch of the bank that had cashed it. As I read the information, I felt my nerves twang. Justine's cheque had found its way halfway across the country to Lunenburg, Nova Scotia. Until her recent financial reversals, Lunenburg had been Lucy Blackwell's home town.

CHAPTER

13

It had started to rain by the time Taylor and I chose our library books and set out for Palliser Place. My younger daughter was full of plans. Buoyed by the news of Hilda's recovery, she'd checked out the video of *Anne of Green Gables* to watch when she and I got back from our visit. As our windshield wipers slapped rhythmically at the rain, the notion of losing myself in the blossom-heavy trees and azure skies of Prince Edward Island grew increasingly seductive, but the brutal realities of Justine's life made escape impossible.

The pieces of the puzzle were beginning to fall into place, and the picture that was emerging was a troubling one. There was no doubt in my mind that Larry and Paula Erle, the Chicago couple whose name and address had been in Justine's private papers, were the parents of the boy who had committed suicide because of Signe Rayner's treatment. Justine's reasons for keeping the Erles' address close at hand were less clear, but an unsettling possibility presented itself. If, as Eric Fedoruk had suggested, Justine had been determined to force her daughter to give up her psychiatric practice, the Erles would have been a useful weapon to have at the ready.

There was logic to my theory that Justine was prepared to use the Erles as a lever to pry Signe loose from her profession, but I was still grappling with the significance of the cancelled cheque. The reason for the cheque's journey from Regina to Lunenburg seemed clear enough. Somehow, Lucy had persuaded Tina to sign the money over to her. The endorsed cheque was certainly evidence that Lucy was a deeply flawed human being, but why had Hilda considered it important enough to remove from Justine's other records? By the time we pulled into the parking lot at Palliser Place, I still hadn't come up with a satisfactory answer.

Tonight, the pretty young woman behind the reception desk was wearing a lime-and-black-striped zipper-fronted Fortrel pantsuit. When I asked her where Garnet Dishaw was, she yawned and indicated the area behind her. "The place he always is when he's not in the hallway hitting balls around – in the dining room, watching the Golf Channel on the big-screen TV.

As soon as she turned her back, Taylor whispered, "I really like that girl's clothes."

"I used to have an outfit like that before Mieka was born," I said.

"Wear it again," Taylor said enthusiastically. "You'd look good with that zipper."

The tables in the dining room were set for breakfast, but the chalkboard inside the door still announced the evening meal. The menu was filled with exclamation marks: Beef Surprise!! Buttered Rice!! Garden Green Beans!! But the damp smell of food that had been held too long on steam tables revealed the unpalatable truth. The food at Palliser Place was not just institutional, it was lousy.

Garnet Dishaw had pulled a chair over in front of the biggest TV I'd ever seen. On the screen, two men were talking about a golf course, which was theatrically green and perfect.

"That's Old Head in Ireland," Garnet said. Painfully, he pushed himself to a standing position. "Isn't it a beauty?"

"It's nice," Taylor said. "But grass isn't really that colour."

Garnet looked at her severely. "Only a person born and bred on the short-grass prairie would be that suspicious. Are you a stubble-jumper?"

Taylor glanced up at me, questioningly.

"You were born in Saskatoon, and you've lived in Saskatchewan all your life," I said, "so I guess you qualify."

"Anyway," my daughter said with a shrug, "I'm Taylor Love."

Garnet made a courtly bow. "Garnet Dishaw," he said, "and I'm honoured to make your acquaintance." He turned to me. "Now, under other circumstances, my suggestion would be that we go back to my room and sample that excellent whisky peeking so seductively out of your bag. But I expect Ms. Love might like to eat some ice cream and watch TV."

"I *would* like that," Taylor said agreeably.

"Splendid," he said. "This institution has Dixie Cups by the truckload. Ice cream is their method of quelling potential insurrection from the inmates. And, Mrs. Kilbourn, we have coffee. A poor substitute for Johnny Walker, nonetheless . . ."

"Coffee would be fine," I said.

Despite our offers of help, Garnet Dishaw insisted on bringing the ice cream and coffee from the kitchen himself. The task wasn't easy for him, but he performed it gracefully. When, finally, he had Taylor settled with her ice cream in front of the giant TV, and he and I had found a table out of earshot, he turned to me.

"Let's begin by laying our cards on the table, Mrs. Kilbourn. In my opinion, Justine was as sane as you are. I saw her three days before she died. She was sound as a dollar. Now, where do you stand?"

"I don't know," I said, "but after yesterday, I think I'm moving towards your camp. For me, the piece of evidence that weighed most heavily against Justine was the fact that she'd let strangers be buried in her family's cemetery plot. It just seemed so crazy, but one of Justine's friends at Culhane House offered me a new perspective."

When I'd finished my précis of Wayne J.'s explanation, Garnet Dishaw chuckled. "So Justine thought Dick would be better off spending eternity with the usual suspects than with his nearest and dearest, eh? Still, it's no laughing matter deciding you don't want to buried next to your own children."

"Not much fun seeing yourself as Lear, either," I said.

"'How sharper than a serpent's tooth it is/To have a thankless child.'" Garnet Dishaw's face was grim. "Poor Justine. First that terrible business when Dick died, now this."

"What terrible business? When I was here with Keith, you said Richard Blackwell died of a broken heart. What broke his heart?"

Garnet sipped his coffee. "A lie," he said. "Someone told him Justine was having an affair. It wasn't true, of course, but Justine's accuser made a cruel choice in selecting the putative paramour. Sadly, Richard, who was usually the most perceptive of men, was blind to the motivations of the talebearer. By the time he arrived at my apartment with the story, he was a beaten man. He loved his family, and he made me promise never to tell a living soul. Forty-eight hours after Richard's midnight visit, he was dead." Garnet Dishaw's clever old face grew thoughtful. "There's nothing like death to give a casual promise the force of a blood oath."

"Who was Justine supposed to be having an affair with?"

Garnet Dishaw shuddered. "The boy next door."

"But there's only one house next door to Justine, and Eric Fedoruk said he'd lived there all his life."

"He had," Garnet said simply.

It took a moment before the penny dropped. "But Richard Blackwell died in 1967," I said. "Hilda told me he had his heart attack at a Centennial dinner. Eric Fedoruk couldn't have been more than . . ."

"Fifteen," Garnet Dishaw said. "Justine was forty and Richard was sixty-five."

"Who would make up something like that?"

Garnet's face closed in on itself. "No," he said, "that's one part of the story I won't tell. It may have been thirty years ago, but I have to honour my word to Richard there."

I sipped my coffee. "That's all right," I said. "I have a pretty good idea who told him. All I need to know is whether you're certain there was no truth to the accusation."

"I'm certain," Garnet said. "I've known Eric since he articled with our firm. There's not a chance in the world he would have had a sexual encounter with Justine. He had as little interest in physical intimacy as she did."

Taylor and I didn't stay long. After his revelation, Garnet Dishaw seemed somehow spent, and I was increasingly anxious to get in touch with Alex. Besides, we were no longer alone. The Saskatchewan–Toronto football game was being televised, and the residents of Palliser Place, decked out in the green and white, were arriving to cheer on the Roughriders.

We walked Garnet back to his room. Before he went inside, he shook hands with Taylor, then he took both my hands in his. "Be careful, Mrs. Kilbourn. We've already sacrificed one fine woman to this madness."

"I'll be careful," I said. I took the bottle of Johnny Walker out of my bag and passed it to him. "And I'll come back to help you make a dent in this."

His voice was firm. "Do I have your word on that?"

"You have my word," I said.

In the time we had been inside Palliser Place, the wind had picked up and the rain had grown heavier. Taylor and I had a soggy run to our car. As we drove home, Taylor, keyed-up by her visit and by the wildness of the night, prattled happily, but I was suddenly exhausted. It had been a long day, and the ache in my muscles and the soreness in my throat now made undeniable a fact I had spent the day denying: I was sick.

Spurred on by our agreement that she could watch half an hour of *Anne of Green Gables* after she'd had her bath, Taylor went straight upstairs. As soon as I heard the water running, I went into the family room to call Alex. When I picked up the phone, the beep indicating that I had a message was insistent. I tapped in our password. At first there was silence, and I thought the call was a prank. Then I heard Eli's voice, very agitated. "I'm a bad person," he said. "I've done bad things. It was her mother who died. I saw it on TV. I had to tell her about the blood. There was so much blood. It was everywhere." The line went dead. I replayed the message. Even when I was prepared for Eli's words, they chilled me. I dialled the number of the apartment. Alex answered on the first ring.

"It's me," I said. "Is Eli there with you?"

"I don't know where he is, Jo. When I came home the door to the apartment was open, but he was gone."

"He called us," I said. "There was a message on the

machine when Taylor and I got home tonight." I relayed Eli's words.

"But he didn't say anything about where he was going?"

"No, but, Alex, I think I understand part of this. The six o'clock news showed that press conference announcing Terrence Ducharme's release. There was some file footage on Justine's murder. Eli must have seen it. I guess he hadn't realized till tonight that Justine was Signe's mother."

"And he called Signe Rayner to talk about it? God, Jo, I hope you're wrong. After I saw you today, I called her to tell her we thought it was time Eli tried another therapist. She went nuts. I'm no expert, Jo, but I would think that patients change therapists all the time. Signe Rayner acted as if I was betraying her. She told me I was ruining Eli's chances for recovery, then she started in about how Eli had done all these terrible things and how nothing he said could be believed."

"But she was his doctor. She was supposed to be on his side."

Alex's voice was tense. "I've got to find him, Jo."

"I'll come with you."

"No, stay there," he said. "Eli tried to get in touch with you once. He might try again."

I hung up. Tense and restless, I walked to the window. Even through the glass, I could hear the wind keening as it tossed leaves and litter through the air. Eli was out there somewhere, alone in the unforgiving night. Rose, who hated storms so much she never left my side until the weather calmed, whimpered. I reached down to rub her head. "It'll be over soon, Rose," I said, but as I gazed at the darkness, I wondered if the fear and the uncertainty ever truly would be over.

Miserable, I turned away. Propped on the mantel till it

dried was Taylor's painting of the dragon-boat crew that would never be. It seemed that a hundred years had passed since that perfect night when Alex and the kids and I had walked home from the lake and made our plans for next year.

I repeated Eli's words aloud. "I've done bad things. There was so much blood." Two sentences, but they opened the floodgate. Details I'd been struggling to hold back since Labour Day overwhelmed me: Eli at the football game telling Angus, "Sometimes I'd just like to kill you all." Alex's memory of Eli showering and changing into fresh clothes hours after Justine's murder. Eli's inability to remember anything that happened from the time he disappeared at the football game until he walked into Dan Kasperski's office. The crude brutality of the decapitated horse splashed over Taylor's dragon-boat painting. The recklessness with which Eli whirled our croquet mallet above his head, the same mallet that would be brought with such force against Hilda's skull that it would almost kill her.

Juxtaposed, the pictures formed a montage, dark with potential violence, but the composite was incomplete. There were other images of Eli, not the terrifying spectre of my worst imaginings, but the gentle boy with the shy smile who had worried about Mieka's unborn baby and looked at me with hopeful eyes the night I'd visited him in the hospital and talked about a school where he might feel safe. This Eli had worried that Taylor might feel left out and had brought Dilly Bars for dinner so I wouldn't have the bother of cleaning up. Something had gone terribly wrong Labour Day weekend. But remembering the Eli I knew, I was as certain as I could be of anything that, whatever Eli's connection was with those unknown events, he had been more sinned against than sinner.

I was still transfixed by the dragon-boat picture when Taylor ran into the room. Sweet-smelling and rosy from her bath, she came over, stood by me, and looked up at her painting. "Which one do you like better, this one or the one we gave Eli?"

"Well, I like the way Mieka and Greg and Madeleine and Hilda are in this one."

"You're in it, too," Taylor said.

"So I am. And guess what? I may have an idea about somebody to sit in that empty place next to me."

"Who?"

"Alex."

"Good," she said. "I miss him." She narrowed her eyes at the picture. "This one's okay, but I like the way the water looked in the other one."

"That's because the perspective was different. You painted the race the way it looked from higher up."

She gave me a look of exasperation. "I know," she said. "I was standing on that hill up by that Boy Scout thing."

I whirled to face her. "What?"

"That thing with the stones. From up there it looked like Angus and Eli had a wall of water in front of them. So that's what I painted, and I put me in too. Now, let's watch the movie." She slipped the video into the VCR and scrambled onto the couch. "Come on," she said. "It's starting."

From the time the opening credits rolled, Taylor was rapt, but my brain was racing as I ran through the sequence of events that fateful Labour Day weekend. Until that moment, I had seen the area in which we watched the races and the Boy Scout memorial where Justine was murdered as the focal points of two different tales. In fact, the places were separated from one another by less than fifty metres.

"There was so much blood." That's what Eli had said.

What if . . . ? As *Anne of Green Gables* opened, I began to put together a hypothesis. Within half an hour, Taylor had fallen asleep in my arms, and I had a conjecture worth testing. All I had to do was wait for Eli to show up, so we could test it together.

At 9:30, I heard a car pull into the driveway. I leapt up and ran to the window, but it wasn't Eli and Alex, it was my son.

Angus was in an expansive mood. "It was the *best* evening. I didn't think it was going to be, but Rabbi Drache is a great guy. He knows everything. He's so smart, Mum, and he likes football. We watched the game."

"Who won?" I said.

"The Argos," Angus said. "But I didn't mind. Rabbi Drache was like a little kid. He was so wired." He stood up. "Anyway, I have a quiz in English tomorrow, so I should probably read the story."

"What's the story?" I asked.

"'The Painted Door,'" he said. "It's not bad. Do you want me to carry Taylor up to bed?"

"Oh, Angus, would you?" My voice sounded uncharacteristically plaintive.

For the first time since he'd walked into the room, my son really looked at me. "Is everything okay?"

"We don't know where Eli is," I said.

Angus's body tensed. "Should I go look for him?"

"No, stay here. If he calls, I might need to go and pick him up." I began coughing, and I couldn't seem to stop.

"Are you getting a cold, Mum?"

"I'm not getting a cold, Angus. I've *got* a cold, but at the moment, I'm not planning to do anything more strenuous than make myself some tea and sit around waiting for the phone to ring." I smiled at my son. "Don't look so worried, it'll take me back to my college days."

Rose stayed glued to me when I walked into the kitchen to fill the kettle. "You really are a major-league suck," I said. She looked wounded, but she didn't move. "Well, at least let's sit down while we wait for the water to boil." Rose started to follow me to the table, but suddenly she stopped, veered towards the back door, and began to bark. She and I had been together for a long time; as a rule, she trusted me to get the message after a couple of perfunctory woofs, but this time she was adamant. I went over to her, flicked on the yard lights, and opened the back door. The wind was still howling, and it blew a scattering of sodden leaves onto my kitchen floor. I nudged Rose with my toe. "Go on," I said. "If you have to go, *go*. The sooner you get out there, the sooner you can come back in."

My tone was sharp, but Rose, who was usually preternaturally sensitive, didn't budge; she just stood on the threshold, barking.

"There's nothing out there," I said, but as I started to shut the door, I saw that I was wrong. A slender figure in blue-jeans and a white T-shirt was shinnying over the back fence. Even a quick glance was enough for me to recognize Eli's lithe grace. I walked out on the deck and called his name, but he'd already disappeared into the laneway. I ran down the deck stairs to the lawn. When I opened the back gate, the wind caught it and banged it against the fence. I stepped out into the alley. The creek was racing the way it did during spring run-off, and the wind was howling, but there wasn't a living creature in sight. I dashed back inside my yard, grabbed the gate with both hands and pulled it shut. It was only when I latched it that I felt the stickiness on my hands and smelled the paint. As I moved closer to the gate, I was able to see the outline of the black horse. Its message was as clear as a cry for help.

The Lavoline Taylor used to remove paint from her hands was in the carport. After I'd got off most of the black spray paint, I ran back inside, grabbed my coat, and called Angus. "Eli's out there," I said. "If Alex checks in, tell him I've gone out to look for him."

"Are you going to bring him back here?"

I shook my head. "I think when we've worked everything out, Eli will just want to go home."

When I pulled out onto Regina Avenue, I decided that, instead of heading directly for Albert Street, I'd double-back along the lane. Somehow, I couldn't believe that, having worked up the courage to come to our house, Eli would simply run away again. The decision was a good one. The gravel of our alley was spongy from the rain, and I had to keep the Volvo moving at a snail's pace. Nonetheless, it didn't take long to find Eli. As I'd anticipated, he hadn't gone far. My headlights picked him out, curled up between my neighbour's back fence and our communal garbage bin. I jumped out of the car and ran to him.

"Come on, Eli. You and I have things we need to talk about."

"Just leave me."

"I'm not going to leave you."

"You don't know what I've done."

"You didn't do anything."

"You don't know."

"But I do know. Get in the car with me, and I'll explain. If you'll give me a chance, I can show you that you didn't do anything wrong."

After a few seconds, he slowly got to his feet and headed for the car. Without a word, he slid into the passenger seat, closed the door, and sat, staring straight ahead. I glanced over at him. "Are you okay?"

Eli nodded. The light from the alley threw the carved beauty of his profile into sharp relief. Except for the trembling of his lower lip, he was absolutely still.

The road that winds through Wascana Park offers few places to pull over, so I drove straight to the cul-de-sac Justine had parked in the night of her death. It was behind an information booth that heralded the pleasures of Regina, the Queen City. The booth wasn't much: a Plexiglas-protected map of the area; a display case filled with posters of past and future events; a public telephone; and a clear view of both the Boy Scout memorial and the shoreline from which we'd watched the races.

I turned to Eli. "Look down there and tell me what happened that night after you decided you couldn't stay at the football game with us."

"Noooooo." The word ululated into a moan.

"Okay," I said quickly. "Let's go back to a better time. We're at the game. All of us. We were having fun. Then you and Angus went off for nachos."

"Just a fucking Indian," he said furiously.

I took his hand. "That's what the man said, and you were hurt and angry. Eli, tell me what happened next."

"I walked down Winnipeg Street – found some guys. They were doing solvent. They wanted me to do it too, but I wouldn't."

"Good for you," I said. "Then what happened?"

"I didn't know where to go." His voice broke. "I couldn't go home. I didn't want to disappoint my uncle again."

"He loves you, Eli. You couldn't disappoint him."

"Don't make me do this," he said miserably.

I stroked his hand. "We have to," I said. "Now, you decided you couldn't go home, so you came back here to where we watched the races."

"Not on purpose," he said. "At least I don't think so. I was just walking, and I ended up here." He smiled. "But it *was* nice to remember. I guess I fell asleep."

To this point, Eli's voice had been dreamy, the voice of someone whose mind was travelling through another time and place. Suddenly, his body grew rigid, and he began to breathe heavily. "When I woke up, the woman was screaming. I heard her. 'No. No. No. Don't do it. No, don't. Don't.' She sounded so scared. Just the way my mum did. . . . I went to help her. So much blood. There was so much blood." He had started to hyperventilate.

"Take a deep breath," I said. "You did everything right, Eli. Someone was hurt, and you went to help. That's the truth. All you did was try to help someone who needed you."

His body relaxed; his eyes met mine, and his question was urgent. "I didn't do anything wrong?"

"No," I said. "You didn't do anything wrong."

"I don't want to remember any more."

"That's all right," I said.

"Can we just go home now?"

"We can go home," I said.

He gave me a small smile and lay back against the seat.

I got a parking spot in front of the apartment building, which was a stroke of real luck because my adrenaline level had dropped dramatically. Even walking up the stairs to the third floor seemed to take every ounce of energy I could summon. Eli was tired too. When we got to the apartment, he reached into the old-fashioned milk chute to the left of the door, pulled out a key, and exhaled with relief. "I always forget my key, so my uncle leaves one in here for me." He looked at it curiously. "I think this one is his."

"We'll be here when he gets home," I said.

"I'm still scared," he said.

"Of what?" I asked.

"Of everything."

"We'll work on that," I said. "Now, let's go inside. I'm going to call our house so, when your uncle checks in, he'll know where we are."

"You're not going to leave me, are you?"

"No," I said. "I'm going to stay here till you boot me out. Now, why don't you have a shower and get into some dry clothes. Could I heat you up some soup or something?"

He shook his head. "I just want to go to bed."

I knew how he felt, but I still had miles to go before I slept. After Eli started his shower, I called home. Angus said that Alex had been checking in every half-hour or so from the cellphone in his car, and he was expecting a call any minute. When I told Angus that Eli and I were safe at the apartment on Lorne Street, my son's relief was apparent.

After I hung up, I grabbed a quilt, sat down in an old easy chair Alex loved, closed my eyes, and listened to the reassuringly ordinary sounds of rainy night traffic and Eli's shower. When I heard the knock, I was so certain it was Alex that I opened the door without a second's hesitation.

She was in the apartment before I could even think of a strategy to stop her.

"Where's Eli?" she said.

"He's not here," I said.

She looked towards the bathroom. "Don't lie to me," she said. "I was waiting across the street. I saw you come in. Call him."

"No," I said.

"What's the point? I'm going to get him sooner or later." She shook her head sadly. "Music Woman, why did you have to get involved in this?"

"I don't know what you're talking about," I said. "I just came by tonight to stay with Eli. He wasn't feeling well."

Lucy Blackwell's turquoise eyes were cold. "I understand he's a very sick boy," she said. "My sister says he's delusional."

"That may be," I said carefully. "He's had a lot of trauma in his life. It's quite possible he's confused about many things." I took a step towards her. "Lucy, why don't you leave and let me take care of him."

"Has he said anything to you about me?"

"No," I said. "He's never once mentioned your name."

"I hear he's been talking about my mother's death."

"I wouldn't worry about that," I said. "As your sister pointed out, Eli is delusional. Nobody will put much credence in anything he says." I took a step closer to her. "If I were you, I'd walk out that door right now. At this point, there's no proof of anything. You can grab your passport and be on the first plane out of here."

She was wearing a silvery raincoat with a hood, and she pulled the hood down to reveal her dark honey hair. "I don't get it," she said. "Why are you offering me a way out, Music Woman?"

"I've loved your music for thirty years. Maybe I just want to see your life have a happy ending." My heart was pounding so loud, I was amazed she didn't hear it. "Just go, Lucy."

"You'd be on the phone to the police as soon as I started downstairs."

"There's nothing to tell them," I said. "It's all perfectly innocent: you knocked at the door; we talked; I asked you to leave; you left."

She looked at me thoughtfully. "You really would let this be our little secret?"

I nodded. "Just leave us alone," I said.

She pulled her hood up. "Okay," she said. "Maybe you're right. Maybe I can still get away." She smiled her wonderful dazzling smile. "Many thanks, Music Woman."

"No!" Eli's scream was atavistic. I whirled around to face him. He was wearing a white robe and his long black hair fell loosely to his shoulders. He looked like an acolyte in a religious order, but there was no peace in his face. His eyes were wide with terror, and his mouth was a rictus. "You did it," he said. "You killed her. I saw. I saw. She kept crying and asking you to stop." His voice grew higher. "'Lucy. Lucy, No. No.' There was so much blood," he screamed. "So much blood!"

Lucy's hands shot up, and she lunged at him. I stepped between them. In an instant, she changed her target. Suddenly, her hands were around my throat, and she was squeezing. I tried to call out, but the only sound that came from my throat was a strangled sob. When I reached up to unclasp her fingers, it was like grappling with steel. I kicked at her legs, but she didn't falter. Lucy Blackwell had the strength of someone engaged in mortal combat. Wildly, I looked around the room I knew so well, but there was nothing there to save me. My vision blurred. I saw red, then black. I felt the sensation of falling, and I knew I was dying.

Then, miraculously, it was over. The fingers loosened. I fell against a chair and gulped air thirstily. When I was able to focus, I saw what had happened. Eli had grabbed Lucy from behind. His arm was around her neck in a kind of stranglehold. Slowly but inexorably, he brought her to the floor and pinned her there.

A few seconds later, when Alex came through the door, everything was taken care of. He nodded at Eli. "Good job," he said.

Eli gave him a small smile. "Just the way you taught me." Then his face broke into misery. "She killed her Mum," he said. "She killed her own Mum."

"I know," Alex said. He went over to Lucy, pushed her arms behind her back, and handcuffed her. "Stay there," he said. "And don't move." He looked up at me. "Could you call headquarters, Jo? Get them to send some backup."

As the three of us waited, Lucy's eyes never left my face. It was obvious that, despite the events of the past few minutes, she still saw me as someone with the potential to be her advocate. "You shouldn't have got involved," she said in her low and thrilling voice. "Should have just stayed home with your rocking chair and your kids."

"Why did you do it, Lucy?" I said.

Lucy shifted position and groaned a little. She was obviously in pain. "Justine never invited us to the party. No matter how hard we tried or how perfect we looked or how much we accomplished, it was never enough. She never invited us to the party." Her voice was heartbreakingly sad. "'Three little girls in virgin's white, swimming through darkness, longing for light.' I killed my mother because she never once invited us to come in out of the dark. And do you know what? If I had the chance, I'd kill her again."

"And Hilda?" I asked. "Would you try to kill Hilda again?"

Confusion flickered across her face. "That was a mistake. Everybody makes mistakes, right?" She tried a gallant smile. "I just make more than most people."

For the next few minutes, Lucy rambled through her *apologia pro vita sua*. Much of the time she was incoherent, but two key points emerged. Lucy herself had been the one who went to Richard Blackwell with the lie about Justine's affair with Eric Fedoruk; nonetheless, she blamed Justine for her father's death. "He loved her too much," she said. "It didn't leave enough for me." Lucy held her mother responsible for Tina Blackwell's botched medical procedure too. Although Justine had given Lucy a substantial amount of money to get *The Sorcerer's Smile* produced, when the boxed set of Lucy's musical legacy failed to take off, Justine refused to write the cheque that would have given her daughter the saturation ad campaign Lucy believed would salvage her dream.

"The only option she left me was Tina," Lucy said sulkily. "How do you think it makes me feel every time I have to look at my sister's face?"

The rest of Lucy's tale was equally ugly, equally filled with self-pity and bitterness. I was relieved when the sounds of a siren split the night. For three decades, I had loved Lucy Blackwell's voice, but I never wanted to hear it again. When the uniformed police arrived, it was over quickly. Two officers helped Lucy to her feet and led her towards the front door. As she walked by me, she gave me a sidelong smile. "So, are you still my number-one fan, Music Woman?"

"Not a chance, Lucy," I said. "Not a chance."

When the door closed behind her, Eli turned to me. "I want to watch them take her away," he said.

We walked out to the balcony together. The rain had stopped. The plaster owl which Alex and I had designated as our sentinel sat jauntily on his railing perch, and the air smelled fresh-washed. Down the street, the bells at the United Church were ringing. It was a good evening to be alive. Eli and I watched silently as Lucy was put into the squad car. Just before Alex got into the front seat, he called up to us. "I love you," he said.

Eli looked at me. "Did he mean me or you?"

"Both of us," I said. "Now, come on. Let's get inside. You and I have a lot to talk about."

"Like what?"

"Oh, like when you think you'll be ready to get together with Dan Kasperski and when you think you'd like to meet Ms. Greyeyes and get started at school."

"I'd like to come by your house some time again, to see the kids."

"That shouldn't be too difficult to arrange."

"I'll need to tell Taylor I'm sorry about what I did to her painting, won't I?"

"Yes," I said, "you will."

"Do you think she'll listen to me?"

"She'll listen. She's a good little kid."

I could see the relief in his face. For a moment he was silent, then he turned to me. "Do you know what I wish?" he said softly.

"What?"

"I wish we could have that dragon-boat team we talked about – the one with all of us."

"There's no reason we can't," I said. "But, Eli, do you really think Taylor's up to taking on all the obligations of being our drummer?"

Eli grinned. "Sure she is. We just have to let her know we think she can do it, and give her time."

* * *

A few days later, when Angus and I were helping Hilda move from the hospital to the Wascana Rehabilitation Centre, I remembered Eli's words about the importance of faith and time. Angus was wheeling Hilda out to our car, and we were talking about what she might need in her new home.

"A good poetry anthology," Hilda said. "Do you have one, Joanne?"

Angus screwed up his face with distaste. "Why would you want to read poetry? It's all about death."

Hilda touched his hand. "It's not about death, Angus. It's about time. All poetry is about time."

Therapy was about time, too. At least, that's what Dr. Dan Kasperski believed. There were no quick fixes for Eli. When Alex and I had gone to talk to him about Eli's prognosis, Dan Kasperski had been realistic. "He's got a lot going for him. He's smart and he's strong. He's come through far more than anyone should be expected to endure. The fact he acted heroically with Lucy Blackwell was a big move forward. But it's up to him. He has to decide what he's going to do with the time ahead. If he wants to give it up to anger and self-pity, he'll be screwed. If he uses his time wisely and bravely . . ." Dan Kasperski shrugged. "Who knows? Sky's the limit."

My horizons weren't sky-high. On our shared fifty-second birthday, Keith Harris and I went out for dinner, and I told him that Alex and I were going to try again. Keith didn't seem surprised, but he didn't offer congratulations. "I want what's best for you, Jo, but even if I can't be in the picture, I'm not sure if Alex is the right one. Somehow I can't see a future for you two."

"Maybe there isn't one," I said. "Alex and I may have to be content with the present."

Keith smiled. "Then let's drink to that." He raised his glass. "To the present. I hope it will be enough for you, Jo."

I raised my glass. "So do I," I said.

By Thanksgiving, Justine Blackwell's tragedy had reached its dénouement. Lucy Blackwell was awaiting trial; Eric Fedoruk had brokered an agreement between Culhane House and Tina Blackwell about Justine's estate; and the College of Physicians and Surgeons had set in motion procedures to revoke Dr. Signe Rayner's licence. There was, however, one piece of business still to be finished.

Thanksgiving Monday, I picked up Garnet Dishaw at Palliser Place, and together we drove to the Wascana Rehabilitation Centre to get Hilda. The day was grey and still, a day for remembering. As we made our way to the cemetery where Justine was buried, Garnet and Hilda traded memories of the woman they had known and cared for. When we turned onto the road that led to Justine's burial plot, I spotted Eric Fedoruk's Eurobrute pulled up beside Wayne J. Waters' elaborately painted van. As soon as we parked, the two men came over. Wayne J. reached into the back seat, pulled out Hilda's wheelchair, snapped it smartly into place, and helped her into it; Eric, after greeting Hilda warmly, helped Garnet Dishaw over the uneven ground to Justine's grave. Tina Blackwell, dressed in black, was waiting by the new headstone. She acknowledged us with a shy smile, then turned to Wayne J.

"Are we ready, Wayne?" she asked.

"Ready as we'll ever be," he said. The tombstone was covered with a beach towel. "I hope you don't think this is in bad taste," he pointed to the towel. "I should have thought ahead, found something appropriate. But I like the idea of an unveiling."

"I do too," Hilda said. "It gives the moment a sense of importance."

"Okay," Wayne J. said. "Here goes." He grabbed the corner of the towel between his thumb and forefinger. "This is a present from Tina and from all of us at Culhane House. Hilda chose the words. They're from Proverbs." He flicked aside the towel to reveal a creamy marble headstone. On it were chiselled Justine's full name and a simple inscription: THE MEMORY OF THE JUST IS BLESSED.